Penguin Books
Connoisseur's Science

Tom Boardman Jr was born in 1930 in New York State and went to England two months later. He was educated in England, in the United States, and in Argentina. In 1949 he went into publishing, but in 1951 he returned to the United States to join the army; he has been active in the Reserve ever since. He returned to England in 1954 and continued his publishing career. He is now editor and publisher of the house bearing his name, and sales manager for a publishing group. He lives in Berkshire with his wife and two children.

Tom Boardman was the first reviewer in Britain to have a regular monthly column on science fiction books, in *Books and Bookmen*; he has been literary adviser on science fiction to three publishers and in 1962 was guest of honour at the British Science Fiction Convention. He is co-founder of the first magazine of sf criticism and comment, *S.F. Horizons*. However, he still has time for golf, cooking, and jazz.

Connoisseur's Science Fiction

An anthology edited by
Tom Boardman

Penguin Books

Penguin Books Ltd, Harmondsworth,
Middlesex, England
Penguin Books Inc., 7110 Ambassador Road,
Baltimore, Maryland 21207, U.S.A.
Penguin Books Australia Ltd, Ringwood,
Victoria, Australia
Penguin Books Canada Ltd, 41 Steelcase Road West,
Markham, Ontario, Canada
Penguin Books (N.Z.) Ltd, 182–190 Wairau Road,
Auckland 10, New Zealand

First published 1964
Reprinted 1966, 1976

Printed in the United States of America by Colonial Press Inc.,
Clinton, Massachusetts

Contents

Acknowledgements

The following acknowledgements are gratefully made for permission to reprint copyright material:

THE FUN THEY HAD, by Isaac Asimov, copyright 1951 by N.E.A. Services Inc. Reprinted by permission of the author and Doubleday & Co., Inc., from *Earth Is Room Enough*.

MADE IN U.S.A., by J. T. McIntosh, copyright 1953 by Galaxy Publishing Corporation Inc., for *Galaxy Science Fiction*. Reprinted by permission of the author.

DIABOLOGIC, by Eric Frank Russell, copyright 1955 by Street & Smith Publications, Inc., for *Astounding Science Fiction* (now *Analog Science Fact – Science Fiction*). Reprinted by permission of the author's agent, Laurence Pollinger Ltd.

THE WIZARDS OF PUNG'S CORNERS, by Frederik Pohl, copyright 1959 by Galaxy Publishing Corporation. Reprinted by permission of the author and his literary agent, E. J. Carnell.

BUILD-UP, by J. G. Ballard, copyright 1960 by Nova Publications Ltd, for *New Worlds Science Fiction*. Reprinted by permission of the author and the author's agent, Scott Meredith Literary Agency, Inc.

THE WAVERIES, by Fredric Brown, copyright 1945 by Street & Smith Publications, Inc., for *Astounding Science Fiction* (now *Analog Science Fact – Science Fiction*). Reprinted by permission of the author and the author's literary agent, Scott Meredith Literary Agency, Inc.

MR COSTELLO, HERO, by Theodore Sturgeon, copyright 1953

Acknowledgements

by Galaxy Publishing Corporation, for *Galaxy Science Fiction*. Reprinted by permission of the author and his literary agent, E. J. Carnell.

DISAPPEARING ACT, by Alfred Bester, copyright 1953 by Ballantine Books Inc., for *Star Science Fiction No. 2*. Reprinted by permission of the author.

TOMORROW AND TOMORROW AND TOMORROW, by Kurt Vonnegut, copyright 1954 by Galaxy Publishing Corporation, for *Galaxy Science Fiction*. Reprinted by permission of the author and his literary agent, John Farquharson Ltd.

QUIT ZOOMIN' THOSE HANDS THROUGH THE AIR, by Jack Finney, copyright 1957 by Jack Finney, from *The Third Level* (Rinehart & Co. Inc.) as *The Clock of Time* (Eyre & Spottiswoode Ltd, 1958). Reprinted by permission of the author's literary agent, A. D. Peters.

Introduction

To too many people science fiction still means rockets to the moon, flying through space, intergalactic wars, bug-eyed monsters, and mad scientists. Science fiction still has to live down the sensational magazine covers of twenty years ago when scantily-clad females in fishbowl helmets fought off the unwanted attentions of eight-tentacled venusians.

This anthology sets out to prove this picture wrong, to show that a great deal of original, literate, imaginative writing is being published under the soubriquet science fiction. It is also exciting and vigorous – maintaining, through the several magazines, a responsive audience for short stories of quality. While the detective story has reached a dead end, and more and more formula stories are published as the authors' invention dries up, sf magazines offer a free market for ideas. Several established authors have turned to sf where, now, there is more freedom to write on controversial subjects than anywhere else. (In Russia this is particularly true.) Want to write about race relations? Religious prejudice? Birth control? Political ideology? – set the story in the future, or on another planet and you offend nobody officially; though the perceptive reader still gets the message.

What then *is* science fiction?

This question has vexed *aficionados* since May 1929 when Hugo Gernsback first used the term. Definitions have been coined and discarded frequently because of inadequacy. Kingsley Amis described it (in 1960) as a *genre* 'in which speculation about the future is satire about the present in disguise, satire that covers a wide range – from politics to sex to subliminal advertising', while it could also be put more brutally, paraphrasing Louis Armstrong on the definition of jazz – 'If you've got to ask what it is, you'll never know.' To my mind, science fiction (the title) is the hopelessly inadequate description of a *genre* which is simply any speculation about what may happen (or may have happened) to Mankind.

This collection of sf attempts to put before the reader, newcomer, or addict a selection of good stories covering a wide variety of themes, showing some of the passionate interests of science fiction authors. Broken down to essentials, each is a *cri de coeur*, for the sf writers are never people with tepid interests – as a group they form as opiniated a body of men and women as will be found anywhere. The authors represented here are amongst the best sf writers in English on both sides of the Atlantic. All served their apprenticeship in the sf magazines, and over the years they have helped to steer sf away from the epic of gadgetry and superficial adventure to a deeper, more meaningful, introverted approach. Science fiction of the fifties and sixties has tended towards sociological satire, examining the problems of mid twentieth century life extrapolated into the future along the lines we are going now.

But, lest this seems to be too serious, the reader will soon discover that there is one thing the stories in this collection have in common: they are told in a wryly comic, sometimes almost tragic, way. They show how conditioned we are becoming to our environment, taking for granted things that should be questioned if we are to keep a balanced attitude to life. What would happen if we suddenly lost our electric power? If we allowed our consuming habits to be dictated by advertisers? If we continue to specialize in one occupation to the exclusion of all other interests? If cities keep on expanding? If we manage, medically, to double our life span?

Each of the stories in this collection is a favourite – if you like, my personal top-ten, the only qualification being that no two stories have the same basic theme. It would be invidious to make further distinction of merit, but two stories deserve special mention. Of all topics in sf today, time-travel seems to be the least likely of being realized. (For one thing, if time travel is invented in the future, why haven't we met anyone from the future yet?) However, it is a subject that has fascinated writers for years. In this volume Jack Finney tells with delicious humour the story of the world's first aeroplane pilot, a private of the Union Army who flew during the American Civil War.

Theodore Sturgeon is considered by many to be the most imaginative of all writers in this essentially imaginative *genre*. No two stories of his are alike and in *Mr Costello, Hero* he introduces an unforgettable character with a terrifying penchant for bringing out the worst in our natures. *Caveat lector!*

In an introduction to another Penguin anthology of sf, the editor, Brian Aldiss makes the felicitous remark 'Science fiction is no more written for scientists than ghost stories are written for ghosts.' If this present anthology shows anything, it shows that good sf need not even be about science. And, although the themes of these stories show sociological awareness, they are by no means tracts. I suspect they were written mainly for the enjoyment they gave the authors in working out the ideas. I am sure they will be read for the same reason. And if they do make us take another look at ourselves, our way of life, our beliefs, only those with closed minds will complain. And they will not like science fiction anyway.

Sunningdale, April 1964   TOM BOARDMAN

Alfred Bester

Disappearing Act

This one wasn't the last war or a war to end war. They called it the War for the American Dream. General Carpenter struck that note and sounded it constantly.

There are fighting generals (vital to an army), political generals (vital to an administration), and public relations generals (vital to a war). General Carpenter was a master of public relations. Forthright and Four-Square, he had ideals as high and as understandable as the mottoes on money. In the mind of America he *was* the army, the administration, the nation's shield and sword and stout right arm. His ideal was the American Dream.

'We are not fighting for money, for power, or for world domination,' General Carpenter announced at the Press Association dinner.

'We are fighting solely for the American dream,' he said to the 162nd Congress.

'Our aim is not aggression or the reduction of nations to slavery,' he said at the West Point Annual Officers' Dinner.

'We are fighting for the Meaning of civilization,' he told the San Francisco Pioneers' Club.'

'We are struggling for the Ideal of civilization; for Culture, for Poetry, for the Only Things Worth Preserving,' he said at the Chicago Wheat Pit Festival.

'This is a war for survival,' he said. 'We are not fighting for ourselves, but for our Dreams; for the Better Things in Life which must not disappear from the face of the earth.'

America fought. General Carpenter asked for one hundred million men. The army was given one hundred million men. General Carpenter asked for ten thousand U-Bombs. Ten thousand U-Bombs were delivered and dropped. The enemy also dropped ten thousand U-Bombs and destroyed most of America's cities.

'We must dig in against the hordes of barbarism,' General Carpenter said. 'Give me a thousand engineers.'

One thousand engineers were forthcoming, and a hundred cities were dug and hollowed out beneath the rubble.

'Give me five hundred sanitation experts, eight hundred traffic managers, two hundred air-conditioning experts, one hundred city managers, one thousand communication chiefs, seven hundred personnel experts . . .'

The list of General Carpenter's demand for technical experts was endless. America did not know how to supply them.

'We must become a nation of experts,' General Carpenter informed the National Association of American Universities. 'Every man and woman must be a specific tool for a specific job, hardened and sharpened by your training and education to win the fight for the American Dream.'

'Our Dream,' General Carpenter said at the Wall Street Bond Drive Breakfast, 'is at one with the gentle Greeks of Athens, with the noble Romans of . . . er . . . Rome. It is a dream of the Better Things in Life. Of Music and Art and Poetry and Culture. Money is only a weapon to be used in the fight for this dream. Ambition is only a ladder to climb to this dream. Ability is only a tool to shape this dream.'

Wall Street applauded. General Carpenter asked for one hundred and fifty billion dollars, fifteen hundred dedicated dollar-a-year men, three thousand experts in mineralogy, petrology, mass production, chemical warfare, and air-traffic time study. They were delivered. The country was in high gear. General Carpenter had only to press a button and an expert would be delivered.

In March of A.D. 2112 the war came to a climax and the American Dream was resolved, not on any one of the seven fronts where millions of men were locked in bitter combat, not in any of the staff headquarters or any of the capitals of the warring nations, not in any of the production centres spewing forth arms and supplies, but in Ward T of the United States

Army Hospital buried three hundred feet below what had once been St Albans, New York.

Ward T was something of a mystery at St Albans. Like all army hospitals, St Albans was organized with specific wards reserved for specific injuries. Right arm amputees were gathered in one ward; left arm amputees in another. Radiation burns, head injuries, eviscerations, secondary gamma poisonings, and so on were each assigned their specific location in the hospital organization. The Army Medical Corps had established nineteen classes of combat injury which included every possible kind of damage to brain and tissue. These used up letters A to S. What then, was in Ward T?

No one knew. The doors were double locked. No visitors were permitted to enter. No patients were permitted to leave. Physicians were seen to arrive and depart. Their perplexed expressions stimulated the wildest speculations but revealed nothing. The nurses who ministered to Ward T were questioned eagerly but they were close-mouthed.

There were dribs and drabs of information, unsatisfying and self-contradictory. A charwoman asserted that she had been in to clean up and there had been no one in the ward. Absolutely no one. Just two dozen beds and nothing else. Had the beds been slept in? Yes. They were rumpled, some of them. Were there signs of the ward being in use? Oh yes. Personal things on the tables and so on. But dusty, kind of. Like they hadn't been used in a long time.

Public opinion decided it was a ghost ward. For spooks only.

But a night orderly reported passing the locked ward and hearing singing from within. What kind of singing? Foreign language, like. What language? The orderly couldn't say. Some of the words sounded like ... well, like: Cow dee on us eager tour ...

Public opinion started to run a fever and decided it was an alien ward. For spies only.

St Albans enlisted the help of the kitchen staff and checked the food trays. Twenty-four trays went into Ward T three times a day. Twenty-four came out. Sometimes the returning trays were emptied. Most times they were untouched.

Public opinion built up pressure and decided that Ward T was a racket. It was an informal club for goldbricks and staff grafters who caroused within. Cow dee on us eager tour indeed!

For gossip, a hospital can put a small town sewing circle to shame with ease, but sick people are easily goaded into passion by trivia. It took just three months for idle speculation to turn into downright fury. In January, 2112, St Albans was a sound, well-run hospital. By March, 2112, St Albans was in a ferment, and the psychological unrest found its way into the official records. The percentage of recoveries fell off. Malingering set in. Petty infractions increased. Mutinies flared. There was a staff shake-up. It did no good. Ward T was inciting the patients to riot. There was another shake-up, and another, and still the unrest fumed.

The news finally reached General Carpenter's desk through official channels.

'In our fight for the American Dream,' he said, 'we must not ignore those who have already given of themselves. Send me a Hospital Administration expert.'

The expert was delivered. He could do nothing to heal St Albans. General Carpenter read the reports and fired him.

'Pity,' said General Carpenter, 'is the first ingredient of civilization. Send me a Surgeon General.'

A Surgeon General was delivered. He could not break the fury of St Albans and General Carpenter broke him. But by this time Ward T was being mentioned in the dispatches.

'Send me,' General Carpenter said, 'the expert in charge of Ward T.'

St Albans sent a doctor, Captain Edsel Dimmock. He was a stout young man, already bald, only three years out of medical school but with a fine record as an expert in psychotherapy. General Carpenter liked experts. He liked Dimmock. Dimmock adored the general as the spokesman for a culture which he had been too specially trained to seek up to now, but which he hoped to enjoy after the war was won.

'Now look here, Dimmock,' General Carpenter began. 'We're all of us tools, today – hardened and sharpened to do a specific job. You know our motto: A job for everyone and everyone on the job. Somebody's not on the job at Ward T and we've got to kick him out. Now, in the first place what the hell is Ward T?'

Dimmock stuttered and fumbled. Finally he explained that it was a special ward set up for special combat cases. Shock cases.

'Then you do have patients in the ward?'

'Yes, sir. Ten women and fourteen men.'

Carpenter brandished a sheaf of reports. 'Says here the St Albans patients claim nobody's in Ward T.'

Dimmock was shocked. That was untrue, he assured the general.

'All right, Dimmock. So you've got your twenty-four crocks in there. Their job's to get well. Your job's to cure them. What the hell's upsetting the hospital about that?'

'W-well, sir. Perhaps it's because we keep them locked up.'

'You keep Ward T locked?'

'Yes, sir.'

'Why?'

'To keep the patients in, General Carpenter.'

'Keep 'em in? What d'you mean? Are they trying to get out? They violent, or something?'

'No, sir. Not violent.'

'Dimmock, I don't like your attitude. You're acting damned sneaky and evasive. And I'll tell you something else I don't like. That T classification. I checked with a Filing Expert from the Medical Corps and there is no T classification. What the hell are you up to at St Albans?'

'W-well, sir ... We invented the T classification. It ... They ... They're rather special cases, sir. We don't know what to do about them or how to handle them. W-We've been trying to keep it quiet until we've worked out a modus operandi, but it's brand-new, General Carpenter. Brand-new!' Here the expert in Dimmock triumphed over discipline. 'It's sensational. It'll make medical history, by God! It's the biggest damned thing ever.'

'What is it, Dimmock? Be specific.'

'Well, sir, they're shock cases. Blanked out. Almost catatonic. Very little respiration. Slow pulse. No response.'

'I've seen thousands of shock cases like that,' Carpenter grunted. 'What's so unusual?'

'Yes, sir, so far it sounds like the standard Q or R classification. But here's something unusual. They don't eat and they don't sleep.'

'Never?'

'Some of them never.'

'Then why don't they die?'

'We don't know. The metabolism cycle's broken, but only on the anabolism side. Catabolism continues. In other words, sir, they're eliminating waste products but they're not taking anything in. They're eliminating fatigue poisons and rebuilding worn tissue, but without food and sleep. God knows how. It's fantastic.'

'That why you've got them locked up? Mean to say ... D'you suspect them of stealing food and cat naps somewhere else?'

'N-No, sir.' Dimmock looked shamefaced. 'I don't know how to tell you this, General Carpenter. I ... We lock them up because of the real mystery. They ... Well, they disappear.'

'They what?'

'They disappear, sir. Vanish. Right before your eyes.'

'The hell you say.'

'I do say, sir. They'll be sitting on a bed or standing around. One minute you see them, the next minute you don't. Sometimes there's two dozen in Ward T. Other times none. They disappear and reappear without rhyme or reason. That's why we've got the ward locked, General Carpenter. In the entire history of combat and combat injury there's never been a case like this before. We don't know how to handle it.'

'Bring me three of those cases,' General Carpenter said.

Nathan Riley ate French toast, eggs benedict; consumed two pints of brown ale, smoked a John Drew, belched delicately and arose from the breakfast table. He nodded quietly to Gentleman Jim Corbett, who broke off his conversation with Diamond Jim Brady to intercept him on the way to the cashier's desk.

'Who do you like for the pennant this year, Nat?' Gentleman Jim inquired.

'The Dodgers,' Nathan Riley answered.

'They've got no pitching.'

'They've got Snider and Furillo and Campanella. They'll take the pennant this year, Jim. I'll bet they take it earlier than any team ever did. By September 13. Make a note. See if I'm right.'

'You're always right, Nat,' Corbett said.

Riley smiled, paid his check, sauntered out into the street and caught a horsecar bound for Madison Square Garden. He got off at the corner of Fiftieth Street and Eighth Avenue and walked upstairs to a handbook office over a radio repair shop. The bookie glanced at him, produced an envelope and counted out fifteen thousand dollars.

'Rocky Marciano by a TKO over Roland La Starza in the eleventh,' he said. 'How the hell do you call them so accurate, Nat?'

'That's the way I make a living,' Riley smiled. 'Are you making book on the elections?'

'Eisenhower twelve to five. Stevenson – '

'Never mind Adlai.' Riley placed twenty thousand dollars on the counter. 'I'm backing Ike. Get this down for me.'

He left the handbook office and went to his suite in the Waldorf where a tall, thin young man was waiting for him anxiously.

'Oh yes,' Nathan Riley said. 'You're Ford, aren't you? Harold Ford?'

'Henry Ford, Mr Riley.'

'And you need financing for that machine in your bicycle shop. What's it called?'

'I call it an Ipsimobile, Mr Riley.'

'Hmmm. Can't say I like that name. Why not call it an automobile?'

'That's a wonderful suggestion, Mr Riley. I'll certainly take it.'

'I like you, Henry. You're young, eager, adaptable. I believe in your future and I believe in your automobile. I'll invest two hundred thousand dollars in your company.'

Riley wrote a cheque and ushered Henry Ford out. He glanced at his watch and suddenly felt impelled to go back and look around for a moment. He entered his bedroom, undressed, put on a grey shirt and grey slacks. Across the pocket of the shirt were large blue letters: U.S.A.H.

He locked the bedroom door and disappeared.

He reappeared in Ward T of the United States Army Hospital in St Albans, standing alongside his bed which was one of twenty-four lining the walls of a long, light steel barracks. Before he could draw another breath, he was seized by three pairs of hands. Before he could struggle, he was shot by a pneumatic syringe and poleaxed by $1\frac{1}{2}$ cc of sodium thiomorphate.

'We've got one,' someone said.

'Hang around,' someone else answered. 'General Carpenter said he wanted three.'

After Marcus Junius Brutus left her bed, Lela Machan clapped her hands. Her slave women entered the chamber and prepared her bath. She bathed, dressed, scented herself, and breakfasted on Smyrna figs, Rose oranges, and a flagon of Lachryma Christi. Then she smoked a cigarette and ordered her litter.

The gates of her house were crowded as usual by adoring hordes from the Twentieth Legion. Two centurions removed her chair-bearers from the poles of the litter and bore her on their stout shoulders. Lela Machan smiled. A young man in a sapphire-blue cloak thrust through the mob and ran towards her. A knife flashed in his hand. Lela braced herself to meet death bravely.

'Lady!' he cried. 'Lady Lela!'

He slashed his left arm with the knife and let the crimson blood stain her robe.

'This blood of mine is the least I have to give you,' he cried.

Lela touched his forehead gently.

'Silly boy,' she murmured. 'Why?'

'For love of you, my lady.'

'You will be admitted tonight at nine,' Lela whispered. He

stared at her until she laughed. 'I promise you. What is your name, pretty boy?'

'Ben Hur.'

'Tonight at nine, Ben Hur.'

The litter moved on. Outside the forum, Julius Caesar passed in hot argument with Savonarola. When he saw the litter he motioned sharply to the centurions, who stopped at once. Caesar swept back the curtains and stared at Lela, who regarded him languidly. Caesar's face twitched.

'Why?' he asked hoarsely. 'I have begged, pleaded, bribed, wept, and all without forgiveness. Why, Lela? Why?'

'Do you remember Boadicea?' Lela murmured.

'Boadicea? Queen of the Britons? Good God, Lela, what can she mean to our love? I did not love Boadicea. I merely defeated her in battle.'

'And killed her, Caesar.'

'She poisoned herself, Lela.'

'She was my mother, Caesar!' Suddenly Lela pointed her finger at Caesar. 'Murderer. You will be punished. Beware the Ides of March, Caesar!'

Caesar recoiled in horror. The mob of admirers that had gathered around Lela uttered a shout of approval. Amidst a shower of rose petals and violets she continued on her way across the Forum to the Temple of the Vestal Virgins where she abandoned her adoring suitors and entered the sacred temple.

Before the altar she genuflected, intoned a prayer, dropped a pinch of incense on the altar flame and disrobed. She examined her beautiful body reflected in a silver mirror, then experienced a momentary twinge of homesickness. She put on a grey blouse and a grey pair of slacks. Across the pocket of the blouse was lettered U.S.A.H.

She smiled once at the altar and disappeared.

She reappeared in Ward T of the United States Army Hospital where she was instantly felled by $1\frac{1}{2}$ cc of sodium thiomorphate injected subcutaneously by a pneumatic syringe.

'That's two,' somebody said.

'One more to go.'

George Hanmer paused dramatically and stared around ... at the opposition benches, at the Speaker on the woolsack, at the silver mace on a crimson cushion before the Speaker's chair. The entire House of Parliament, hypnotized by Hanmer's fiery oratory, waited breathlessly for him to continue.

'I can say no more,' Hanmer said at last. His voice was choked with emotion. His face was blanched and grim. 'I will fight for this bill at the beach-heads. I will fight in the cities, the towns, the fields and the hamlets. I will fight for this bill to the death and, God willing, I will fight for it after death. Whether this be a challenge or a prayer, let the consciences of the right honorable gentlemen determine; but of one thing I am sure and determined: England must own the Suez Canal.'

Hanmer sat down. The house exploded. Through the cheering and applause he made his way out into the division lobby where Gladstone, Churchill, and Pitt stopped him to shake his hand. Lord Palmerston eyed him coldly, but Pam was shouldered aside by Disraeli who limped up, all enthusiasm, all admiration.

'We'll have a bite at Tattersall's,' Dizzy said. 'My car's waiting.'

Lady Beaconsfield was in the Rolls-Royce outside the Houses of Parliament. She pinned a primrose on Dizzy's lapel and patted Hanmer's cheek affectionately.

'You've come a long way from the schoolboy who used to bully Dizzy, Georgie,' she said.

Hanmer laughed. Dizzy sang: *'Gaudeamus igitur ... '* and Hanmer chanted the ancient scholastic song until they reached Tattersall's. There Dizzy ordered Guinness and grilled bones while Hanmer went upstairs in the club to change.

For no reason at all he had the impulse to go back for a last look. Perhaps he hated to break with his past completely. He divested himself of his surtout, nankeen waistcoat, pepper and salt trousers, polished Hessians, and undergarments. He put on a grey shirt and grey trousers and disappeared.

He reappeared in Ward T of the St Albans hospital where he was rendered unconscious by $1\frac{1}{2}$ cc of sodium thiomorphate.

'That's three,' somebody said.

'Take 'em to Carpenter.'

So there they sat in General Carpenter's office, PFC Nathan Riley, M/Sgt Lela Machan, and Corp/2 George Hanmer. They were in their hospital greys. They were torpid with sodium thiomorphate.

The office had been cleared and it blazed with light. Present were experts from Espionage, Counter-Espionage, Security, and Central Intelligence. When Captain Edsel Dimmock saw the steel-faced ruthless squad awaiting the patients and himself, he started. General Carpenter smiled grimly.

'Didn't occur to you that we mightn't buy your disappearance story, eh Dimmock?'

'S-Sir?'

'I'm an expert too, Dimmock. I'll spell it out for you. The war's going badly. Very badly. There've been intelligence leaks. The St Albans mess might point to you.'

'B-But they do disappear, sir. I – '

'My experts want to talk to you and your patients about this disappearing act, Dimmock. They'll start with you.'

The experts worked over Dimmock with preconscious softeners, id releases and super-ego blocks. They tried every truth serum in the books and every form of physical and mental pressure. They brought Dimmock, squealing, to the breaking point three times, but there was nothing to break.

'Let him stew for now,' Carpenter said. 'Get on to the patients.'

The experts appeared reluctant to apply pressure to the sick men and the woman.

'For God's sake, don't be squeamish,' Carpenter raged. 'We're fighting a war for civilization. We've got to protect our ideals no matter what the price. Get to it!'

The experts from Espionage, Counter-Espionage, Security and Central Intelligence got to it. Like three candles, PFC Nathan Riley, M/Sgt Lela Machan and Corp/2 George Hanmer snuffed out and disappeared. One moment they were seated in chairs surrounded by violence. The next moment they were not.

The experts gasped. General Carpenter did the handsome thing. He stalked to Dimmock. 'Captain Dimmock, I apologize. Colonel Dimmock, you've been promoted for making an important discovery ... only what the hell does it mean? We've got to check ourselves first.'

Carpenter snapped up the intercom. 'Get me a combat-shock expert and an alienist.'

The two experts entered and were briefed. They examined the witnesses. They considered.

'You're all suffering from a mild case of shock,' the combat-shock expert said. 'War jitters.'

'You mean we didn't see them disappear?'

The shock expert shook his head and glanced at the alienist who also shook his head.

'Mass illusion,' the alienist said.

At that moment PFC Riley, M/Sgt Machan and Corp/2 Hanmer reappeared. One moment they were a mass illusion; the next, they were back sitting in their chairs surrounded by confusion.

'Dope 'em again, Dimmock,' Carpenter cried. 'Give 'em a gallon.' He snapped up his intercom. 'I want every expert we've got. Emergency meeting in my office at once.'

Thirty-seven experts, hardened and sharpened tools all, inspected the unconscious shock cases and discussed them for three hours. Certain facts were obvious: This must be a new fantastic syndrome brought on by the new and fantastic horrors of the war. As combat technique develops, the response of victims of this technique must also take new roads. For every action there is an equal and opposite reaction. Agreed.

This new syndrome must involve some aspects of teleportation ... the power of mind over space. Evidently combat shock, while destroying certain known powers of the mind must develop other latent powers hitherto unknown. Agreed.

Obviously, the patients must only be able to return to the point of departure, otherwise they would not continue to return to Ward T, nor would they have returned to General Carpenter's office. Agreed.

Obviously, the patients must be able to procure food and

sleep wherever they go, since neither was required in Ward T. Agreed.

'One small point,' Colonel Dimmock said. 'They seem to be returning to Ward T less frequently. In the beginning they would come and go every day or so. Now most of them stay away for weeks and hardly ever return.'

'Never mind that,' Carpenter said. 'Where do they go?'

'Do they teleport behind the enemy lines?' someone asked. 'There's those intelligence leaks.'

'I want Intelligence to check,' Carpenter snapped. 'Is the enemy having similar difficulties with, say, prisoners of war who appear and disappear from their POW camps? They might be some of ours from Ward T.'

'They might simply be going home,' Colonel Dimmock suggested.

'I want Security to check,' Carpenter ordered. 'Cover the home life and associations of every one of those twenty-four disappearers. Now . . . about our operations in Ward T. Colonel Dimmock has a plan.'

'We'll set up six extra beds in Ward T,' Edsel Dimmock explained. 'We'll send in six experts to live there and observe. Information must be picked up indirectly from the patients. They're catatonic and nonresponsive when conscious, and incapable of answering questions when drugged.'

'Gentlemen,' Carpenter summed it up. 'This is the greatest potential weapon in the history of warfare. I don't have to tell you what it can mean to us to be able to teleport an entire army behind enemy lines. We can win the war for the American Dream in one day if we can win this secret hidden in those shattered minds. We must win!'

The experts hustled, Security checked, Intelligence probed. Six hardened and sharpened tools moved into Ward T in St Albans Hospital and slowly got acquainted with the disappearing patients who reappeared less and less frequently. The tension increased.

Security was able to report that not one case of strange appearance had taken place in America in the past year.

Intelligence reported that the enemy did not seem to be having similar difficulties with their own shock cases or with POWS.

Carpenter fretted. 'This is all brand new. We've got no specialists to handle it. We've got to develop new tools.' He snapped up his intercom. 'Get me a college,' he said.

They got him Yale.

'I want some experts in mind over matter. Develop them,' Carpenter ordered. Yale at once introduced three graduate courses in Thaumaturgy, Extra-sensory Perception, and Tele-kinesis.

The first break came when one of the Ward T experts re-quested the assistance of another expert. He needed a Lapidary.

'What the hell for?' Carpenter wanted to know.

'He picked up a reference to a gem stone,' Colonel Dimmock explained. 'He's a personnel specialist and he can't relate it to anything in his experience.'

'And he's not supposed to,' Carpenter said approvingly. 'A job for every man and every man on the job.' He flipped up the intercom. 'Get me a Lapidary.'

An expert Lapidary was given leave of absence from the army arsenal and asked to identify a type of diamond called Jim Brady. He could not.

'We'll try it from another angle,' Carpenter said. He snapped up his intercom. 'Get me a Semanticist.'

The Semanticist left his desk in the War Propaganda Depart-ment but could make nothing of the words Jim Brady. They were names to him. No more. He suggested a Genealogist.

A Genealogist was given one day's leave from his post with the Un-American Ancestors Committee but could make nothing of the name Brady beyond the fact that it had been a common name in America for five hundred years. He suggested an Archaeologist.

An Archaeologist was released from the Cartography Divi-sion of Invasion Command and instantly identified the name Diamond Jim Brady. It was a historic personage who had been famous in the city of Little Old New York some time between Governor Peter Stuyvesant and Governor Fiorello La Guardia.

'Christ!' Carpenter marvelled. 'That's ages ago. Where the

hell did Nathan Riley get that? You'd better join the experts in Ward T and follow this up.'

The Archaeologist followed it up, checked his references and sent in his report. Carpenter read it and was stunned. He called an emergency meeting of his staff of experts.

'Gentlemen,' he announced, 'Ward T is something bigger than teleportation. Those shock patients are doing something far more incredible . . . far more meaningful. Gentlemen, they're travelling through time.'

The staff rustled uncertainly. Carpenter nodded emphatically.

'Yes, gentlemen. Time travel is here. It has not arrived the way we expected it . . . as a result of expert research by qualified specialists; it has come as a plague . . . an infection . . . a disease of the war . . . a result of combat injury to ordinary men. Before I continue, look through these reports for documentation.'

The staff read the stencilled sheets. PFC Nathan Riley . . . disappearing into the early twentieth century in New York; M/Sgt Lela Machan . . . visiting the first century in Rome; Corp/2 George Hanmer . . . journeying into the nineteenth century in England. And all the rest of the twenty-four patients, escaping the turmoil and horrors of modern war in the twenty-second century by fleeing to Venice and the Doges, to Jamaica and the buccaneers, to China and the Han Dynasty, to Norway and Eric the Red, to any place and any time in the world.

'I needn't point out the colossal significance of this discovery,' General Carpenter pointed out. 'Think what it would mean to the war if we could send an army back in time a week or a month or a year. We could win the war before it started. We could protect our Dream . . . Poetry and Beauty and the Culture of America . . . from barbarism without ever endangering it.'

The staff tried to grapple with the problem of winning battles before they started.

'The situation is complicated by the fact that these men and women of Ward T are *non compos*. They may or may not know how they do what they do, but in any case they're incapable of communicating with the experts who could reduce this

27

miracle to method. It's for us to find the key. They can't help us.'

The hardened and sharpened specialists looked around uncertainly.

'We'll need experts,' General Carpenter said.

The staff relaxed. They were on familiar ground again.

'We'll need a Cerebral Mechanist, a Cyberneticist, a Psychiatrist, an Anatomist, an Archaeologist, and a first-rate Historian. They'll go into that world and they won't come out until their job is done. They must learn the technique of time travel.'

The first five experts were easy to draft from other war departments. All America was a tool chest of hardened and sharpened specialists. But there was trouble locating a first-class Historian until the Federal Penitentiary cooperated with the army and released Dr Bradley Scrim from his twenty years at hard labour. Dr Scrim was acid and jagged. He had held the chair of Philosophic History at a Western university until he spoke his mind about the war for the American Dream. That got him the twenty years hard.

Scrim was still intransigent, but induced to play ball by the intriguing problem of Ward T.

'But I'm not an expert,' he snapped. 'In this benighted nation of experts, I'm the last singing grasshopper in the ant heap.'

Carpenter snapped up the intercom. 'Get me an Entomologist,' he said.

'Don't bother,' Scrim said. 'I'll translate. You're a nest of ants ... all working and toiling and specializing. For what?'

'To preserve the American Dream,' Carpenter answered hotly. 'We're fighting for Poetry and Culture and Education and the Finer Things in Life.'

'Which means you're fighting to preserve me,' Scrim said. 'That's what I've devoted my life to. And what do you do with me? Put me in jail.'

'You were convicted of enemy sympathizing and fellow-travelling,' Carpenter said.

'I was convicted of believing in *my* American Dream,' Scrim said. 'Which is another way of saying I was jailed for having a mind of my own.'

Scrim was also intransigent in Ward T. He stayed one night, enjoyed three good meals, read the reports, threw them down and began hollering to be let out.

'There's a job for everyone and everyone must be on the job,' Colonel Dimmock told him. 'You don't come out until you've got the secret of time travel.'

'There's no secret I can get,' Scrim said.

'Do they travel in time?'

'Yes and no.'

'The answer has to be one or the other. Not both. You're evading the –'

'Look,' Scrim interrupted wearily. 'What are you an expert in?'

'Psychotherapy.'

'Then how the hell can you understand what I'm talking about? This is a philosophic concept. I tell you there's no secret here that the army can use. There's no secret any group can use. It's a secret for individuals only.'

'I don't understand you.'

'I didn't think you would. Take me to Carpenter.'

They took Scrim to Carpenter's office where he grinned at the general malignantly, looking for all the world like a red-headed, underfed devil.

'I'll need ten minutes,' Scrim said. 'Can you spare them out of your tool box?'

Carpenter nodded.

'Now listen carefully. I'm going to give you the clues to something so vast and so strange that it will need all your fine edge to cut into it.'

Carpenter looked expectant.

'Nathan Riley goes back in time to the early twentieth century. There he lives the life of his fondest dreams. He's a big-time gambler, the friend of Diamond Jim Brady and others. He wins money betting on events because he always knows the outcome in advance. He won money betting on Eisenhower to win an election. He won money betting on a prize fighter

29

named Marciano to beat another prize fighter named La Starza. He made money investing in an automobile company owned by Henry Ford. There are the clues. They mean anything to you?'

'Not without a Sociological Analyst,' Carpenter answered. He reached for the intercom.

'Don't order one, I'll explain later. Let's try some more clues. Lela Machan, for example. She escapes into the Roman Empire where she lives the life of her dreams as a *femme fatale*. Every man loves her. Julius Caesar, Savonarola, the entire Twentieth Legion, a man named Ben Hur. Do you see the fallacy?'

'No.'

'She also smokes cigarettes.'

'Well?' Carpenter asked after a pause.

'I continue,' Scrim said. 'George Hanmer escapes into England of the nineteenth century where he's a member of Parliament and the friend of Gladstone, Winston Churchill, and Disraeli, who takes him riding in his Rolls-Royce. Do you know what a Rolls-Royce is?'

'No.'

'It was the name of an automobile.'

'So?'

'You don't understand yet?'

'No.'

Scrim paced the floor in exaltation. 'Carpenter, this is a bigger discovery than teleportation or time travel. This can be the salvation of man. I don't think I'm exaggerating. Those two dozen shock victims in Ward T have been H-Bombed into something so gigantic that it's no wonder your specialists and experts can't understand it.'

'What the hell's bigger than time travel, Scrim?'

'Listen to this, Carpenter. Eisenhower did not run for office until the middle of the twentieth century. Nathan Riley could not have been a friend of Diamond Jim Brady's and bet on Eisenhower to win an election ... not simultaneously. Brady was dead a quarter of a century before Ike was President. Marciano defeated La Starza fifty years after Henry Ford started his automobile company. Nathan Riley's time travelling is full of similar anachronisms.'

Carpenter looked puzzled.

'Lela Machan could not have had Ben Hur for a lover. Ben Hur never existed in Rome. He never existed at all. He was a character in a novel. She couldn't have smoked. They didn't have tobacco then. You see? More anachronisms. Disraeli could never have taken George Hanmer for a ride in a Rolls-Royce because automobiles weren't invented until long after Disraeli's death.'

'The hell you say,' Carpenter exclaimed. 'You mean they're all lying?'

'No. Don't forget, they don't need sleep. They don't need food. They're not lying. They're going back in time all right. They're eating and sleeping back there.'

'But you just said their stories don't stand up. They're full of anachronisms.'

'Because they travel back into a time of their own imagination. Nathan Riley has his own picture of what America was like in the early twentieth century. It's faulty and anachronistic because he's no scholar, but it's real for him. He can live there. The same is true for the others.'

Carpenter goggled.

'The concept is almost beyond understanding. These people have discovered how to turn dreams into reality. They know how to enter their dream realities. They can stay there, live there, perhaps forever. My God, Carpenter, *this* is your American dream. It's miracle-working, immortality, Godlike creation, mind over matter ... It must be explored. It must be studied. It must be given to the world.'

'Can you do it, Scrim?'

'No, I cannot. I'm a historian. I'm non-creative, so it's beyond me. You need a poet ... an artist who understands the creation of dreams. From creating dreams on paper it oughtn't to be too difficult to take the step to creating dreams in actuality.'

'A poet? Are you serious?'

'Certainly I'm serious. Don't you know what a poet is?

31

You've been telling us for five years that this war is being fought to save the poets.'

'Don't be facetious, Scrim, I – '

'Send a poet into Ward T. He'll learn how they do it. He's the only man who can. A poet is half doing it anyway. Once he learns, he can teach your psychologists and anatomists. Then they can teach us; but the poet is the only man who can interpret between those shock cases and your experts.'

'I believe you're right, Scrim.'

'Then don't delay, Carpenter. Those patients are returning to this world less and less frequently. We've got to get at that secret before they disappear forever. Send a poet to Ward T.'

Carpenter snapped up his intercom. 'Send me a poet,' he said.

He waited, and waited ... and waited ... while America sorted feverishly through its two hundred and ninety millions of hardened and sharpened experts, its specialized tools to defend the American Dream of Beauty and Poetry and the Better Things in Life. He waited for them to find a poet, not understanding the endless delay, the fruitless search; not understanding why Bradley Scrim laughed and laughed and laughed at this final, fatal disappearance.

Frederik Pohl

The Wizards of Pung's Corners

I

This is the way it happened in the old days. Pay attention now. I'm not going to repeat myself.

There was this old man. A wicked one. Coglan was his name, and he came into Pung's Corners in a solid-lead car. He was six feet seven inches tall. He attracted a lot of attention.

Why? Why, because nobody had ever seen a solid-lead car before. Nobody much had ever seen a stranger. It wasn't usual. That was how Pung's Corners was in the old days, a little pocket in the middle of the desert, and nobody came there. There weren't even planes overhead, or not for a long time; but there had been planes just before old man Coglan showed up. It made people nervous.

Old man Coglan had snapping black eyes and a loose and limber step. He got out of his car and slammed the door closed. It didn't go *tchik* like a Volkswagen or *perclack* like a Buick. It went woomp. It was heavy, since, as I mentioned, it was solid lead.

'Boy!' he bellowed, standing in front of Pung's Inn. 'Come get my bags!'

Charley Frink was the bell-boy at that time – yes, the Senator. Of course, he was only fifteen years old then. He came out for Coglan's bags and he had to make four trips. There was a lot of space in the back of that car, with its truck tyres and double-thick glass, and all of it was full of baggage.

While Charley was hustling the bags in, Coglan was parading back and forth on Front Street. He winked at Mrs Churchwood and ogled young Kathy Flint. He nodded to the boys in front

33

of the barber shop. He was a character, making himself at home like that.

In front of Andy Grammis's grocery store, Andy tipped his chair back. Considerately, he moved his feet so his yellow dog could get out the door. 'He seems like a nice feller,' he said to Jack Tighe. (Yes, *that* Jack Tighe.)

Jack Tighe stood in the shelter of the door and he was frowning. He knew more than any of the rest of them, though it wasn't time to say anything yet. But he said: 'We don't get any strangers.'

Andy shrugged. He leaned back in his chair. It was warm in the sun.

'Pshaw, Jack,' he said. 'Maybe we ought to get a few more. Town's going to sleep.' He yawned drowsily.

And Jack Tighe left him there, left him and started down the street for home, because he knew what he knew.

Anyway, Coglan didn't hear them. If he had heard, he wouldn't have cared. It was old man Coglan's great talent that he didn't care what people had to say about him, and the others like him. He couldn't have been what he was if that hadn't been so.

So he checked in at Pung's Inn. 'A suite, boy!' he boomed. 'The best. A place where I can be comfortable, *real* comfortable.'

'Yes, sir, Mister – '

'Coglan, boy! Edsel T. Coglan. A proud name at both ends, and I'm proud to wear it!'

'Yes, *sir*, Mr Coglan. Right away. Now let's see.' He pored over his room ledgers, although, except for the Willmans and Mr Carpenter when his wife got mad at him, there weren't any guests, as he certainly knew. He pursed his lips. He said: 'Ah, good! The bridal suite's vacant, Mr Coglan. I'm sure you'll be very comfortable there. Of course, it's eight-fifty a day.'

'The bridal suite it is, boy!' Coglan chucked the pen into its holder with a fencer's thrust. He grinned like a fine old Bengal tiger with white crew-cut hair.

And there was something to grin about, in a way, wasn't there? The bridal suite. That was funny.

Hardly anybody ever took the bridal suite at Pung's Inn,

34

unless they had a bride. You only had to look at Coglan to know that he was a long way from taking a bride – a long way, and in the wrong direction. Tall as he was, snapping-eyed and straight-backed as he was, he was clearly on the far side of marrying. He was at least eighty. You could see it in his creepy skin and his gnarled hands.

The room clerk whistled for Charley Frink. 'Glad to have you with us, Mr Coglan,' he said. 'Charley'll have your bags up in a jiffy. Will you be staying with us long?'

Coglan laughed out loud. It was the laugh of a relaxed and confident man. 'Yes,' he said. 'Quite long.'

Now what did Coglan do when he was all alone in the bridal suite?

Well, first he paid off the bell-boy with a ten dollar bill. That surprised Charley Frink, all right. He wasn't used to that kind of tipping. He went out and Coglan closed the door behind him in a very great good humour.

Coglan was happy.

So he peered around, grinning a wolf's grin. He looked at the bathroom, with its stall shower and bright white porcelain. 'Quaint,' he murmured. He amused himself with the electric lights, switching them on and off. 'Delicious,' he said. 'So *manual*.' In the living-room of the suite, the main light was from an overhead six-point chandelier, best Grand Rapids glass. Two of the pendants were missing. 'Ridiculous,' chuckled old Mr Coglan, 'but very, very sweet.'

Of course, you know what he was thinking. He was thinking of the big caverns and the big machines. He was thinking of the design wobblators and the bomb-shielded power sources, the self-contained raw material lodes and the unitized distribution pipelines. But I'm getting ahead of the story. It isn't time to talk about those things yet. So don't ask.

Anyway, after old man Coglan had a good look around, he opened one of his bags.

He sat down in front of the desk.

He took a Kleenex out of his pocket and with a fastidious expression picked up the blotter with it, and dumped it on the floor.

He lifted the bag on to the bare desk top and propped it, open, against the wall.

You never saw a bag like that! It looked like a kind of electronic tool kit, I swear. Its back was a panel of pastel lucite with sparks embedded in it. It glittered. There was a cathode screen. There was a scanner, a microphone, a speaker. All those things and lots more. How do I know this? Why, it's all written down in a book called *My Eighteen Years at Pung's Hall*, by Senator C. T. Frink. Because Charley was in the room next door and there was a keyhole.

So then what happened was that a little tinkly chime sounded distantly within the speaker, and the cathode screen flickered and lit up.

'Coglan,' boomed the tall old man. 'Reporting in. Let me speak to V. P. Maffity.'

2

Now you have to know what Pung's Corners was like in those days.

Everybody knows what it is now, but then it was small. Very small. It sat on the bank of the Delaware River like a fat old lady on the edge of a spindly chair.

General 'Retreating Johnnie' Estabrook wintered there before the Battle of Monmouth and wrote pettishly to General Washington: 'I can obtain no Provision here, as the inhabitants are so averse to our Cause, that I cannot get a Man to come near me.'

During the Civil War, a small draft riot took place in its main square, in which a recruiting colonel of the IXth Volunteer Pennsylvania Zouaves was chased out of town and the son of the town's leading banker suffered superficial scalp wounds. (He fell off his horse. He was drunk.)

These were only little wars, you know. They had left only little scars.

Pung's Corners missed all the big ones.

For instance, when the biggest of all got going, why, Pung's

Corners had a ticket on the fifty-yard line but never had to carry the ball.

The cobalt bomb that annihilated New Jersey stopped short at the bank of the Delaware, checked by a persistent easterly wind.

The radio-dust that demolished Philadelphia went forty-some miles up the river. Then the drone that was spreading it was rammed down by a suicide pilot in a shaky jet. (Pung's Corners was one mile farther on.)

The H-bombs that scattered around the New York megalopolis bracketed Pung's Corners, but it lay unscathed between.

You see how it was? They never laid a glove on us. But after the war, we were marooned.

Now that wasn't a bad way to be, you know? Read some of the old books, you'll see. The way Pung's Corners felt, there was a lot to be said for being marooned. People in Pung's Corners were genuinely sorry about the war, with so many people getting killed and all. (Although we won it. It was worse for the other side.) But every cloud has its silver lining and so on, and being surrounded at every point of the compass by badlands that no one could cross had a few compensating features.

There was a Nike battalion in Pung's Corners, and they say they shot down the first couple of helicopters that tried to land because they thought they were the enemy. Maybe they did. But along about the fifth copter, they didn't think that any more, I guarantee. And then the planes stopped coming. Outside, they had plenty to think about, I suppose. They stopped bothering with Pung's Corners.

Until Mr Coglan came in.

After Coglan got his line of communication opened up – because that was what the big suitcase was, a TV communications set – he talked for a little while. Charley had a red dent on his forehead for two days, he pressed against the doorknob so hard, trying to see.

'Mr Maffity?' boomed Coglan, and a pretty girl's face lighted up on the screen.

'This is Vice President Maffity's secretary,' she said sweetly. 'I see you arrived safely. One moment, please, for Mr Maffity.'

And then the set flickered and another face showed up, the blood brother to Coglan's own. It was the face of an elderly and successful man who recognized no obstacles, the face of a man who knew what he wanted and got it. 'Coglan, boy! Good to see you got there!'

'No sweat, L.S.,' said Coglan. 'I'm just about to secure my logistics. Money. This is going to take money.'

'No trouble?'

'No trouble, Chief. I can promise you that. There isn't *going* to be any trouble.' He grinned and picked up a nested set of little metallic boxes out of a pouch in the suitcase. He opened one, shook out a small disc-shaped object, silver and scarlet plastic. 'I'm using this right away.'

'And the reservoir?'

'I haven't checked yet, Chief. But the pilots said they dumped the stuff in. No opposition from the ground either, did you notice that? These people used to shoot down every plane that came near. They're softening. They're ripe.'

'Good enough,' said L. S. Maffity from the little cathode screen. 'Make it so, Coglan. Make it so.'

Now, at the Shawanganunk National Bank, Mr LaFarge saw Coglan come in and knew right away something was up.

How do I know that? Why, that's in a book too. *The Federal Budget and How I Balanced It: A Study in Surplus Dynamics,* by Treasury Secretary (Retired) Wilbur Otis LaFarge. Most everything is in a book, if you know where to look for it. That's something you young people have got to learn.

Anyway, Mr LaFarge, who was then only an Assistant Vice-President, greeted old man Coglan effusively. It was his way. 'Morning, sir!' he said. 'Morning! In what way can we serve you here at the bank?'

'We'll find a way,' promised Mr Coglan.

'Of course, sir. Of course!' Mr LaFarge rubbed his hands. 'You'll want a checking account. Certainly! And a savings account? And a safety deposit box? Absolutely! Christmas

Club, I suppose. Perhaps a short-term auto loan, or a chattel loan on your household effects for the purpose of consolidating debts and reducing – '

'Don't have any debts,' said Coglan. 'Look, what's-your-name – '

'LaFarge, sir! Wilbur LaFarge. Call me Will.'

'Look, Willie. Here are my credit references.' And he spilled a manila envelope out on the desk in front of LaFarge.

The banker looked at the papers and frowned. He picked one up. 'Letter of credit,' he said. 'Some time since I saw one of those. From Danbury, Connecticut, eh?' He shook his head and pouted. 'All from outside, sir.'

'I'm from outside.'

'I see.' LaFarge sighed heavily after a second. 'Well, sir, I don't know. What is it you wanted?'

'What I want is a quarter of a million dollars, Willie. In cash. And make it snappy, will you?'

Mr LaFarge blinked.

You don't know him, of course. He was before your time. You don't know what a request like that would do to him.

When I say he blinked, I mean, man, he *blinked*. Then he blinked again and it seemed to calm him. For a moment, the veins had begun to stand out in his temples; for a moment, his mouth was open to speak. But he closed his mouth and the veins receded.

Because, you see, old man Coglan took that silvery scarlet thing out of his pocket. It glittered. He gave it a twist and he gave it a certain kind of squeeze, and it hummed, a deep and throbbing note. But it didn't satisfy Mr Coglan.

'Wait a minute,' he said, offhandedly, and he adjusted it and squeezed it again. 'That's better,' he said.

The note was deeper, but still not quite deep enough to suit Coglan. He twisted the top a fraction more, until the pulsing note was too deep to be heard, and then he nodded.

There was silence for a second.

Then: 'Large bills?' cried Mr LaFarge. 'Or small?' He leaped up and waved to a cashier. 'Two hundred and fifty thousand dollars! You there, Tom Fairleigh! Hurry it up now. What?

39

No, I don't care where you get it. Go out to the vault, if there isn't enough in the cages. But bring me two hundred and fifty thousand dollars!'

He sank down at his desk again, panting. 'I am really sorry, sir,' he apologized to Mr Coglan. 'The clerks you get these days! I almost wish that old times would come back.'

'Perhaps they will, friend,' said Coglan, grinning widely to himself. 'Now,' he said, not unkindly, 'shut up.'

He waited, tapping the desk top, humming to himself, staring at the blank wall. He completely ignored Mr LaFarge until Tom Fairleigh and another teller brought four canvas sacks of bills. They began to dump them on the desk to count them.

'No, don't bother,' said Coglan cheerfully, his black eyes snapping with good humour. 'I trust you.' He picked up the sacks, nodded courteously to Mr LaFarge, and walked out.

Ten seconds later, Mr LaFarge suddenly shook his head, rubbed his eyes and stared at the two tellers. 'What –'

'You just gave him a quarter of a million dollars,' said Tom Fairleigh. 'You made me get it out of the vault.'

'I *did?*'

'You did.'

They looked at each other.

Mr LaFarge said at last: 'It's been a long time since we had any of *that* in Pung's Corners.'

3

Now I have to tell a part that isn't so nice. It's about a girl named Marlene Groshawk. I positively will not explain any part of it. I probably shouldn't mention it at all, but it's part of the history of our country. Still –

Well, this is what happened. Yes, it's in a book too – *On Call*, by One Who Knows. (And we know who 'One Who Knows' is, don't we?)

She wasn't a bad girl. Not a bit of it. Or, anyway, she didn't mean to be. She was too pretty for her own good and not very smart. What she wanted out of life was to be a television star.

Well, that was out of the question, of course. We didn't use live television at all in Pung's Corners those days, only a few old tapes. They left the commercials in, although the goods the old, dead announcers were trying to sell were not on the market anywhere, much less in Pung's Corners. And Marlene's idol was a TV saleslady named Betty Furness. Marlene had pictures of her, dubbed off the tapes, pasted all over the walls of her room.

At the time I'm talking about, Marlene called herself a public stenographer. There wasn't too much demand for her services. (And later on, after things opened up, she gave up that part of her business entirely.) But if anybody needed a little extra help in Pung's Corners, like writing some letters or getting caught up on the back filing and such, they'd call on Marlene. She'd never worked for a stranger before.

She was rather pleased when the desk clerk told her that there was this new Mr Coglan in town, and that he needed an assistant to help him run some new project he was up to. She didn't know what the project was, but I have to tell you that if she knew, she would have helped anyhow. Any budding TV star, of course.

She stopped in the lobby of Pung's Inn to adjust her make-up. Charley Frink looked at her with that kind of a look, in spite of being only fifteen. She sniffed at him, tossed her head, and proudly went upstairs.

She tapped on the carved oak door of Suite 41 – that was the bridal suite; she knew it well – and smiled prettily for the tall old man with snapping eyes who swung it open.

'Mr Coglan? I'm Miss Groshawk, the public stenographer. I understand you sent for me.'

The old man looked at her piercingly for a moment.

'Yes,' he said, 'I did. Come in.'

He turned his back on her and let her come in and close the door by herself.

Coglan was busy. He had the suite's television set in pieces all over the floor.

He was trying to fix it some way or another, Marlene judged. And that was odd, mused Marlene in her cloudy young way, because even if she wasn't really *brainy*, she knew that he was no television repairman, or anything like that. She knew exactly what he was. It said so on his card, and Mr LaFarge had shown the card around town. He was a research and development counsellor.

Whatever *that* was.

Marlene was conscientious, and she knew that a good public stenographer took her temporary employer's work to heart. She said: 'Something wrong, Mr Coglan?'

He looked up, irritably. 'I can't get Danbury on this thing.'

'Danbury, Connecticut? Outside? No, sir. It isn't supposed to get Danbury.'

He straightened up and looked at her. 'It isn't supposed to get Danbury.' He nodded thoughtfully. 'This forty-eight-inch twenty-seven tube full-colour suppressed sideband UHF-VHF General Electric wall model with static suppressors and self-compensating tuning strips, it isn't supposed to get Danbury, Connecticut.'

'That's right, sir.'

'Well,' he said, 'that's going to be a big laugh on the cavern in Schenectady.'

Marlene said helpfully: 'It hasn't got any antenna.'

Coglan frowned and corrected her. 'No, that's impossible. It's got to have an antenna. These leads go somewhere.'

Marlene shrugged attractively.

He said: 'Right after the war, of course, you couldn't get Danbury at all. I agree. Not with all those fission products, eh? But that's down to a negligible count now. Danbury should come in loud and clear.'

Marlene said: 'No, it was after that. I used to, uh, date a fellow named Timmy Horan, and he was in that line of business, making television repairs, I mean. A couple years after the war, I was just a kid, they began to get pictures once in a while. Well, they passed a law, Mr Coglan.'

'A *law*?' His face looked suddenly harsh.

'Well, I think they did. Anyway, Timmy had to go around taking the antennas off all the sets. He really did. Then they hooked them up with TV tape recorders, like.' She thought hard for a second. 'He didn't tell me why,' she volunteered.

'I know why,' he said flatly.

'So it only plays records, Mr Coglan. But if there's anything you want, the desk clerk'll get it for you. He's got lots. Dinah Shores and Jackie Gleasons and *Medic*. Oh, and Westerns. You tell him what you want.'

'I see.' Coglan stood there for a second, thinking. Not to her but to himself, he said: 'No wonder we weren't getting through. Well, we'll see about that.'

'What, Mr Coglan?'

'Never mind, Miss Groshawk. I see the picture now. And it isn't a very pretty one.'

He went back to the television set.

He wasn't a TV mechanic, no, but he knew a little something about what he was doing for sure, because he had it all back together in a minute. Oh, less than that. And not just the way it was. He had it improved. Even Marlene could see that. Maybe not *improved*, but different; he'd done something to it.

'Better?' he demanded, looking at her.

'I beg your pardon?'

'I mean does looking at the picture do anything to you?'

'I'm sorry, Mr Coglan, but I honestly don't care for *Studio One*. It makes me think too hard, you know?'

But she obediently watched the set.

He had tuned in on the recorded wire signal that went out to all of Pung's Corners TV sets. I don't suppose you know how we did it then, but there was a central station where they ran off a show all the time, for people who didn't want to bother with tapes. It was all old stuff, of course. And everybody had seen all of them already.

But Marlene watched, and funnily, in a moment she began to giggle.

'Why, Mr *Coglan*,' she said, though he hadn't done anything at all.

'Better,' he said, and he was satisfied.

He had every reason to be.

'However,' said Mr Coglan, 'first things come first. I need your help.'

'All right, Mr Coglan,' Marlene said in a silky voice.

'I mean in a business way. I want to hire some people. I

want you to help me locate them, and to keep the records straight. Then I shall need to buy certain materials. And I'll need an office, perhaps a few buildings for light industrial purposes, and so on.'

'That will take a lot of money, won't it?'

Coglan chuckled.

'Well, then,' said Marlene, satisfied, 'I'm your girl, Mr Coglan. I mean in a business way. Would you mind telling me what the business is?'

'I intend to put Pung's Corners back on its feet.'

'Oh, sure, Mr Coglan. But how, I mean?'

'Advertising,' said old man Coglan, with a devil's smile and a demon's voice.

Silence. There was a moment of silence.

Marlene said faintly: 'I don't think they're going to like it.'

'Who?'

'The bigwigs. They aren't going to like that. Not advertising, you know. I mean I'm for *you*. I'm in favour of advertising. I *like* it. But –'

'There's no question of liking it!' Coglan said in a terrible voice. 'It's what has made our country great! It tooled us up to fight in a great war, and when the war was over, it put us back together again!'

'I understand that, Mr Coglan,' she said. 'But –'

'I don't want to hear that word from you, Miss Groshawk,' he snapped. 'There is no question. Consider America after the war, ah? You don't remember, perhaps. They kept it from you. But the cities all were demolished. The buildings were ruins. It was only advertising that built them up again – advertising, and the power of research! For I remind you of what a great man once said: "Our chief job in research is to keep the customer reasonably dissatisfied with what he has." '

Coglan paused, visibly affected. 'That was Charles F. Kettering of General Motors,' he said, 'and the beauty of it, Miss Groshawk, is that he said this in the Twenties! Imagine! So clear a perception of what Science means to all of us. So comprehensive a grasp of the meaning of American Inventiveness!'

Marlene said brokenly: 'That's beautiful.'

Coglan nodded. 'Of course. So, you see, there is nothing at all that your bigwigs can do, like it or not. We Americans – we *real* Americans – know that without advertising there is no industry; and accordingly we have shaped advertising into a tool that serves us well. Why, here, look at that television set!'

Marlene did, and in a moment began again to giggle. Archly she whispered: 'Mr. Coglan!'

'You see? And if that doesn't suffice, well, there's always the law. Let's see what the bigwigs of Pung's Corners can do against the massed might of the United States Army!'

'I do hope there won't be any fighting, Mr Coglan.'

'I doubt there will,' he said sincerely. 'And now to work, eh? Or – ' he glanced at his watch and nodded – 'after all, there's no real hurry this afternoon. Suppose we order some dinner, just for the two of us. And some wine? And – '

'Of course, Mr Coglan.'

Marlene started to go to the telephone, but Mr Coglan stopped her. 'On second thought, Miss Groshawk,' he said, beginning to breathe a little hard, 'I'll do the ordering. You just sit there and rest for a minute. Watch the television set, eh?'

4

Now I have to tell you about Jack Tighe.

Yes, indeed. Jack Tighe. The Father of the Second Republic. Sit tight and listen and don't interrupt, because what I have to tell you isn't exactly what you learned in school.

The apple tree? No, that's only a story. It couldn't have happened, you see, because apple trees don't grow on upper Madison Avenue, and that's where Jack Tighe spent his youth. Because Jack Tighe wasn't the President of the Second Republic. For a long time, he was something else, something called V.P. in charge of S.L. division, of the advertising firm of Yust and Ruminant.

That's right. Advertising.

Don't cry. It's all right. He'd given it up, you see, long before – oh, *long* before, even before the big war; given it up and come to Pung's Corners, to retire.

Jack Tighe had his place out on the marshland down at the bend of the Delaware River. It wasn't particularly healthy there. All the highlands around Pung's Corners drained into the creeks of that part of the area, and a lot of radio-activity had come down. But it didn't bother Jack Tighe, because he was too old.

He was as old as old man Coglan, in fact. And what's more, they had known each other, back at the agency.

Jack Tighe was also big, not as big as Coglan but well over six feet. And in a way he looked like Coglan. You've seen his pictures. Same eyes, same devil-may-care bounce to his walk and snap to his voice. He could have been a big man in Pung's Corners. They would have made him mayor any time. But he said he'd come there to retire, and retire he would; it would take a major upheaval to make him come out of retirement, he said.

And he got one.

The first thing was Andy Grammis, white as a sheet.

'Jack!' he whispered, out of breath at the porch steps, for he'd run almost all the way from his store.

Jack Tighe took his feet down off the porch rail. 'Sit down, Andy,' he said kindly. 'I suppose I know why you're here.'

'You do, Jack?'

'I think so.' Jack Tighe nodded. Oh, he was a handsome man. He said: 'Aircraft dumping neoscopalamine in the reservoir, a stranger turning up in a car with a sheet-lead body. And we all know what's outside, don't we? Yes, it has to be that.'

'It's him, all right,' babbled Andy Grammis, plopping himself down on the steps, his face chalk. 'It's him and there's nothing we can do! He came into the store this morning. Brought Marlene with him. We should have done something about that girl, Jack. I knew she'd come to no good –'

'What did he want?'

'Want? Jack, he had a pad and a pencil like he wanted to take down *orders*, and he kept asking for – asking for – "Breakfast foods," he says, "what've you got in the way of breakfast foods?" So I told him. Oatmeal and corn flakes. Jack, he *flew* at me! "You don't stock Coco-Wheet?" he says. "Or

Treets, Eets, Neets, or Elixo-Wheets? How about Hunny-Yummies, or Prune-Bran Whippets, The Cereal with the Zip-Gun in Every Box?" "No, sir," I tell him.'

'But he's mad by then. "Potatoes?" he hollers. "What about potatoes?" Well, we've got plenty of potatoes, a whole cellar full. But I tell him and *that* doesn't satisfy him. "*Raw*, you mean?" he yells. "Not Tater-Fluff, Pre-Skortch Mickies, or Uncle Everett's Converted Spuds?" And then he shows me his card.'

'I know,' said Jack Tighe kindly, for Grammis seemed to find it hard to go on. 'You don't have to say it, if you don't want to.'

'Oh, I can say it all right, Jack,' said Andy Grammis bravely. 'This Mr Coglan, he's an adver – '

'No,' said Jack Tighe, standing up, 'don't make yourself do it. It's bad enough as it is. But it had to come. Yes, count it that it had to come, Andy. We've had a few good years, but we couldn't expect them to last forever.'

'But what are we going to *do*?'

'Get up, Andy,' said Jack Tighe strongly. 'Come inside! Sit down and rest yourself. And I'll send for the others.'

'You're going to fight him? But he has the whole United States Army behind him.'

Old Jack Tighe nodded. 'So he has, Andy,' he said, but he seemed wonderfully cheerful.

Jack Tighe's place was a sort of ranch house, with fixings. He was a great individual man, Jack Tighe was. All of you know that, because you were taught it in school; and maybe some of you have been to the house. But it's different now; I don't care what they say. The furniture isn't just the same. And the grounds –

Well, during the big war, of course, that was where the radio-dust drained down from the hills, so nothing grew. They've prettied it up with grass and trees and flowers. Flowers! I'll tell you what's wrong with that. In his young days, Jack Tighe was an account executive on the National Floral account. Why, he wouldn't have a flower in the house, much less plant and tend them.

But it was a nice house, all the same. He fixed Andy Grammis

47

a drink and sat him down. He phoned down-town and invited half a dozen people to come in to see them. He didn't say what it was about, naturally. No sense in starting a panic.

But everyone pretty much knew. The first to arrive was Timmy Horan, the fellow from the television service, and he'd given Charley Frink a ride on the back of his bike. He said, breathless: 'Mr Tighe, they're on our lines. I don't know how he's done it, but Coglan is transmitting on our wire TV circuit. And the stuff he's transmitting, Mr Tighe!'

'Sure,' said Tighe soothingly. 'Don't worry about it, Timothy. I imagine I know what sort of stuff it is, eh?'

He got up, humming pleasantly, and snapped on the television set. 'Time for the afternoon movie, isn't it? I suppose you left the tapes running.'

'Of course, but he's interfering with it!'

Tighe nodded. 'Let's see.'

The picture on the TV screen quavered, twisted into slanting lines of pale dark, and snapped into shape.

'I remember that one!' Charley Frink exclaimed. 'It's one of my favourites, Timmy!'

On the screen, Number Two Son, a gun in his hand was backing away from a hooded killer. Number Two Son tripped over a loose board and fell into a vat. He came up grotesquely comic, covered with plaster and mud.

Tighe stepped back a few paces. He spread the fingers of one hand and moved them rapidly up and down before his eyes.

'Ah,' he said, 'yes. See for yourself, gentlemen.'

Andy Grammis hesitatingly copied the older man. He spread his fingers and, clumsily at first, moved them before his eyes, as though shielding his vision from the cathode tube. Up and down he moved his hand, making a sort of stroboscope that stopped the invisible flicker of the racing electronic pencil.

And, yes, there it was!

Seen without the stroboscope, the screen showed bland-faced Charlie Chan in his white Panama hat. But the stroboscope showed something else. Between the consecutive images of the old movie there was another image – flashed for only a tiny fraction of a second, too quick for the conscious brain to comprehend, but, oh, how it struck into the subconscious!

Andy blushed.

'That – that girl,' he stammered, shocked. 'She hasn't got any –'

'Of course she hasn't,' said Tighe pleasantly. 'Subliminal compulsion, eh? The basic sex drive; you don't know you're seeing it, but the submerged mind doesn't miss it. No. And notice the box of Prune-Bran Whippets in her hand.'

Charley Frink coughed. 'Now that you mention it, Mr Tighe,' he said, 'I notice that I've just been thinking how tasty a dish of Prune-Bran Whippets would be right now.'

'Naturally,' agreed Jack Tighe. Then he frowned. 'Naked women, yes. But the female audience should be appealed to also. I wonder.' He was silent for a couple of minutes, and held the others silent with him, while tirelessly he moved the spread hand before his eyes.

Then *he* blushed.

'Well,' he said amiably, 'that's for the female audience. It's all there. Subliminal advertising. A product, and a key to the basic drives, and all flashed so quickly that the brain can't organize its defences. So when you think of Prune-Bran Whippets, you think of sex. Or more important, when you think of sex, you think of Prune-Bran Whippets.'

'Gee, Mr Tighe. I think about sex a lot.'

'Everybody does,' said Jack Tighe comfortingly, and he nodded.

There was a gallumphing sound from outside then and Wilbur LaFarge from the Shawanganunk National came trotting in. He was all out of breath and scared.

'He's done it again, he's done it again, Mr Tighe, sir! That Mr Coglan, he came and demanded more money! Said he's going to build a real TV network slave station here in Pung's Corners. Said he's opening up a branch agency for Yust and Ruminant, whoever they are. Said he was about to put Pung's Corners back on the map and needed money to do it.'

'And you gave it to him?'

'I couldn't *help* it.'

Jack Tighe nodded wisely. 'No, you couldn't. Even in my day, you couldn't much help it, not when the agency had you in its sights and the finger squeezing down on the trigger. Neo-scop in the drinking water, to make every living soul in Pung's Corners a little more suggestible, a little less stiff-backed. Even me, I suppose, though perhaps I don't drink as much water as most. And subliminal advertising on the wired TV, and subsonic compulsives when it comes to man-to-man talk. Tell me, La-Farge, did you happen to hear a faint droning sound? I thought so; yes. They don't miss a trick. Well,' he said, looking somehow pleased, 'there's no help for it. We'll have to fight.'

'Fight?' whispered Wilbur LaFarge, for he was no brave man, no, not even though he later became the Secretary of the Treasury.

'Fight!' boomed Jack Tighe.

Everybody looked at everybody else.

'There are hundreds of us,' said Jack Tighe, 'and there's only one of him. Yes, we'll fight! We'll distil the drinking water. We'll rip Coglan's little transmitter out of our TV circuit. Timmy can work up electronic sniffers to see what else he's using; we'll find all his gadgets, and we'll destroy them. The subsonics? Why, he has to carry that gear with him. We'll just take it away from him. It's either that or we give up our heritage as free men!'

Wilbur LaFarge cleared his throat. 'And then –'

'Well you may say "and then," ' agreed Jack Tighe. 'And then the United States Cavalry comes charging over the hill to rescue him. Yes. But you must have realized by now, gentlemen, that this means war.'

And so they had, though you couldn't have said that any of them seemed very happy about it.

5

Now I have to tell you what it was like outside in those days.

The face of the Moon is no more remote. Oh, you can't imagine it, you really can't. I don't know if I can explain it to you, either, but it's all in a book and you can read it if you want to . . . a book that was written by somebody important, a major, who later on became a general (but that was *much* later and in another army) and whose name was T. Wallace Commaigne.

The book? Why, that was called *The End of the Beginning*, and it is Volume One of his twelve-volume set of memoirs entitled: *I Served with Tighe: The Struggle to Win the World*.

War had been coming, war that threatened more, until it threatened everything, as the horrors in its supersonic pouches grew beyond even the dreads of hysteria. But there was time to guesstimate, as *Time* Magazine used to call it.

The dispersal plan came first. Break up cities, spread them apart, diffuse population and industry to provide the smallest possible target for even the largest possible bomb.

But dispersal increased another vulnerability – more freight trains, more cargo ships, more boxcar planes carrying raw materials to and finished products from an infinity of production points. Harder, yes, to hit and destroy, easier to choke off coming and going.

Then dig in, the planners said. Not dispersal but bomb shelter. But more than bomb shelter – make the factories mine for their ores, drill for their fuels, pump for their coolants and steams – and make them independent of supplies that may never be delivered, of workers who could not live below ground for however long the unpredictable war may last, seconds or forever – even of brains that might not reach the drawing boards and research labs and directors' boards, brains that might either be dead or concussed into something other than brains.

So the sub-surface factories even designed for themselves, always on a rising curve.

Against an enemy presupposed to grow smarter and slicker and quicker with each advance, just as we and our machines do. Against our having fewer and fewer fighting men; pure logic that, as war continues, more and more are killed, fewer and fewer left to operate the killer engines. Against the destruction or capture of even the impregnable underground factories, guarded as no dragon of legend ever was – by all that Man could devise at first in the way of traps and cages, blast and ray – and then by the slip-leashed invention of machines ordered always to speed up – more and more, deadlier and deadlier.

And the next stage – the fortress factoriese hooked to each other, so that the unthinkably defended plants, should they inconceivably fall, would in the dying message pass their responsibilities to the next of kin – survivor factories to split up their work, increase output, step up the lethal pace of invention and perfection, still more murderous weapons to be operated by still fewer defenders.

And another, final plan – gear the machines to feed and house and clothe and transport a nation, a hemisphere, a world recovering from no one could know in advance what bombs and germs and poisons and – name it and it probably would happen if the war lasted long enough.

With a built-in signal of peace, of course: the air itself. Pure once more, the atmosphere, routinely tested moment by moment, would switch production from war to peace.

And so it did.

But who could have known beforehand that the machines might not *know* war from peace?

Here's Detroit: a hundred thousand rat-inhabited manless acres, blind windows and shattered walls. From the air, it is dead. But underneath it – ah, the rapid pulse of life! The hammering systole and diastole of raw-material conduits sucking in fuel and ore, pumping out finished autos. Spidery passages stretched out to the taconite beds under the Lakes. Fleets of barges issued from concrete pens to match the U-boat nests at Lorient and, unmanned, swam the Lakes and the canals to their distribution points, bearing shiny new Buicks and Plymouths.

What made them new?

Why, industrial design! For the model years changed. The Dynaflow '61 gave place to the Super-Dynaflow Mark Eight of 1962; twin-beam headlights became triple; white-wall tyres turned to pastel and back to solid ebony black.

It was a matter of design efficiency.

What the Founding Fathers learned about production was essentially this: It doesn't much matter what you build, it only matters that people should want to buy it. What they learned was: Never mind the judgematical faculties of the human race. They are a frail breed. They move no merchandise. They boost no sales. Rely, instead, on the monkey trait of curiosity.

And curiosity, of course, feeds on secrecy.

So generations of automotivators created new cosmetic gimmicks for their cars in secret laboratories staffed by sworn mutes. No atomic device was half so classified! And all Detroit echoed their security measures; fleets of canvas-swathed mysteries swarmed the highways at new-model time each year; people talked. Oh, yes – they laughed; it was comic; but though they were amused, they were piqued; it was good to make a joke of the mystery, but the capper to the joke was to own one of the new models oneself.

The appliance manufacturers pricked up their ears. Ah, so. Curiosity, eh? So they leased concealed space to design new ice-tray compartments and brought them out with a flourish of trumpets. Their refrigerators sold like mad. Yes, like mad.

R C A brooded over the lesson and added a fillip of their own; there was the vinylite record, unbreakable, colourful, new. They designed it under wraps and then, the crowning touch, they leaked the secret; it was the trick that Manhattan Project hadn't learned – a secret that concealed the real secret. For all the vinylite programme was only a façade; it was security in its highest manifestation; the vinylite programme was a mere cover for the submerged L P.

It moved goods. But there was a limit. The human race is a blabbermouth.

Very well, said some great unknown, eliminate the human race! Let a *machine* design the new models! Add a design unit. Set it, by means of wobblators and random-choice circuits, to make its changes in an unforeseeable way. Automate the factories; conceal them underground; programme the machine to programme itself. After all, why not? As Coglan had quoted Charles F. Kettering, 'Our chief job in research is to keep the customer reasonably dissatisfied with what he has,' and proper machines can do *that* as well as any man. Better, if you really want to know.

And so the world was full of drusy caverns from which wonders constantly poured. The war had given industry its start by starting the dispersal pattern; bomb shelter had embedded the factories in rock; now industrial security made the factories independent. Goods flowed out in a variegated torrent.

But they couldn't stop. And nobody could get inside to shut them off or even slow them down. And that torrent of goods, made for so many people who didn't exist, had to be moved. The advertising men had to do the moving, and they were excellent at the job.

So that was the outside, a very, very busy place and a very, very big one. In spite of what happened in the big war.

I can't begin to tell you how busy it was or how big; I can only tell you about a little bit of it. There was a building called the Pentagon and it covered acres of ground. It had five sides, of course; one for the Army, one for the Navy, one for the Air Force, one for the Marines, and one for the offices of Yust & Ruminant.

So here's the Pentagon, this great building, the nerve centre of the United States in every way that mattered. (There was also a 'Capitol', as they called it, but that doesn't matter much. Didn't then, in fact.)

And here's Major Commaigne, in his scarlet dress uniform with his epaulettes and his little gilt sword. He's waiting in the anteroom of the Director's Office of Yust & Ruminant, nervously watching television. He's been waiting there for an hour, and then at last they send for him.

He goes in.

Don't try to imagine his emotions as he walks into that pigskin panelled suite. You can't. But understand that he believes that the key to all of his future lies in this room; he believes that with all his heart and in a way, as it develops, he is right.

'Major,' snaps an old man, a man very like Coglan and very like Jack Tighe, for they were all pretty much of a breed, those Ivy-League charcoal greys, 'Major, he's coming through. It's just as we feared. There has been trouble.'

'Yes, sir!'

Major Commaigne is very erect and military in his bearing, because he has been an Army officer for fifteen years now and this is his first chance at combat. He missed the big war – well, the whole Army missed the big war; it was over too fast for moving troops – and fighting has pretty much stopped since then. It isn't *safe* to fight, except under certain conditions. But maybe the conditions are right now, he thinks. And it can mean a lot to a major's career, these days, if he gets an expeditionary force to lead and acquits himself well with it!

So he stands erect, alert, sharp-eyed. His braided cap is tucked in the corner of one arm, and his other hand rests on the hilt of his sword, and he looks fierce. Why, that's natural enough, too. What comes in over the TV communicator in that pigskin-panelled office would make any honest Army officer look fierce. The authority of the United States has been flouted!

'L.S.,' gasps the image of a tall, dark old man in the picture tube, 'they've turned against me! They've seized my transmitter, neutralized my drugs, confiscated my subsonic gear. All I have left is this transmitter!'

And he isn't urbane any more, this man Coglan whose picture is being received in this room; he looks excited and he looks mad.

'Funny,' comments Mr Maffity, called 'L.S.' by his intimate staff, 'that they didn't take the transmitter away too. They must have known you'd contact us and that there would be reprisals.'

'But they *wanted* me to contact you!' cries the voice from the picture tube. 'I told them what it would mean L.S., they're going crazy. They're spoiling for a fight.'

And after a little more talk, L.S. Maffity turns off the set.

'We'll give it to them, eh, Major?' he says, as stern and straight as a ramrod himself.

'We will, sir!' says the major, and he salutes, spins around and leaves. Already he can feel the eagles on his shoulders – who knows, maybe even stars!

And this is how the punitive expedition came to be launched; and it was exactly what Pung's Corners could have expected as a result of their actions – could have, and did.

Now I already told you that fighting had been out of fashion for some time, though getting *ready* to fight was a number-one preoccupation of a great many people. You must understand that there appeared to be no contradiction in these two contradictory facts, outside.

The big war had pretty much discouraged anybody from doing anything very violent. Fighting in the old-fashioned way – that is, with missiles and radio-dust and atomic cannon – had turned out to be expensive and for other reasons impractical. It was only the greatest of luck then that stopped things before the planet was wiped off, nice and clean, of everything more advanced than the notochord, ready for the one-celled beasts of the sea to start over again. Now things were different.

First place, all atomic explosives were under *rigid* interdiction. There were a couple of dozen countries in the world that owned A-bombs or better, and every one of them had men on duty, twenty-four hours a day, with their fingers held ready over buttons that would wipe out for once and all whichever one of them might first use an atomic weapon again. So that was out.

And aircraft, by the same token, lost a major part of their usefulness. The satellites with their beady little TV eyes scanned every place every second, so that you didn't dare drop even an ordinary HE bomb as long as some nearsighted chap watching through a satellite relay might mistake it for something nuclear – and give the order to push one of those buttons.

This left, generally speaking, the infantry.

But what infantry it was! A platoon of riflemen was twenty-three men and it owned roughly the firepower of all of Napoleon's legions. A company comprised some twelve hundred and fifty, and it could single-handed have won World War One.

Hand weapons spat out literally sheets of metal, projectiles firing so rapidly one after another that you didn't so much try to shoot a target as to slice it in half. As far as the eye could see, a rifle bullet could fly. And where the eye was blocked by darkness, by fog, or by hills, the sniperscope, the radar-screen, and the pulse-beam interferometer sights could locate the target as though it were ten yards away at broad noon.

They were, that is to say, very modern weapons. In fact, the weapons that this infantry carried were so modern that half of each company was in process of learning to operate weapons that the other half had already discarded as obsolete. Who wanted a Magic-Eye Self-Aiming All-Weather Gunsight, Mark XII, when a Mark XIII, With Dubl-Jewelled Bearings, was available?

For it was one of the triumphs of the age that at last the planned obsolescence and high turnover of, say, a TV set or a Detroit car had been extended to carbines and bazookas.

It was wonderful and frightening to see.

It was these heroes, then, who went off to war, or to whatever might come.

Major Commaigne (so he says in his book) took a full company of men, twelve hundred and fifty strong, and started out for Pung's Corners. Air brought them to the plains of Lehigh County, burned black from radiation but no longer dangerous. From there, they journeyed by wheeled vehicles.

Major Commaigne was coldly confident. The radioactivity of the sands surrounding Pung's Corners was no problem. Not with the massive and perfect equipment he had for his force. What old Mr Coglan could do, the United States Army could do better; Coglan drove inside sheet lead, but the expeditionary force cruised in solid iridium steel, with gamma-ray baffles fixed in place.

Each platoon had its own half-track personnel carrier. Not only did the men have their hand weapons, but each vehicle mounted a 105-mm explosive cannon, with Zip-Fire Auto-Load and Wizardtrol Safety Interlock. Fluid mountings sustained the gimbals of the cannon. Radar picked out its target. Automatic digital computers predicted and outguessed the flight of its prey.

In the lead personnel carrier, Major Commaigne barked a last word to his troops:

'This is it, men! The chips are down! You have trained for this a long time and now you're in the middle of it. I don't know how we're going to make out *in there* –' and he swung an arm in the direction of Pung's Corners, a gesture faithfully reproduced in living three-dimensional colour on the intercoms of each personnel carrier in his fleet – 'but win or lose, and I know we're going to win, I want every one of you to know that you belong to the best Company in the best Regiment of the best Combat Infantry Team of the best Division of –'

Crump went the 105-mm piece on the lead personnel carrier as radar range automatically sighted in and fired upon a moving object outside, thus drowning out the tributes he had intended to pay to Corps, to Army, to Group, and to Command.

The battle for Pung's Corners had begun.

6

Now that first target, it wasn't any *body*.

It was only a milch cow, and one in need of freshening at that. She shouldn't have been on the baseball field at all, but there she was, and since that was the direction from which the invader descended on the town, she made the supreme sacrifice. Without even knowing she'd done it, of course.

Major Commaigne snapped at his adjutant: 'Lefferts! Have the ordnance sections put the one-oh-fives on safety. Can't have this sort of thing.' It had been a disagreeable sight, to see that poor old cow become hamburger, well ketchuped, so rapidly. Better chain the big guns until one saw, at any rate, whether Pung's Corners was going to put up a fight.

So Major Commaigne stopped the personnel carriers and ordered everybody out. They were past the dangerous radioactive area anyway.

The troops fell out in a handsome line of skirmish; it was very, very fast and very, very good. From the top of the Presbyterian Church steeple in Pung's Corners, Jack Tighe and Andy Grammis watched through field glasses, and I can tell you that Grammis was pretty near hysterics. But Jack Tighe only hummed and nodded.

Major Commaigne gave an order and every man in the line of skirmish instantly dug in. Some were in marsh and some in mud; some had to tunnel into solid rock and some – nearest where that first target had been – through a thin film of beef. It didn't much matter, because they didn't use the entrenching spades of World War II; they had Power-Pakt Diggers that clawed into anything in seconds, and, what's more, lined the pits with a fine ceramic glaze. It was magnificent.

And yet, on the other hand –

Well, look. It was this way. Twenty-six personnel carriers had brought them here. Each carrier had its driver, its relief driver, its emergency alternate driver, and its mechanic. It had its radar-and-electronics repairman, and its radar-and-electronics repairman's assistant. It had its ordnance staff of four, and its liaison communications officer to man the intercom and keep in touch with the P.C. commander.

Well, they needed all those people, of course. Couldn't get along without them.

But that came to two hundred and eighty-two men.

Then there was the field kitchen, with its staff of forty-seven, plus administrative detachment and dietetic staff; the headquarters detachment, with paymaster's corps and military police platoon; the meteorological section, a proud sight as they began setting up their field teletypes and fax receivers and launching their weather balloons; the field hospitality with eighty-one medics and nurses, nine medical officers and attached medical administrative staff; the special services detachment, prompt to begin setting up a three-D motion-picture screen in the lee of the parked personnel carriers and to commence organizing a hand-ball tournament among the off-duty men; the four chaplains and chaplains' assistants, plus the Wiseham Counsellor for Ethical Culturists, agnostics and waverers; the Historical officer and his eight trained clerks already going from foxhole to foxhole bravely carrying tape recorders, to take down history as it was being made in the form of first-hand impressions of the battle that had yet to be fought; military observers from Canada, Mexico, Uruguay, the Scandinavian Confederation, and the Soviet Socialist Republic of Inner Mongolia, with their orderlies and attachés; and, of course, field correspondents from *Stars & Stripes*, the New York

Times, the *Christian Science Monitor*, the Scripps-Howard chain, five wire services, eight television networks, an independent documentary motion-picture producer, and one hundred and twenty-seven other newspapers and allied public information outlets.

It was a stripped-down combat command, naturally. Therefore, there was only one Public Information Officer per reporter.

Still . . .

Well, it left exactly forty-six riflemen in line of skirmish.

Up in the Presbyterian belfry, Andy Grammis wailed: 'Look at them, Jack! I don't know, maybe letting advertising back into Pung's Corners wouldn't be so bad. All right, it's a rat race, but –'

'Wait,' said Jack Tighe quietly, and hummed.

They couldn't see it very well, but the line of skirmish was in some confusion. The word had been passed down that all the field pieces had been put on safety and that the entire firepower of the company rested in their forty-six rifles. Well, that wasn't so bad; but after all, they had been equipped with E-Z Fyre Revolv-a-Clip Carbines until ten days before the expeditionary force had been mounted. Some of the troops hadn't been fully able to familiarize themselves with the new weapons.

It went like this:

'Sam,' called one private to the man in the next foxhole. 'Sam, listen, I can't figure this something rifle out. When the something green light goes on, does that mean that the something safety is off?'

'Beats the something hell out of me,' rejoined Sam, his brow furrowed as he pored over the full-coloured glossy-paper operating manual, alluringly entitled, *The Five-Step Magic-Eye Way to New Combat Comfort and Security*. 'Did you see what it says here? It says, "Magic-Eye in Off position is provided with positive Fayl-Sayf action, thus assuring Evr-Kleen Cartridge of dynamic ejection and release, when used in combination with Shoulder-Eez Anti-Recoil Pads."'

'What did you say, Sam?'

'I said it beats the something hell out of me,' said Sam, and pitched the manual out into no-man's-land before him.

But he was sorry and immediately crept out to retrieve it, for although the directions seemed intended for a world that had no relation to the rock-and-mud terra firma around Pung's Corners, all of the step-by-step instructions in the manual were illustrated by mock-up photographs of starlets in Bikinis – for the cavern factories produced instruction manuals as well as weapons. They had to, obviously, and they were good at it; the more complicated the directions, the more photographs they used. The vehicular ones were downright shocking.

Some minutes later: 'They don't seem to be doing anything,' ventured Andy Grammis, watching from the steeple.

'No, they don't, Andy. Well, we can't sit up here for ever. Come along and we'll see what's what.'

Now Andy Grammis didn't want to do that, but Jack Tighe was a man you didn't resist very well, and so they climbed down the winding steel stairs and picked up the rest of the Pung's Corners Independence Volunteers, all fourteen of them, and they started down Front Street and out across the baseball diamond.

Twenty-six personnel carriers electronically went *ping*, and the turrets of their one-oh-fives swivelled to zero in on the Independence Volunteers.

Forty-six riflemen, swearing, attempted to make Akur-A-C Greenline Sighting Strip cross Horizon Blue True-Site Band in the Up-Close radar screens of their rifles.

And Major Commaigne, howling mad, waved a sheet of paper under the nose of his adjutant. 'What kind of something nonsense is *this*?' he demanded, for a soldier is a soldier regardless of his rank. 'I can't take those men out of line with the enemy advancing on us!'

'Army orders, sir,' said the adjutant impenetrably. He had got his doctorate in Military Jurisprudence at Harvard Law and he knew whose orders meant what to whom. 'The rotation plan isn't my idea, sir. Why not take it up with the Pentagon?'

'But, Lefferts, you idiot, I can't get through to the Pentagon!

61

Those something newspapermen have the channels sewed up solid! And now you want me to take every front-line rifleman out and send him to a rest camp for three weeks –'

'No, sir,' corrected the adjutant, pointing to a line in the order. 'Only for twenty days, sir, *including* travel time. But you'd best do it right away, sir, I expect. The order's marked "priority".'

Well, Major Commaigne was no fool. Never mind what they said later. He had studied the catastrophe of Von Paulus at Stalingrad and Lee's heaven-sent escape from Gettysburg, and he knew what could happen to an expeditionary force in trouble in enemy territory. Even a big one. And his, you must remember, was very small.

He knew that when you're on your own, everything becomes your enemy; frost and diarrhoea destroyed more of the Nazi Sixth Army than the Russians did; the jolting wagons of Lee's retreat put more of his wounded and sick out of the way than Meade's cannon. So he did what he had to do.

'Sound the retreat!' he bawled. 'We're going back to the barn.'

Retire and regroup; why not? But it wasn't as simple as that. The personnel carriers backed and turned like a fleet in manoeuvres. Their drivers were trained for that. But one P.C. got caught in Special Service's movie screen and blundered into another, and a flotilla of three of them found themselves stymied by the spreading pre-fabs of the field hospital. Five of them, doing extra duty in running electric generators from the power take-offs at their rear axles, were immobilized for fifteen minutes and then boxed in.

What it came down to was that four of the twenty-six were in shape to move right then. And obviously that wasn't enough, so it wasn't a retreat at all; it was a disaster.

'There's only one thing to do,' brooded Major Commaigne amid the turmoil, with manly tears streaming down his face, 'but how I wish I'd never tried to make lieutenant colonel!'

So Jack Tighe received Commaigne's surrender. Jack Tighe

didn't act surprised. I can't say the same for the rest of the Independence Volunteers.

'No, Major, you may keep your sword,' said Jack Tighe kindly. 'And all of the officers may keep their Pinpoint Levl-Site No-Jolt sidearms.'

'Thank you, sir,' wept the major, and blundered back into the officer's club which the Headquarters Detachment had never stopped building.

Jack Tighe looked after him with a peculiar and thoughtful expression.

William LaFarge, swinging a thirty-inch hickory stick – it was all he'd been able to pick up as a weapon – babbled: 'It's a great victory! Now they'll leave us alone, I bet!'

Jack Tighe didn't say a single word.

'Don't you think so, Jack? Won't they stay away now?'

Jack Tighe looked at him blankly, seemed about to answer and then turned to Charley Frink. 'Charley. Listen. Don't you have a shotgun put away somewhere?'

'Yes, Mr Tighe. And a .22. Want me to get them?'

'Why, yes, I think I do.' Jack Tighe watched the youth run off. His eyes were hooded. And then he said: 'Andy, do something for us. Ask the major to give us a P.O.W. driver who knows the way to the Pentagon.'

And a few minutes later, Charley came back with the shotgun and the .22; and the rest, of course, is history.

Kurt Vonnegut

Tomorrow and Tomorrow and Tomorrow

The year was 2158 A.D., and Lou and Emerald Schwartz were whispering on the balcony outside of Lou's family's apartment on the 76th floor of Building 257 in Alden Village, a New York housing development that covered what had once been known as Southern Connecticut. When Lou and Emerald had married, Em's parents had tearfully described the marriage as being between May and December; but now, with Lou 112 and Em 93, Em's parents had to admit that the match had worked out surprisingly well.

But Em and Lou weren't without their troubles, and they were out in the nippy air of the balcony because of them. What they were saying was bitter and private.

'Sometimes I get so mad, I feel like just up and diluting his anti-gerasone,' said Em.

'That'd be against Nature, Em,' said Lou, 'it'd be murder. Besides, if he caught us tinkering with his anti-gerasone, not only would he disinherit us, he'd bust my neck. Just because he's 172 doesn't mean Gramps isn't strong as a bull.'

'Against Nature,' said Em. 'Who knows what Nature's like any more? Ohhhhh – I don't guess I could ever bring myself to dilute his anti-gerasone or anything like that, but, gosh, Lou, a body can't help thinking Gramps is never going to leave if somebody doesn't help him along a little. Golly – we're so crowded a person can hardly turn around, and Verna's dying for a baby, and Melissa's gone thirty years without one.' She stamped her feet. 'I get so sick of seeing his wrinkled old face, watching him take the only private room and the best chair and the best food, and getting to pick out what to watch on TV, and running everybody's life by changing his will all the time.'

'Well, after all,' said Lou bleakly, 'Gramps *is* head of the family. And he can't help being wrinkled like he is. He was 70 before anti-gerasone was invented. He's going to leave, Em. Just give him time. It's his business. I know he's tough to live with, but be patient. It wouldn't do to do anything that'd rile him. After all, we've got it better'n anybody else, there on the day-bed.'

'How much longer do you think we'll get to sleep on the day-bed before he picks another pet? The world's record's two months, isn't it?'

'Mom and Pop had it that long once, I guess.'

'When *is* he going to leave, Lou?' said Emerald.

'Well, he's talking about giving up anti-gerasone right after the 500-mile Speedway Race.'

'Yes – and before that it was the Olympics, and before that the World's Series, and before that the Presidential Elections, and before that I-don't-know-what. It's been just one excuse after another for fifty years now. I don't think we're ever going to get a room to ourselves or an egg or anything.'

'All right – call me a failure!' said Lou. 'What can I do? I work hard and make good money, but the whole thing practically is taxed away for defence and old age pensions. And if it wasn't taxed away, where you think we'd find a vacant room to rent? Iowa, maybe? Well, who wants to live on the outskirts of Chicago?'

Em put her arms around his neck. 'Lou, hon, I'm not calling you a failure. The Lord knows you're not. You just haven't had a chance to be anything or have anything because Gramps and the rest of his generation won't leave and let somebody else take over.

'Yeah, yeah,' said Lou gloomily. 'You can't exactly blame 'em, though, can you? I mean, I wonder how quick we'll knock off the anti-gerasone when we get Gramps' age.'

'Sometimes I wish there wasn't any such thing as anti-gerasone!' said Emerald passionately. 'Or I wish it was made out of something real expensive and hard-to-get instead of mud and dandelions. Sometimes I wish folks just up and died regular as clockwork, without anything to say about it, instead of deciding themselves how long they're going to stay around. There ought to be a law against selling the stuff to anybody over 150.'

'Fat chance of that,' said Lou, 'with all the money and votes the old people've got.' He looked at her closely. 'You ready to up and die, Em?'

'Well, for heaven's sakes, what a thing to say to your wife. Hon! I'm not even 100 yet.' She ran her hands lightly over her firm, youthful figure, as though for confirmation. 'The best years of my life are still ahead of me. But you can bet that when 150 rolls around, old Em's going to pour her anti-gerasone down the sink, and quit taking up room, and she'll do it smiling.'

'Sure, sure,' said Lou, 'you bet. That's what they all say. How many you heard of doing it?'

'There was that man in Delaware.'

'Aren't you getting kind of tired of talking about him, Em? That was five months ago.'

'All right, then – Gramma Winkler, right here in the same building.'

'She got smeared by a subway.'

'That's just the way she picked to go,' said Em.

'Then what was she doing carrying a carton of anti-gerasone when she got it?'

Emerald shook her head wearily and covered her eyes. 'I dunno, I dunno, I dunno. All I know is, something's just got to be done.' She sighed. 'Sometimes I wish they'd left a couple of diseases kicking around somewhere, so I could get one and go to bed for a little while. Too many people!' she cried, and her words cackled and gabbled and died in a thousand asphalt-paved, skyscraper-walled courtyards.

Lou laid his hand on her shoulder tenderly. 'Aw, hon, I hate to see you down in the dumps like this.'

'If we just had a car, like the folks used to in the old days,' said Em, 'we could go for a drive, and get away from people for a little while. Gee – if *those* weren't the days!'

'Yeah,' said Lou, 'before they'd used up all the metal.'

'We'd hop in, and Pop'd drive up to a filling station and say, "Fillerup!"'

'That was the nuts, wasn't it – before they'd used up all the gasoline.'

'And we'd go for a carefree ride in the country.'

'Yeah – all seems like a fairyland now, doesn't it, Em? Hard to believe there really used to be all that space between cities.'

'And when we got hungry,' said Em, 'we'd find ourselves a restaurant, and walk in, big as you please and say, "I'll have a steak and French-fries, I believe," or, "How are the pork chops today?"' She licked her lips, and her eyes glistened.

'Yeah man!' growled Lou. 'How'd you like a hamburger with the works, Em?'

'Mmmmmmmmm.'

'If anybody'd offered us processed seaweed in those days, we would have spit right in his eye, huh, Em?'

'Or processed sawdust,' said Em.

Doggedly, Lou tried to find the cheery side of the situation. 'Well, anyway, they've got the stuff so it tastes a lot less like seaweed and sawdust than it did at first; and they say it's actually better for us than what we used to eat.'

'I felt fine!' said Em fiercely.

Lou shrugged. 'Well, you've got to realize the world wouldn't be able to support twelve billion people if it wasn't for processed seaweed and sawdust. I mean, it's a wonderful thing, really. I guess. That's what they say.'

'They say the first thing that pops into their heads,' said Em. She closed her eyes. 'Golly – remember shopping, Lou? Remember how the stores used to fight to get our folks to buy something? You didn't have to wait for somebody to die to get a bed or chairs or a stove or anything like that. Just went in – bing! – and bought whatever you wanted. Gee whiz that was nice, before they used up all the raw materials. I was just a little kid then, but I can remember so plain.'

Depressed, Lou walked listlessly to the balcony's edge, and looked at the clean, cold, bright stars against the black velvet of infinity. 'Remember when we used to be bugs on science fiction, Em? Flight seventeen, leaving for Mars, launching ramp twelve. "Board! All non-technical personnel kindly remain in bunkser, Ten seconds ... nine ... eight ... seven ... six ... five

... four ... three ... two ... *one! Main Stage! Barrrrrroooom!*'

'Why worry about what was going on on Earth?' said Em, looking up at the stars with him. 'In another few years, we'd all be shooting through space to start life all over again on a new planet.'

Lou sighed. 'Only it turns out you need something about twice the size of the Empire State Building to get one lousy colonist to Mars. And for another couple of trillion bucks he could take his wife and dog. *That's* the way to lick overpopulation – *emigrate!*'

'Lou –?'

'Hmmm?'

'When's the 500-mile Speedway Race?'

'Uh – Memorial Day, 30 May.'

She bit her lip. 'Was that awful of me to ask?'

'Not very, I guess. Everybody in the apartment's looked it up to make sure.'

'I don't want to be awful,' said Em, 'but you've just got to talk over these things now and then, and get them out of your system.'

'Sure you do. Feel better?'

'Yes – and I'm not going to lose my temper any more, and I'm going to be just as nice to him as I know how.'

'That's my Em.'

They squared their shoulders, smiled bravely, and went back inside.

Gramps Schwartz, his chin resting on his hands, his hands on the crook of his cane, was staring irascibly at the five-foot television screen that dominated the room. On the screen, a news commentator was summarizing the day's happenings. Every thirty seconds or so, Gramps would jab the floor with his cane-tip and shout, 'Hell! We did that a hundred years ago!'

Emerald and Lou, coming in from the balcony, were obliged to take seats in the back row, behind Lou's father and mother, brother and sister-in-law, son and daughter-in-law, grandson and wife, granddaughter and husband, great-grandson and wife, nephew and wife, grandnephew and wife, great-grandniece and husband, great-grandnephew and wife, and, of course, Gramps, who was in front of everybody. All, save Gramps, who was somewhat withered and bent, seemed, by pre-anti-gerasone standards, to be about the same age – to be somewhere in their late twenties or early thirties.

'*Meanwhile*,' the commentator was saying, '*Council Bluffs, Iowa, was still threatened by stark tragedy. But 200 weary rescue workers have refused to give up hope, and continue to dig in an effort to save Elbert Haggedorn, 183, who has been wedged for two days in a . . .*'

'I wish he'd get something more cheerful,' Emerald whispered to Lou.

'Silence!' cried Gramps. 'Next one shoots off his big bazoo while the TV's on is gonna find hisself cut off without a dollar –' and here his voice suddenly softened and sweetened – 'when they wave that checkered flag at the Indianapolis Speedway, and old Gramps gets ready for the Big Trip Up Yonder.' He sniffed sentimentally, while his heirs concentrated desperately on not making the slightest sound. For them, the poignancy of the prospective Big Trip had been dulled somewhat by its having been mentioned by Gramps about once a day for fifty years.

'*Dr Brainard Keyes Bullard*,' said the commentator, '*President of Wyandotte College, said in an address tonight that most of the world's ills can be traced to the fact that Man's knowledge of himself has not kept pace with his knowledge of the physical world.*'

'Hell!' said Gramps. 'We said that a hundred years ago!'

'*In Chicago tonight*,' said the commentator, '*a special celebration is taking place in the Chicago Lying-in Hospital. The guest of honour is Lowell W. Hitz, age zero. Hitz, born this morning, is the twenty-five millionth child to be born in the hospital.*' The commentator faded, and was replaced on the screen by young Hitz, who squalled furiously.

'Hell,' whispered Lou to Emerald, 'we said that a hundred years ago.'

'I heard that!' shouted Gramps. He snapped off the

television set, and his petrified descendants stared silently at the screen. 'You, there, boy –'

'I didn't mean anything by it, sir,' said Lou.

'Get me my will. You know where it is. You kids *all* know where it is. Fetch, boy!'

Lou nodded dully, and found himself going down the hall, picking his way over bedding to Gramps' room, the only private room in the Schwartz apartment. The other rooms were the bathroom, the living-room, and the wide, windowless hallway, which was originally intended to serve as a dining area, and which had a kitchenette in one end. Six mattresses and four sleeping bags were dispersed in the hallway and living-room, and the daybed, in the living-room, accommodated the eleventh couple, the favourites of the moment.

On Gramps' bureau was his will, smeared, dog-eared, perforated, and blotched with hundreds of additions, deletions, accusations, conditions, warnings, advice, and homely philosophy. The document was, Lou reflected, a fifty-year diary, all jammed onto two sheets – a garbled, illegible log of day after day of strife. This day, Lou would be disinherited for the eleventh time, and it would take him perhaps six months of impeccable behaviour to regain the promise of a share in the estate.

'Boy!' called Gramps.

'Coming, sir.' Lou hurried back into the living-room, and handed Gramps the will.

'Pen!' said Gramps.

He was instantly offered eleven pens, one from each couple.

'Not *that* leaky thing,' he said, brushing Lou's pen aside. 'Ah, there's a nice one. Good boy, Willy.' He accepted Willy's pen. That was the tip they'd all been waiting for. Willy, then, Lou's father, was the new favourite.

Willy, who looked almost as young as Lou, though 142, did a poor job of concealing his pleasure. He glanced shyly at the daybed, which would become his, and from which Lou and Emerald would have to move back into the hall, back to the worst spot of all by the bathroom door.

Gramps missed none of the high drama he'd authored, and he

gave his own familiar role everything he had. Frowning and running his finger along each line, as though he were seeing the will for the first time, he read aloud in a deep, portentous mono-tone, like a bass tone on a cathedral organ:

'I, Harold D. Schwartz, residing in Building 257 of Alden Village, New York City, do hereby make, publish and declare this to be my last Will and Testament, hereby revoking any and all former wills and codicils by me at any time heretofore made.' He blew his nose importantly, and went on, not missing a word, and repeating many for emphasis – repeating in partic-ular his ever-more-elaborate specifications for a funeral.

At the end of these specifications, Gramps was so choked with emotion that Lou thought he might forget why he'd gotten out the will in the first place. But Gramps heroically brought his powerful emotions under control, and, after erasing for a full minute, he began to write and speak at the same time. Lou could have spoken his lines for him, he'd heard them so often.

'I have had many heartbreaks ere leaving this vale of tears for a better land,' Gramps said and wrote. 'But the deepest hurt of all has been dealt me by – ' He looked around the group, trying to remember who the malefactor was.

Everyone looked helpfully at Lou, who held up his hand resignedly.

Gramps nodded, remembering, and completed the sentence: 'my great-grandson, Louis J. Schwartz.'

'Grandson, sir,' said Lou.

'Don't quibble. You're in deep enough now, young man,' said Gramps, but he changed the trifle. And from there he went without a mis-step through the phrasing of the disinherit-ance, causes for which were disrespectfulness and quibbling.

In the paragraph following, the paragraph that had belonged to everyone in the room at one time or another, Lou's name was scratched out and Willy's substituted as heir to the apartment and, the biggest plum of all, the double bed in the private bed-room. 'So!' said Gramps, beaming. He erased the date at the foot of the will, and substituted a new one, including the time of day. 'Well – time to watch the McGarvey Family.' The McGarvey Family was a television serial that Gramps had been following since he was 60, or for 112 years. 'I can't wait to see what's going to happen next,' he said.

Lou detached himself from the group, and lay down on his bed of pain by the bathroom door. He wished Em would join him, and he wondered where she was.

He dozed for a few moments, until he was disturbed by someone's stepping over him to get into the bathroom. A moment later, he heard a faint gurgling sound, as though something were being poured down the washbasin drain. Suddenly, it entered his mind that Em had cracked up, and that she was in there doing something drastic about Gramps.

'Em – ?' he whispered through the panel. There was no reply, and Lou pressed against the door. The worn lock, whose bolt barely engaged its socket, held for a second, then let the door swing inward.

'Morty!' gasped Lou.

Lou's great-grandnephew, Mortimer, who had just married and brought his wife home to the Schwartz ménage, looked at Lou with consternation and surprise. Morty kicked the door shut, but not before Lou had glimpsed what was in his hand – Gramps' enormous economy-size bottle of anti-gerasone, which had been half-emptied, and which Morty was refilling to the top with tap water.

A moment later, Morty came out, glared defiantly at Lou, and brushed past him wordlessly to rejoin his pretty bride.

Shocked, Lou didn't know what on earth to do. He couldn't let Gramps take the mouse-trapped anti-gerasone; but if he warned Gramps about it, Gramps would certainly make life in the apartment, which was merely insufferable now, harrowing.

Lou glanced into the living-room, and saw that the Schwartzes, Emerald among them, were momentarily at rest, relishing the botches that the McGarveys had made of *their* lives. Stealthily, he went into the bathroom, locked the door as well as he could, and began to pour the contents of Gramps' bottle down the drain. He was going to refill it with full-strength anti-gerasone from the 22 smaller bottles on the shelf. The bottle contained a half-gallon, and its neck was small, so it seemed to Lou that the emptying would take for ever. And the almost imperceptible smell of anti-gerasone, like Worcestershire sauce, now seemed to Lou, in his nervousness, to be pouring out into the rest of the apartment through the keyhole and under the door.

'*Gloog-gloog-gloog-gloog-*,' went the bottle monotonously. Suddenly, up came the sound of music from the living-room, and there were murmurs and the scraping of chairlegs on the floor. '*Thus ends*,' said the television announcer, '*the 29,121st chapter in the life of your neighbours and mine, the Mc-Garveys.*' Footsteps were coming down the hall. There was a knock on the bathroom door.

'Just a sec,' called Lou cheerily. Desperately, he shook the big bottle, trying to speed up the flow. His palms slipped on the wet glass, and the heavy bottle smashed to splinters on the tile floor.

The door sprung open, and Gramps, dumbfounded, stared at the incriminating mess.

Lou felt a hideous prickling sensation on his scalp and the back of his neck. He grinned engagingly through his nausea, and, for want of anything remotely resembling a thought, he waited for Gramps to speak.

'Well, boy,' said Gramps at last, 'looks like you've got a little tidying up to do.'

And that was all he said. He turned around, elbowed his way through the crowd, and locked himself in his bedroom.

The Schwartzes contemplated Lou in incredulous silence for a moment longer, and then hurried back to the living-room, as though some of his horrible guilt would taint them, too, if they looked too long. Morty stayed behind long enough to give Lou a quizzical, annoyed glance. Then he, too, went into the living-room, leaving only Emerald standing in the doorway.

Tears streamed over her cheeks. 'Oh, you poor lamb – please don't look so awful. It was my fault. I put you up to this.'

'No,' said Lou, finding his voice, 'really you didn't. Honest, Em, I was just –'

'You don't have to explain anything to me, hon. I'm on your side no matter what.' She kissed him on his cheek, and whispered in his ear. 'It wouldn't have been murder, hon. It wouldn't

73

have killed him. It wasn't such a terrible thing to do. It just would have fixed him up so he'd be able to go any time God decided He wanted him.'

'What's gonna happen next, Em?' said Lou hollowly. 'What's he gonna do?'

Lou and Emerald stayed fearfully awake almost all night, waiting to see what Gramps was going to do. But not a sound came from the sacred bedroom. At two hours before dawn, the pair dropped off to sleep.

At six o'clock they arose again, for it was time for their generation to eat breakfast in the kitchenette. No one spoke to them. They had twenty minutes in which to eat, but their reflexes were so dulled by the bad night that they had hardly swallowed two mouthfuls of egg-type processed seaweed before it was time to surrender their places to their son's generation.

Then, as was the custom for whoever had been most recently disinherited, they began preparing Gramps' breakfast, which would presently be served to him in bed, on a tray. They tried to be cheerful about it. The toughest part of the job was having to handle the honest-to-God eggs and bacon and margarine on which Gramps spent almost all of the income from his fortune.

'Well,' said Emerald, 'I'm not going to get all panicky until I'm sure there's something to be panicky about.'

'Maybe he doesn't know what it was I busted,' said Lou hopefully.

'Probably thinks it was your watch crystal,' said Eddie, their son, who was toying apathetically with his buckwheat-type processed sawdust cakes.

'Don't get sarcastic with your father,' said Em, 'and don't talk with your mouth full, either.'

'I'd like to see anybody take a mouthful of this stuff and *not* say something,' said Eddie, who was 73. He glanced at the clock. 'It's time to take Gramps his breakfast, you know.'

'Yeah, it is, isn't it,' said Lou weakly. He shrugged. 'Let's have the tray, Em.'

'We'll both go.'

Walking slowly, smiling bravely, they found a large semi-circle of long-faced Schwartzes standing around the bedroom door.

Em knocked. 'Gramps,' she said brightly, 'break-fast is rea-dy.'

There was no reply, and she knocked again, harder.

The door swung open before her fist. In the middle of the room, the soft, deep, wide, canopied bed, the symbol of the sweet by-and-by to every Schwartz, was empty.

A sense of death, as unfamiliar to the Schwartzes as Zoro-astrianism or the causes of the Sepoy Mutiny, stilled every voice and slowed every heart. Awed, the heirs began to search gingerly under the furniture and behind the drapes for all that was mortal of Gramps, father of the race.

But Gramps had left not his earthly husk but a note, which Lou finally found on the dresser, under a paper-weight which was a treasured souvenir from the 2000 World's Fair. Unstead-ily, Lou read it aloud:

'"Somebody who I have sheltered and protected and taught the best I know how all these years last night turned on me like a mad dog, and diluted my anti-gerasone, or tried to. I am no longer a young man. I can no longer bear the crushing burden of life as I once could. So, after last night's bitter ex-perience, I say good-bye. The cares of this world will soon drop away like a cloak of thorns, and I shall know peace. By the time you find this, I will be gone."'

'Gosh,' said Willy brokenly, 'he didn't even get to see how the 500-mile Speedway Race was going to come out.'

'Or the World's Series,' said Eddie.

'Or whether Mrs McGarvey got her eyesight back,' said Morty.

'There's more,' said Lou, and he began reading aloud again: '"I, Harold D. Schwartz ... do hereby make, publish and de-clare this to be my last Will and Testament, hereby revoking any and all former wills and codicils by me at any time hereto-fore made."'

'No!' cried Willy. 'Not another one!'

'"I do stipulate,"' read Lou, '"that all of my property, of

75

whatsoever kind and nature, not be divided, but do devise and bequeath it to be held in common by my issue, without regard for generation, equally, share and share alike." '

'Issue?' said Emerald.

Lou included the multitude in a sweep of his hand. 'It means we all own the whole damn shootin' match.'

All eyes turned instantly to the bed.

'Share and share alike?' said Morty.

'Actually,' said Willy, who was the oldest person present, 'it's just like the old system, where the oldest people head up things with their headquarters in here, and –'

'I like *that*!' said Em. 'Lou owns as much of it as you do, and I say it ought to be for the oldest one who's still working. You can snooze around here all day, waiting for your pension cheque, and poor Lou stumbles in here after work, all tuckered out, and –'

'How about letting somebody who's never had any privacy get a little crack at it?' said Eddie hotly. 'Hell, you old people had plenty of privacy back when you were kids. I was born and raised in the middle of the goddam barracks in the hall! How about –'

'Yeah?' said Morty. 'Sure, you've all had it pretty tough, and my heart bleeds for you. But try honeymooning in the hall for a real kick.'

'Silence!' shouted Willy imperiously. 'The next person who opens his mouth spends the next six months by the bathroom. Now clear out of my room. I want to think.'

A vase shattered against the wall, inches above his head. In the next moment, a free-for-all was under way, with each couple battling to eject every other couple from the room. Fighting coalitions formed and dissolved with the lightning changes of the tactical situation. Em and Lou were thrown into the hall, where they organized others in the same situation, and stormed back into the room.

After two hours of struggle, with nothing like a decision in sight, the cops broke in.

For the next half-hour, patrol wagons and ambulances hauled away Schwartzes, and then the apartment was still and spacious.

An hour later, films of the last stages of the riot were being televised to 500,000,000 delighted viewers on the Eastern Seaboard.

In the stillness of the three-room Schwartz apartment on the 76th floor of Building 257, the television set had been left on. Once more the air was filled with the cries and grunts and crashes of the fray, coming harmlessly now from the loudspeaker.

The battle also appeared on the screen of the television set in the police station, where the Schwartzes and their captors watched with professional interest.

Em and Lou were in adjacent four-by-eight cells, and were stretched out peacefully on their cots.

'Em –' called Lou through the partition, 'you got a washbasin all your own too?'

'Sure. Washbasin, bed, light – the works. Ha! And we thought Gramps' room was something. How long's this been going on?' She held out her hand. 'For the first time in forty years, hon, I haven't got the shakes.'

'Cross your fingers,' said Lou, 'the lawyer's going to try to get us a year.'

'Gee,' said Em dreamily, 'I wonder what kind of wires you'd have to pull to get solitary?'

'All right, pipe down,' said the turnkey, 'or I'll toss the whole kit and caboodle of you right out. And first one who lets on to anybody outside how good jail is ain't never getting back in!'

The prisoners instantly fell silent.

The living-room of the Schwartz apartment darkened for a moment, as the riot scenes faded, and then the face of the announcer appeared, like the sun coming from behind a cloud. *'And now, friends,'* he said, *'I have a special message from the makers of anti-gerasone, a message for all you folks over 150. Are you hampered socially by wrinkles, by stiffness of joints and discolouration or loss of hair, all because these things came upon you before anti-gerasone was developed? Well, if you are you need no longer suffer, need no longer feel different and out of things.*

77

'After years of research, medical science has now developed super-anti-gerasone! In weeks, yes weeks, you can look, feel, and act as young as your great-great-grandchildren! Wouldn't you pay $5,000 to be indistinguishable from everybody else? Well, you don't have to. Safe, tested super-anti-gerasone costs you only dollars a day. The average cost of regaining all the sparkle and attractiveness of youth is less than fifty dollars.

'Write now for your free trial carton. Just put your name and address on a dollar postcard, and mail it to "Super", Box 500,000, Schenectady, N.Y. Have you got that? I'll repeat it. "Super", Box . . .' Underlining the announcer's words was the scratching of Gramps' fountain-pen, the one Willy had given him the night before. He had come in a few minutes previous from the Idle Hour Tavern, which commanded a view of Building 257 across the square of asphalt known as the Alden Village Green. He had called a cleaning woman to come straighten the place up, and had hired the best lawyer in town to get his descendants a conviction. Gramps had then moved the day-bed before the television screen so that he could watch from a reclining position. It was something he'd dreamed of doing for years.

'Schen-ec-ta-dy,' mouthed Gramps. 'Got it.' His face had changed remarkably. His facial muscles seemed to have relaxed, revealing kindness and equanimity under what had been taut, bad-tempered lines. It was almost as though his trial package of *Super*-anti-gerasone had already arrived. When something amused him on television, he smiled easily, rather than barely managing to lengthen the thin line of his mouth a milimetre. Life was good. He could hardly wait to see what was going to happen next.

Theodore Sturgeon

Mr Costello, Hero

'Come in, Purser. And shut the door.'

'I beg your pardon, sir?' The Skipper never invited anyone in – not to his quarters. His office, yes, but not here.

He made an abrupt gesture, and I came in and closed the door. It was about as luxurious as a compartment on a space-ship can get. I tried not to goggle at it as if it was the first time I had ever seen it, just because it was the first time I had ever seen it.

I sat down.

He opened his mouth, closed it, forced the tip of his tongue through his thin lips. He licked them and glared at me. I'd never seen the Iron Man like this. I decided that the best thing to say would be nothing, which is what I said.

He pulled a deck of cards out of the top-middle drawer and slid them across the desk. 'Deal.'

I said, 'I b –'

'And don't say you beg my pardon!' he exploded.

Well, all right. If the skipper wanted a cosy game of gin rummy to while away the parsecs, far be it from me to ... I shuffled. Six years under this cold-blooded, fish-eyed automatic computer with eyebrows, and this was the first time that he –

'Deal,' he said. I looked up at him. 'Draw, five-card draw. You do play draw poker, don't you, Purser?'

'Yes, sir.' I dealt and put down the pack. I had three threes and a couple of court cards. The skipper scowled at his hand and threw down two. He glared at me again.

I said, 'I got three of a kind, sir.'

He let his cards go as if they no longer existed, slammed out of his chair, and turned his back to me. He tilted his head back

79

and stared up at the see-it-all, with its complex of speed, time, position, and distance-run coordinates. Borinquen, our destination planet, was at spitting distance – only a day or so off – and Earth was a long, long way behind. I heard a sound and dropped my eyes. The Skipper's hands were locked behind him, squeezed together so hard that they crackled.

'Why didn't you draw?' he grated.

'I beg your – '

'When *I* played poker – and I used to play a hell of a lot of poker – as I recall it, the dealer would find out how many cards each player wanted after the deal and give him as many as he discarded. Did you ever hear of that, Purser?'

'Yes, sir, I did.'

'You *did*.' He turned around. I imagine he had been scowling this same way at the see-it-all, and I wondered why it was he hadn't shattered the cover glass.

'Why, then, Purser,' he demanded, 'did you show your three of a kind without discarding, without drawing – without, mister, asking me how many cards I might want?'

I thought about it. 'I – we – I mean, sir, we haven't been playing poker that way lately.'

'You've been playing draw poker without drawing!' He sat down again and beamed that glare at me again. 'And who changed the rules?'

'I don't know, sir. We just – that's the way we've been playing.'

He nodded thoughtfully. 'Now tell me something, Purser. How much time did you spend in the galley during the last watch?'

'About an hour, sir.'

'About an hour.'

'Well, sir,' I explained hurriedly, 'it was my turn.'

He said nothing, and it suddenly occurred to me that these galley-watches weren't in the ship's orders.

I said quickly, 'It isn't *against* your orders to stand such a watch, is it, sir?'

'No,' he said, 'it isn't.' His voice was so gentle, it was ugly. 'Tell me, Purser, doesn't Cooky mind these galley-watches?'

'Oh, no, sir! He's real pleased about it.' I knew he was thinking about the size of the galley. It was true that two men made
quite a crowd in a place like that. I said, 'That way, he knows
everybody can trust him.'

'You mean that way you know he won't poison you.'

'Well – yes, sir.'

'And tell me,' he said, his voice even gentler, 'who suggested
he might poison you?'

'I really can't say, Captain. It's just sort of something that
came up. Cooky doesn't mind.' I added. 'If he's watched all
the time, he knows nobody's going to suspect him. It's all
right.'

Again he repeated my words.

'It's all right.' I wished he wouldn't. I wished he'd stop looking at me like that. 'How long,' he asked, 'has it been customary
for the deck officer to bring a witness with him when he takes
over the watch?'

'I really couldn't say, sir. That's out of my department.'

'You couldn't say. Now think hard, Purser. Did you ever
stand galley-watches, or see deck-officers bring witnesses with
them when they relieve the bridge, or see draw poker played
without drawing – before this trip?'

'Well, no, sir. I don't think I have. I suppose we just never
thought of it before.'

'We never had Mr Costello as a passenger before, did we?'

'No, sir.'

I thought for a moment he was going to say something else,
but he didn't, just: 'Very well, Purser. That will be all.'

I went out and started back aft, feeling puzzled and sort of
upset. The Skipper didn't have to hint things like that about
Mr Costello. Mr Costello was a very nice man. Once, the
Skipper had picked a fight with Mr Costello. They'd shouted at
each other in the day-room. That is, the Skipper had shouted –
Mr Costello never did. Mr Costello was as good-natured as they
come. A good-natured soft-spoken man, with the kind of face
they call open. Open and honest. He'd once been a Triumver
back on Earth – the youngest ever appointed, they said.

You wouldn't think such an easy-going man was as smart as

that. Triumvers are usually life-time appointments, but Mr Costello wasn't satisfied. Had to keep moving, you know. Learning all the time, shaking hands all around, staying close to the people. He loved people.

I don't know why the Skipper couldn't get along with him. Everybody else did. And besides – Mr Costello didn't play poker; why should he care one way or the other how *we* played it? He didn't eat the galley food – he had his own stock in his cabin – so what difference would it make to him if the cook poisoned anyone? Except, of course, that he cared about *us*. People – he *liked* people.

Anyway, it's better to play poker without the draw. Poker's a good game with a bad reputation. And where do you suppose it gets the bad reputation? From cheaters. And how do people cheat at poker? Almost never when they deal. It's when they pass out cards after the discard. That's when a shady dealer knows what he holds, and he knows what to give the others so he can win. All right, remove the discard and you remove nine-tenths of the cheaters. Remove the cheaters and the honest men can trust each other.

That's what Mr Costello used to say, anyhow. Not that he cared one way or the other for himself. He wasn't a gambling man.

I went into the day-room and there was Mr Costello with the Third Officer. He gave me a big smile and a wave, so I went over.

'Come on, sit down, Purser,' he said. 'I'm landing tomorrow. Won't have much more chance to talk to you.'

I sat down. The Third snapped shut a book he'd been holding open on the table and sort of got it out of sight.

Mr Costello laughed at him. 'Go ahead, Third, show the Purser. You can trust him – he's a good man. I'd be proud to be shipmates with the Purser.'

The Third hesitated and then raised the book from his lap. It was the *Space Code* and expanded *Rules of the Road*. Every licensed officer has to bone up on it a lot, to get his licence. But it's not the kind of book you ordinarily kill time with.

'The Third here was showing me all about what a captain can and can't do,' said Mr Costello.

'Well, you asked me to,' the Third said.

'Now just a minute,' said Mr Costello rapidly, 'now just a minute.' He had a way of doing that sometimes. It was part of him, like the thinning hair on top of his head and the big smile and the way he had of cocking his head to one side and asking you what it was you just said, as if he didn't hear so well. 'Now just a minute, you *wanted* to show me this material, didn't you?'

'Well, yes, Mr Costello,' the Third said.

'You're going over the limitations of a spacemaster's power of your own free will, aren't you?'

'Well,' said the Third, 'I guess so. Sure.'

'Sure,' Mr Costello repeated happily. 'Tell the Purser the part you just read to me.'

'The one you found in the book?'

'You know the one. You read it out your own self, didn't you?'

'Oh,' said the Third. He looked at me – sort of uneasily, I thought – and reached for the book.

Mr Costello put his hand on it. 'Oh, don't bother looking it up,' he said. 'You can remember it.'

'Yeah, I guess I do,' the Third admitted. 'It's a sort of safe-guard against letting a skipper's power go to his head, in case it ever does. Suppose a time comes when a captain begins to act up, and the crew gets the idea that a lunatic has taken over the bridge. Well, something has to be done about it. The crew has the power to appoint one officer and send him up to the Captain for an accounting. If the Skipper refuses, or if the crew doesn't like his accounting, then they have the right to confine him to his quarters and take over the ship.'

'I think I heard about that,' I said. 'But the Skipper has rights, too. I mean the crew has to report everything by space-radio the second it happens, and then the Captain has a full hearing along with the crew at the next port.'

Mr Costello looked at us and shook his big head, full of admiration. When Mr Costello thought you were good, it made you feel good all over.

The Third looked at his watch and got up. 'I got to relieve the bridge. Want to come along, Purser?'

'I'd like to talk to him for a while,' Mr Costello said. 'Do you suppose you could get somebody else for a witness?'

'Oh, sure, if you say so,' said the Third.

'But you're going to get someone.'

'Absolutely,' said the Third.

'Safest ship I was ever on,' said Mr Costello. 'Gives a fellow a nice feeling to know that the watch is never going to get the orders wrong.'

I thought so myself and wondered why we never used to do it before. I watched the Third leave and stayed where I was, feeling good, feeling safe, feeling glad that Mr Costello wanted to talk to me. And me just a Purser, him an ex-Triumver.

Mr Costello gave me the big smile. He nodded towards the door. 'That young fellow's going far. A good man. You're all good men here.' He stuck a sucker-cup in the heater and passed it over to me with his own hands. 'Coffee,' he said. 'My own brand. All I ever use.'

I tasted it and it was fine. He was a very generous man. He sat back and beamed at me while I drank it.

'What do you know about Borinquen?' he wanted to know.

I told him all I could. Boriquen's a pretty nice place, what they call 'four-nines Earth Normal' – which means that the climate, gravity, atmosphere, and ecology come within .9999 of being the same as Earth's. There are only about six known planets like that. I told him about the one city it had and the trapping that used to be the main industry. Coats made out of *glunker* fur last for ever. They shine green in white light and a real warm ember-red in blue light, and you can take a full-sized coat and scrunch it up and hide it in your two hands, it's that light and fine. Being so light, the fur made ideal space-cargo.

Of course, there was a lot more on Borinquen now – rare isotope ingots and foodstuffs and seeds for the drug business and all, and I suppose the *glunker* trade could dry right up and Borinquen could still carry its weight. But furs settled the planet, furs supported the city in the early days, and half the population still lived out in the bush and trapped.

Mr Costello listened to everything I said in a way I can only call respectful.

I remember I finished up by saying, 'I'm sorry you have to get off there, Mr Costello. I'd like to see you some more. I'd like to come see you at Borinquen, whenever we put in, though I don't suppose a man like you would have much spare time.'

He put his big hand on my arm. 'Purser, if I don't have time when you're in port, I'll make time. Hear?' Oh, he had a wonderful way of making a fellow feel good.

Next thing you know, he invited me right into his cabin. He sat me down and handed me a sucker full of a mild red wine with a late flavour of cinnamon, which was a new one on me, and he showed me some of his things.

He was a great collector. He had one or two little bits of coloured paper that he said were stamps they used before the Space Age, to prepay carrying charges on paper letters. He said no matter where he was, just one of those things could get him a fortune. Then he had some jewels, not rings or anything, just stones, and a fine story for every single one of them.

'What you're holding in your hand,' he said, 'cost the life of a king and the loss of an empire half again as big as United Earth.' And: 'This one was once so well guarded that most people didn't know whether it existed or not. There was a whole religion based on it – and now it's gone, and so is the religion.'

It gave you a queer feeling, being next to this man who had so much, and him just as warm and friendly as your favourite uncle.

'If you can assure me these bulkheads are soundproof, I'll show you something else I collect,' he said.

I assured him they were, and they were, too. 'If ships' architects ever learned anything,' I told him, 'they learned that a man has just got to be by himself once in a while.'

He cocked his head to one side in that way he had. 'How's that again?'

'A man's just got to be by himself once in a while,' I said. 'So, mass or no, cost or no, a ship's bulkheads are built to give a man his privacy.'

85

'Good,' he said. 'Now let me show you.' He unlocked a hand-case and opened it, and from a little compartment inside he took out a thing about the size of the box a watch comes in. He handled it very gently as he put it down on his desk. It was square, and it had a fine grille on the top and two little silver studs on the side. He pressed one of them and turned to me, smiling. And let me tell you, I almost fell right off the bunk where I was sitting, because here was the Captain's voice as loud and as clear and natural as if he was right there in the room with us. And do you know what he said?

He said, 'My crew questions my sanity – yet you can be sure that if a single man aboard questions my authority, he will learn that I am master here, even if he must learn it at the point of a gun.'

What surprised me so much wasn't only the voice but the words – and what surprised me especially about the words was that I had heard the Skipper say them myself. It was the time he had had the argument with Mr Costello. I remembered it well because I had walked into the dayroom just as the Captain started to yell.

'Mr Costello,' he said in that big heavy voice of his, 'in spite of your conviction that my crew questions my sanity ... ' and all the rest of it, just like on this recording Mr Costello had. And I remember he said, too, 'even if he must learn it at the point of a gun. *That, sir, applies to passengers – the crew has legal means of their own.*'

I was going to mention this to Mr Costello, but before I could open my mouth, he asked me, 'Now tell me, Purser, is that the voice of the Captain of your ship?'

And I said, 'Well, if it isn't, I'm not the Purser here. Why, I heard him speak those words my very own self.'

Mr Costello swatted me on the shoulder. 'You have a good ear. Purser. And how do you like my little toy?'

Then he showed it to me, a little mechanism on the jewelled pin he wore on his tunic, a fine thread of wire to a pushbutton in his side pocket.

'One of my favourite collections,' he told me. 'Voices. Anybody, any time, anywhere.' He took off the pin and slipped a tiny bead out of the setting. He slipped this into a groove in the box and pressed the stud.

And I heard my own voice say, 'I'm sorry you have to get off there, Mr Costello. I'd like to see you some more.' I laughed and laughed. That was one of the cleverest things I ever saw. And just think of my voice in his collection, along with the Captain and space only knows how many great and famous people!

He even had the voice of the Third Officer, from just a few minutes before, saying, 'A lunatic has taken over the bridge. Well, something has to be done about it.'

All in all, I had a wonderful visit with him, and then he asked me to do whatever I had to do about his clearance papers. So I went back to my office and got them out. They are kept in the Purser's safe during a voyage. And I went through them with the okays. There were a lot of them – he had more than most people.

I found one from Earth Central that sort of made me mad. I guess it was a mistake. It was a *Know All Ye* that warned consular officials to report every six months, Earth time, on the activities of Mr Costello.

I took it to him, and it was a mistake, all right – he said so himself. I tore it out of his passport book and adhesed an official note, reporting the accidental destruction of a used page of fully stamped visas. He gave me a beautiful blue gemstone for doing it.

When I said, 'I better not; I don't want you thinking I take bribes from passengers,' he laughed and put one of those beads in his recorder, and it came out, in my voice, 'I take bribes from passengers.' He was a great joker.

We lay at Borinquen for four days. Nothing much happened except I was busy. That's what's tough about pursering. You got nothing to do for weeks in space, and then, when you're in spaceport, you have too much work to do even to go ashore much, unless it's a long layover.

I never really minded much. I'm one of those mathematical geniuses, you know, even if I don't have too much sense otherwise, and I take pride in my work. Everybody has something he's good at, I guess. I couldn't tell you how the gimmick works that makes the ship travel faster than light, but I'd hate to trust the Chief Engineer with one of my interplanetary cargo manifests, or a rate-of-exchange table, *glunker* pelts to U.E. dollars.

Some hard-jawed character with Space Navy Investigator credentials came aboard with a portable voice recorder and made me and the Third Officer recite a lot of nonsense for some sort of test, I don't know what. The S.N.I. is always doing a lot of useless and mysterious things. I had an argument with the Port Agent, and I went ashore with Cooky for a fast drink. The usual thing. Then I had to work overtime signing on a new Third – they transferred the old one to a corvette that was due in, they told me.

Oh, yes, that was the trip the Skipper resigned. I guess it was high time. He'd been acting very nervous. He gave me the damnedest look when he went ashore that last time, like he didn't know whether to kill me or burst into tears. There was a rumour around that he'd gone berserk and threatened the crew with a gun, but I don't listen to rumours. And anyway, the Port Captain signs on new skippers. It didn't mean any extra work for me, so it didn't matter much.

We upshipped again and made the rounds. Boötes Sigma and Nightingale and Caranho and Earth – chemical glassware, black-prints, *sho* seed and glitter crystals; perfume, music tape, *glizzard* skins and Aldebar – all the usual junk for all the usual months. And round we came again to Borinquen.

Well, you wouldn't believe a place could change so much in so short a t' . Borinquen used to be a pretty free-and-easy planet. Ther 'as just the one good-sized city, see, and then trapper camps all through the unsettled area. If you liked people, you settled in the city, and you could go to work in the processing plants or maintenance or some such. If you didn't, you could trap *glunkers*. There was always something for every-body on Borinquen.

But things were way different this trip. First of all, a man with a Planetary Government badge came aboard, by God, to censor the music tapes consigned for the city, and he had the credentials for it, too. Next thing I find out, the municipal authorities have confiscated the warehouses – *my* warehouses – and they were being converted into barracks.

And where were the goods – the pelts and ingots for export? Where was the space for our cargo? Why, in houses – in hundreds of houses, all spread around every which way, all indexed up with a whole big new office full of conscripts and volunteers to mix up and keep mixed up! For the first time since I went to space, I had to request layover so I could get things unwound.

Anyway it gave me a chance to wander around the town, which I don't often get.

You should have seen the place! Everybody seemed to be moving out of the houses. All the big buildings were being made over into hollow shells, filled with rows of mattresses. There were banners strung across the streets: ARE YOU A MAN OR ARE YOU ALONE? A SINGLE SHINGLE IS A SORRY SHELTER! THE DEVIL HATES A CROWD!

All of which meant nothing to me. But it wasn't until I noticed a sign painted in whitewash on the glass front of a bar-room, saying – TRAPPERS STAY OUT! – that I was aware of one of the biggest changes of all.

There were no trappers on the streets – none at all. They used to be one of the tourist attractions of Borinquen, dressed in *glunker* fur, with the long tailwings afloat in the wind of their walking, and a kind of distance in their eyes that not even spacemen had. As soon as I missed them, I began to see the TRAPPERS STAY OUT! signs just about everywhere – on the stores, the restaurants, the hotels, and theatres.

I stood on a street corner, looking around me and wondering what in hell was going on here, when a Borinquen cop yelled something at me from a monowheel prowl car. I didn't understand him, so I just shrugged. He made a U-turn and coasted up to me.

'What's the matter, country boy? Lose your traps?'

I said, 'What?'

He said, 'If you want to go it alone, *glunker*, we got solitary cells over at the Hall that'll suit you fine.'

I just gawked at him. And, to my surprise, another cop poked his head up out of the prowler. A one-man prowler, mind. They were really jammed in there.

This second one said, 'Where's your trap-line, jerker?'

I said, 'I don't have a trap-line.' I pointed to the mighty tower of my ship, looming over the spaceport. 'I'm the Purser off that ship.'

'Oh, for God's sakes!' said the first cop. 'I might have known. Look, Spacer, you'd better double up or you're liable to get yourself mobbed. This is no spot for a soloist.'

'I don't get you, Officer. I was just –'

'I'll take him,' said someone. I looked around and saw a tall Borinqueña standing just inside the open doorway of one of the hundreds of empty houses. She said, 'I came back here to pick up some of my things. When I got done in here, there was nobody on the sidewalks. I've been here an hour, waiting for somebody to go with.' She sounded a little hysterical.

'You know better than to go in there by yourself,' said one of the cops.

'I know – I know. It was just to get my things. I wasn't going to stay.' She hauled up a duffel-bag and dangled it in front of her. 'Just to get my things,' she said again, frightened.

The cops looked at each other. 'Well, all right. But watch yourself. You go along with the Purser here. Better straighten him out – he don't seem to know what's right.'

'I will,' she said thankfully.

But by then the prowler had moaned off, weaving a little under its double load.

I looked at her. She wasn't pretty. She was sort of heavy and stupid.

She said, 'You'll be all right now. Let's go.'

'Where?'

'Well, Central Barracks, I guess. That's where most everybody is.'

'I have to get back to the ship.'

'Oh, dear,' she said, all distressed again. 'Right away?'

'No, not right away. I'll go in town with you, if you want.'

She picked up her duffel-bag, but I took it from her and

heaved it up on my shoulder. 'Is everybody here crazy?' I asked her, scowling.

'Crazy?' She began walking, and I went along. 'I don't *think* so.'

'All this,' I persisted. I pointed to a banner that said. NO LADDER HAS A SINGLE RUNG. 'What's that mean?'

'Just what it says.'

'You have to put up a big thing like that just to tell me ...'

'Oh,' she said. 'You mean what does it *mean*!' She looked at me strangely. 'We've found out a new truth about humanity. Look, I'll try to tell it to you the way the Lucilles said it last night.'

'Who's Lucille?'

'*The* Lucilles,' she said, in a mildly shocked tone. 'Actually, I suppose there's really only one – though, of course, there'll be someone else in the studio at the time,' she added quickly. 'But on trideo it looks like four Lucilles, all speaking at once, sort of in chorus.'

'You just go on talking,' I said when she paused. 'I catch on slowly.'

'Well, here's what they say. They say no one human being ever did *anything*. They say it takes a hundred pairs of hands to build a house, ten thousand pairs to build a ship. They say a single pair is not only useless – it's *evil*. All humanity is a thing made up of many parts. No part is good by itself. Any part that wants to go off by itself hurts the whole main thing – the thing that has become so great. So we're seeing to it that no part ever gets separated. What good would your hand be if a finger suddenly decided to go off by itself?'

I said, 'And you believe this – what's your name?'

'Nola. *Believe* it? Well, it's true, isn't it? Can't you see it's true? Everybody *knows* it's true.'

'Well, it *could* be true,' I said reluctantly. 'What do you do with people who want to be by themselves?'

'We help them.'

'Suppose they don't want help?'

'Then they're trappers,' she said immediately. 'We push them back into the bush, where the evil soloists come from.'

'Well, what about the fur?'

'Nobody uses furs any more!'

So that's what happened to our fur consignment! And I was thinking those amateur red-tapers had just lost 'em somewhere.

She said, as if to herself, 'All sin starts in the lonesome dark,' and when I looked up, I saw she'd read it approvingly off another banner.

We rounded a corner and I blinked at a blaze of light. It was one of the warehouses.

'There's the Central,' she said. 'Would you like to see it?'

'I guess so.'

I followed her down the street to the entrance. There was a man sitting at a table in the doorway. Nola gave him a card. He checked it against a list and handed it back.

'A visitor,' she said. 'From the ship.'

I showed him my Purser's card and he said, 'Okay. But if you want to stay, you'll have to register.'

'I won't want to stay,' I told him. 'I have to get back.'

I followed Nola inside.

The place had been scraped out to the absolute maximum. Take away one splinter of vertical structure more and it wouldn't have held a roof. There wasn't a concealed corner, a shelf, a drape, an overhang. There must have been two thousand beds, cots, and mattresses spread out, cheek by jowl, over the entire floor, in blocks of four, with only a hand's-breadth between them.

The light was blinding – huge floods and spots bathed every square inch in yellow-white fire.

Nola said, 'You'll get used to the light. After a few nights, you don't even notice it.'

'The lights never get turned off?'

'Oh, dear, no!'

Then I saw the plumbing – showers, tubs, sinks, and everything else. It was all lined up against one wall.

Nola followed my eyes. 'You get used to that, too. Better to have everything out in the open than to let the devil in for one secret second. That's what the Lucilles say.'

I dropped her duffel-bag and sat down on it. The only thing

I could think of was, 'Whose idea was all this? Where did it start?'

'The Lucilles,' she said vaguely. Then, 'Before them, I don't know. People just started to realize. Somebody bought a warehouse – no, it was a hangar – I don't know,' she said again, apparently trying hard to remember. She sat down next to me and said in a subdued voice, 'Actually, some people didn't take to it so well at first.' She looked around. '*I* didn't. I mean it, I really didn't. But you believed, or you had to act as if you believed, and one way or another everybody just came to this.' She waved a hand.

'What happened to the ones who wouldn't come to Centrals?'

'People made fun of them. They lost their jobs, the schools wouldn't take their children, the stores wouldn't honour their ration cards. Then the police started to pick up soloists – like they did you.' She looked around again, a sort of contented familiarity in her gaze. 'It didn't take long.'

I turned away from her, but found myself staring at all that plumbing again. I jumped up. 'I have to go, Nola. Thanks for your help. Hey – how do I get back to the ship, if the cops are out to pick up any soloist they see?'

'Oh, just tell the man at the gate. There'll be people waiting to go your way. There's always somebody waiting to go everywhere.'

She came along with me. I spoke to the man at the gate, and she shook hands with me. I stood by the little table and watched her hesitate, then step up to a woman who was entering. They went in together. The doorman nudged me over towards a group of what appeared to be loungers.

'*North!*' he bawled.

I drew a pudgy little man with bad teeth, who said not one single word. We escorted each other two-thirds of the way to the spaceport, and he disappeared into a factory. I scuttled the rest of the way alone, feeling like a criminal, which I suppose I was. I swore I would never go into that crazy city again.

And the next morning, who should come out for me, in an armoured car with six two-man prowlers as escort, but Mr Costello himself!

It was pretty grand seeing him again. He was just like always, big and handsome and good-natured. He was not alone. All spread out in the back corner of the car was the most beautiful blonde woman that ever struck me speechless. She didn't say very much. She would just look at me every once in a while and sort of smile, and then she would look out of the car window and bite on her lower lip a little, and then look at Mr Costello and not smile at all.

Mr Costello hadn't forgotten me. He had a bottle of that same red cinnamon wine, and he talked over old times the same as ever, like he was a special uncle. We got a sort of guided tour. I told him about last night, about the visit to the Central, and he was pleased as could be. He said he knew I'd like it. I didn't stop to think whether I liked it or not.

'Think of it!' he said. 'All humankind, a single unit. You know the principle of cooperation, Purser?'

When I took too long to think it out, he said, 'You know. Two men working together can produce more than two men working separately. Well, what happens when a thousand – a million – work, sleep, eat, think, breathe together?' The way he said it, it sounded fine.

He looked out past my shoulder and his eyes widened just a little. He pressed a button and the chauffeur brought us to a sliding stop.

'Get that one,' Mr Costello said into a microphone beside him.

Two of the prowlers hurtled down the street and flanked a man. He dodged right, dodged left, and then a prowler hit him and knocked him down.

'Poor chap,' said Mr Costello, pushing the Go button. 'Some of 'em just won't learn.'

I think he regretted it very much. I don't know if the blonde woman did. She didn't even look.

'Are you the mayor?' I asked him.

'Oh, no,' he said. 'I'm a sort of broker. A little of this, a little of that. I'm able to help out a bit.'

'Help out?'

'Purser,' he said confidentially, 'I'm a citizen of Borinquen now. This is my adopted land and I love it. I mean to do everything in my power to help it. I don't care about the cost. This is a people that has found the *truth*, Purser. It awes me. It makes me humble.'

'I ...'

'Speak up, man. I'm your *friend*.'

'I appreciate that, Mr Costello. Well, what I was going to say, I saw that Central and all. I just haven't made up my mind. I mean whether it's good or not.'

'Take your time, take your time,' he said in the big soft voice. 'Nobody has to *make* a man see a truth, am I right? A real truth? A man just sees it all by himself.'

'Yeah,' I agreed. 'Yeah, I guess so.' Sometimes it was hard to find an answer to give Mr Costello.

The car pulled up beside a building. The blonde woman pulled herself together. Mr Costello opened the door for her with his own hands. She got out. Mr Costello rapped the trideo screen in front of him.

He said, 'Make it a real good one, Lucille, real good. I'll be watching.'

She looked at him. She gave me a small smile. A man came down the steps and she went with him up into the building.

We moved off.

I said, 'She's the prettiest woman I ever saw.'

He said, 'She likes you fine, Purser.'

I thought about that. It was too much.

He asked, 'How would you like to have her for your very own?'

'Oh,' I said, 'she wouldn't.'

'Purser, I owe you a big favour. I'd like to pay it back.'

'You don't owe me a thing, Mr Costello!'

We drank some of the wine. The big car slid silently along. It went slowly now, headed back out to the spaceport.

'I need some help,' he said after a time. 'I know you, Purser. You're just the kind of man I can use. They say you're a mathematical genius.'

'Not mathematics exactly, Mr Costello. Just numbers –

statistics – conversion tables and like that. I couldn't do astrogation or theoretical physics and such. I got the best job I could have right now.'

'No, you haven't. I'll be frank with you. I don't want any more responsibility on Borinquen than I've got, you understand, but the people are forcing it on me. They want order, peace and order – tidiness. They want to be as nice and tidy as one of your multiple manifests. Now I could organize them, all right, but I need a tidy brain like yours to keep them organized. I want full birth- and death-rate statistics, and then I want them projected so we can get policy. I want calorie-counts and rationing, so we can use the food supply the best way. I want – well, you see what I mean. Once the devil is routed –'

'What devil?'

'The trappers,' he said gravely.

'Are the trappers really harming the city people?'

He looked at me, shocked. 'They go out and spend weeks alone by themselves, with their own evil thoughts. They are wandering cells, wild cells in the body of humanity. They must be destroyed.'

I couldn't help but think of my consignments. 'What about the fur trade, though?'

He looked at me as if I had made a pretty grubby little mistake. 'My dear Purser,' he said patiently, 'would you set the price of a few pelts above the immortal soul of a race?'

I hadn't thought of it that way.

He said urgently, 'This is just the beginning, Purser. Borinquen is only a start. The unity of that great being, Humanity, will become known throughout the Universe.' He closed his eyes. When he opened them, the organ tone was gone. He said in his old, friendly voice, 'And you and I, we'll show 'em how to do it, hey, boy?'

I leaned forward to look up to the top of the shining spire of the spaceship. 'I sort of like the job I've got. But – my contract *is* up four months from now . . .'

The car turned into the spaceport and hummed across the slag area.

'I think I can count on you,' he said vibrantly. He laughed. 'Remember this little joke, Purser?'

He clicked a switch, and suddenly my own voice filled the tonneau. '*I take bribes from passengers.*'

'Oh, that,' I said, and let loose one *ha* of a *ha-ha* before I understood what he was driving at. 'Mr Costello, you wouldn't use that against me.'

'What do you take me for?' he demanded, in wonderment.

Then we were at the ramp. He got out with me. He gave me his hand. It was warm and hearty.

'If you change your mind about the Purser's job when your contract's up, son, just buzz me through the field phone. They'll connect me. Think it over until you get back here. Take your time.' His hand clamped down on my biceps so hard I winced. 'But you're not going to take any longer than that, are you, my boy?'

'I guess not,' I said.

He got into the front, by the chauffeur, and zoomed away.

I stood looking after him and, when the car was just a dark spot on the slag area, I sort of came to myself. I was standing alone on the foot of the ramp. I felt very exposed.

I turned and ran up to the airlock, hurrying, hurrying to get near people.

That was the trip we shipped the crazy man. His name was Hynes. He was United Earth Consul at Borinquen and he was going back to report. He was no trouble at first, because diplomatic passports are easy to process. He knocked on my door the fifth watch out from Borinquen. I was glad to see him. My room was making me uneasy and I appreciated his company.

Not that he was really company. He was crazy. That first time, he came bursting in and said, 'I hope you don't mind, Purser, but if I don't talk to somebody about this, I'll go out of my mind.' Then he sat down on the end of my bunk and put his head in his hands and rocked back and forth for a long time, without saying anything. Next thing he said was, 'Sorry,' and out he went. Crazy, I tell you.

But he was back in again before long. And then you never heard such ravings.

'Do you know what's happened to Borinquen?' he'd demand. But he didn't want any answers. He had the answers. 'I'll tell you what's wrong with Borinquen – Borinquen's gone mad!' he'd say.

I went on with my work, though there wasn't much of it in space, but that Hynes just couldn't get Borinquen out of his mind.

He said, 'You wouldn't believe it if you hadn't seen it done. First the little wedge, driven in the one place it might exist – between the urbans and the trappers. There was never any conflict between them – never! All of a sudden, the trapper was a menace. How it happened, why, God only knows. First, these laughable attempts to show that they were an unhealthy influence. Yes, laughable – how could you take it seriously?

'And then the changes. You didn't have to prove that a trapper had done anything. You only had to prove he was a trapper. That was enough. And the next thing – how could you *anticipate* anything as mad as this?' – he almost screamed – 'the next thing was to take anyone who wanted to be alone and lump him with the trappers. It all happened so fast – it happened in our sleep. And all of a sudden you were afraid to be alone in a room for a *second*. They left their homes. They built barracks. Everyone afraid of everyone else, afraid, afraid ...

'Do you know what they *did*?' he roared. 'They burned the paintings, every painting on Borinquen they could find that had been done by one artist. And the few artists who survived as artists – I've seen them. By twos and threes, they work together on the one canvas.'

He cried. He actually sat there and cried.

He said, 'There's food in the stores. The crops come in. Trucks run, planes fly, the schools are in session. Bellies get full, cars get washed, people get rich. I know a man called Costello, just in from Earth a few months, maybe a year or so, and already owns half the city.'

'Oh, I know Mr Costello,' I said.

'Do you now! How's that?'

I told him about the trip out with Mr Costello. He sort of backed off from me. '*You're* the one!'

'The one what?' I asked in puzzlement.

'*You're* the man who testified against your Captain, broke him, made him resign.'

'I did no such a thing.'

'I'm the Consul. It was my hearing, man! I was *there!* A recording of the Captain's voice, admitting to insanity, declaring he'd take a gun to his crew if they overrode him. Then your recorded testimony that it was his voice, that you were present when he made the statement. And the Third Officer's recorded statement that all was not well on the bridge. The man denied it, but it was his voice.'

'Wait, wait,' I said. 'I don't believe it. That would need a trial. There was no trial. I wasn't called to any trial.'

'There would have been a trial, you idiot! But the Captain started raving about draw poker without a draw, about the crew fearing poisoning from the cook, about the men wanting witnesses even to change the bridge-watch. Maddest thing I ever heard. He realized it suddenly, the Captain did. He was old, sick, tired, beaten. He blamed the whole thing on Costello, and Costello said he got the recordings from you.'

'Mr Costello wouldn't do such a thing!' I guess I got mad at Mr Hynes then. I told him a whole lot about Mr Costello, what a big man he was. He started to tell me how Mr Costello was forced off the Triumverate for making trouble in the high court, but they were lies and I wouldn't listen. I told him about the poker, how Mr Costello saved us from the cheaters, how he saved us from poisoning, how he made the ship safe for us all.

I remember how he looked at me then. He sort of whispered, 'What has happened to human beings? What have we done to ourselves with these centuries of peace, with confidence and cooperation and no conflict? Here's distrust by man for man, waiting under a thin skin to be punctured by just the right vampire, waiting to hate itself and kill itself all over again ...

'My *God*!' he suddenly screamed at me. 'Do you know what I've been hanging onto? The idea that, for all its error, for all its stupidity, this One Humanity idea on Borinquen was a *principle*? I hated it, but because it was a principle, I could respect it. It's Costello — Costello, who doesn't gamble, but who uses fear to change the poker rules — Costello, who doesn't eat your food, but makes you fear poison — Costello, who can see three hundred years of safe interstellar flight, but who through fear makes the watch officers doubt themselves without a witness — Costello, who runs things without being seen!

'My God, Costello doesn't *care*! It isn't a principle at all. It's just Costello spreading fear anywhere, everywhere, to make himself strong!'

He rushed out, crying with rage and hate. I have to admit I was sort of jolted. I guess I might even have thought about the things he said, only he killed himself before we reached Earth. He was crazy.

We made the rounds, same as ever, scheduled like an interurban line: Load, discharge, blastoff, fly and planetfall. Refuel, clearance, manifest. Eat, sleep, work. There was a hearing about Hynes. Mr Costello sent a spacegram with his regrets when he heard the news. I didn't say anything at the hearing, just that Mr Hynes was upset, that's all, and it was about as true as anything could be. We shipped a second engineer who played real good accordion. One of the inboard men got left on Carànho. All the usual things, except I wrote up my termination with no options, ready to file.

So in its turn we made Borinquen again, and what do you know, there was the space fleet of United Earth. I never guessed they had that many ships. They sheered us off, real Navy: all orders and no information. Borinquen was buttoned up tight; there was some kind of fighting going on down there. We couldn't get or give a word of news through the quarantine. It made the skipper mad and he had to use part of the cargo for fuel, which messed up my records six ways from the middle. I stashed my termination papers away for the time being.

And in its turn, Sigma, where we lay over a couple of days to get back in the rut, and, same as always, Nightingale, right on schedule again.

And who should be waiting for me at Nightingale but Barney

Roteel, who was medic on my first ship, years back when I was fresh from the Academy. He had a pot belly now and looked real successful. We got the jollity out of the way and he settled down and looked me over, real sober. I said it's a small Universe – I'd known he had a big job on Nightingale, but imagine him showing up at the spaceport just when I blew in!

'I showed up *because* you blew in, Purser,' he answered.

Then before I could take that apart, he started asking me questions. Like how was I doing, what did I plan to do.

I said, 'I've been a purser for years and years. What makes you think I want to do anything different?'

'Just wondered.'

I wondered, too. 'Well,' I said, 'I haven't exactly made up my mind, you might say – and a couple of things have got in the way – but I did have a kind of offer.' I told him just in a general way about how big a man Mr Costello was on Borinquen now, and how he wanted me to come in with him. 'It'll have to wait, though. The whole damn Space Navy has a cordon around Borinquen. They wouldn't say why. But whatever it is, Mr Costello'll come out on top. You'll see.'

Barney gave me a sort of puckered-up look. I never saw a man look so weird. Yes, I did, too. It was the old Iron Man, the day he got off the ship and resigned.

'Barney, what's the matter?' I asked.

He got up and pointed through the glass door-lights to a white monowheel that stood poised in front of the receiving station. 'Come on,' he said.

'Aw, I can't. I got to –'

'Come *on*!'

I shrugged. Job or no, this was Barney's bailiwick, not mine. He'd cover me.

He held the door open and said, like a mind reader, 'I'll cover you.'

He went down the ramp and climbed in and skimmed off.

'Where are we going?'

But he wouldn't say. He just drove.

Nightingale's a beautiful place. The most beautiful of them

all, I think, even Sigma. It's run by the U.E., one hundred per cent; this is one planet with no local options, but *none*. It's a regular garden of a world and they keep it that way.

We topped a rise and went down a curving road lined with honest-to-God Lombardy poplars from Earth. There was a little lake down there and a sandy beach. No people.

The road curved and there was a yellow line across it and then a red one, and after it a shimmering curtain, almost transparent. It extended from side to side as far as I could see.

'Force-fence,' Barney said and pressed a button on the dash.

The shimmer disappeared from the road ahead, though it stayed where it was at each side. We drove through and it formed behind us, and we went down the hill to the lake.

Just this side of the beach was the cosiest little Sigman cabana I've seen yet, built to hug the slope and open its arms to the sky. Maybe when I get old they'll turn me out to pasture in one half as good.

While I was goggling at it, Barney said, 'Go on.'

I looked at him and he was pointing. There was a man down near the water, big, very tanned, built like a space-tug. Barney waved me on and I walked down there.

The man got up and turned to me. He had the same widespaced, warm deep eyes, the same full, gentle voice. 'Why, it's the Purser! Hi, old friend. So you came, after all!'

It was sort of rough for a moment. Then I got it out. 'Hi, Mr Costello.'

He banged me on the shoulder. Then he wrapped one big hand around my left biceps and pulled me a little closer. He looked uphill to where Barney leaned against the monowheel, minding his own business. Then he looked across the lake, and up in the sky.

He dropped his voice. 'Purser, you're just the man I need. But I told you that before, didn't I?' He looked around again. 'We'll do it yet, Purser. You and me, we'll hit the top. Come with me. I want to show you something.'

He walked ahead of me towards the beach margin. He was wearing only a breech-ribbon, but he moved and spoke as if he still had the armoured car and the six prowlers. I stumbled after him.

He put a hand behind him and checked me, and then knelt. He said, 'To look at them, you'd think they were all the same, wouldn't you? Well, son, you just let me show you something.'

I looked down. He had an anthill. They weren't like Earth ants. These were bigger, slower, blue, and they had eight legs. They built nests of sand tied together with mucus, and tunnelled under them so that the nests stood up an inch or two like on little pillars.

'They look the same, they act the same, but you'll see,' said Mr Costello.

He opened a synthine pouch that lay in the sand. He took out a dead bird and the thorax of what looked like a Caránho roach, the one that grows as long as your fore-arm. He put the bird down here and the roach down yonder.

'Now,' he said, 'watch.'

The ants swarmed to the bird, pulling and crawling. Busy. But one or two went to the roach and tumbled it and burrowed around. Mr Costello picked an ant off the roach and dropped it on the bird. It weaved around and shouldered through the others and scrabbled across the sand and went back to the roach.

'You see, you *see*?' he said, enthusiastic. 'Look.'

He picked an ant off the dead bird and dropped it by the roach. The ant wasted no time or even curiosity on the piece of roach. It turned around once to get its bearings, and then went straight back to the dead bird.

I looked at the bird with its clothing of crawling blue, and I looked at the roach with its two or three voracious scavengers. I looked at Mr Costello.

He said raptly, 'See what I mean? About one in thirty eats something different. And that's all we need. I tell you, Purser, wherever you look, if you look long enough, you can find a way to make most of a group turn on the rest.'

I watched the ants. 'They're not fighting.'

'Now wait a minute,' he said swiftly. 'Wait a minute. All we have to do is let these bird-eaters know that the roach-eaters ·are dangerous.'

'They're not dangerous,' I said. 'They're just different.'

'What's the difference, when you come right down to it? So we'll get the bird-eaters scared and they'll kill all the roach-eaters.'

'Yes, but why, Mr Costello?'

He laughed. 'I like you, boy. I do the thinking, you do the work. I'll explain it to you. They all look alike. So once we've made 'em drive out these –' he pointed to the minority around the roach – 'they'll never know which among 'em might be a roach-eater. They'll get so worried, they'll do anything to keep from being suspected of roach-eating. When they get scared enough, we can make 'em do anything we want.'

He hunkered down to watch the ants. He picked up a roach-eater and put it on the bird. I got up.

'Well, I only just dropped in, Mr Costello,' I said.

'I'm not an ant,' said Mr Costello. 'As long as it makes no difference to me what they eat, I can make 'em do anything in the world I want.'

'I'll see you around,' I said.

He kept on talking quietly to himself as I walked away. He was watching the ants, figuring, and paid no attention to me.

I went back to Barney. I asked, sort of choked, 'What is he doing, Barney?'

'He's doing what he has to do,' Barney said.

We went back to the monowheel and up the hill and through the force-gate. After a while, I asked, 'How long will he be here?'

'As long as he wants to be.' Barney was kind of short about it.

'Nobody wants to be locked up.'

He had that odd look on his face again. 'Nightingale's not a jail.'

'He can't get out.'

'Look, chum, we could start him over. We could even make a purser out of him. But we stopped doing that kind of thing a long time ago. We let a man do what he wants to do.'

'He never wanted to be boss over an anthill.'

'He didn't?'

I guess I looked as if I didn't understand that, so he said, 'All his life he's pretended he's a man and the rest of us are ants. Now it's come true for him. He won't run human anthills any more because he will never again get near one.'

I looked through the windshield at the shining finger that was my distant ship. 'What happened on Borinquen, Barney?'

'Some of his converts got loose around the System. That Humanity One idea had to be stopped.' He drove a while, seeing badly out of a thinking face. 'You won't take this hard, Purser, but you're a thick-witted ape. I can say that if no one else can.'

'All right,' I said. 'Why?'

'We had to *smash* into Borinquen, which used to be so free and easy. We got into Costello's place. It was a regular fort. We got him and his files. We didn't get his girl. He killed her, but the files were enough.'

After a time I said, 'He was always a good friend to me.'

'Was he?'

I didn't say anything. He wheeled up to the receiving station and stopped the machine.

He said, 'He was all ready for you if you came to work for him. He had a voice recording of you large as life, saying "Sometimes a man's just *got* to be by himself." Once you went to work for him, all he needed to do to keep you in line was to threaten to put that on the air.'

I opened the door. 'What did you have to show him to me for?'

'Because we believe in letting a man do what he wants to do, as long as he doesn't hurt the rest of us. If you want to go back to the lake and work for Costello, for instance, I'll take you there.'

I closed the door carefully and went up the ramp to the ship.

I did my work and when the time came, we blasted off. I was mad. I don't think it was about anything Barney told me. I wasn't especially mad about Mr Costello or what happened to him, because Barney's the best Navy psych doc there is and Nightingale's the most beautiful hospital planet in the Universe.

What made me mad was the thought that never again would a man as big as Mr Costello give that big, warm, soft, strong friendship to a lunkhead like me.

Jack Finney

Quit Zoomin' Those Hands Through the Air

Hey, quit zoomin' your *hands* through the air, boy – I know you was a flier! You flew *good* in the war, course you did; I'd expect that from a grandson of mine. But don't get to thinking you know all about war, son, or flying machines either. The war we finished in sixty-five is still the toughest we've fought, and don't you forget it. It was a big war fought by big men, and your Pattons and Arnolds and Stilwells – they were *good*, boy, no denying it – but Grant, there was a general. Never told you about this before, because I was swore to secrecy by the general himself, but I think it's all right, now; I think the oath has expired. Now, *quiet*, boy! Put those hands in your pockets and listen!

Now, the night I'm talking about, the night I met the general, I didn't know we'd see him at all. Didn't know anything except we were riding along Pennsylvania Avenue, me and the major, him not saying where we were going or why, just jogging along, one hand on the reins, a big black box strapped to the major's saddle in front, and that little pointy beard of his stabbing up and down with every step.

It was late, after ten, and everyone was asleep. But the moon was up, bright and full through the trees, and it was nice – the horses' shadows gliding along sharp and clear beside us, and not a sound in the street but their hoofs, hollow on the packed dirt. We'd been riding two days, I'd been nipping some liberated applejack – only we didn't say 'liberated' then; we called it 'foraging' – and I was asleep in the saddle, my trumpet jiggling in the small of my back. Then the major nudged me, and I woke up and saw the White House ahead. 'Yessir,' I said.

He looked at me, the moon shining yellow on his epaulets,

and said, real quiet, 'Tonight, boy, we may win the war. You and I.' He smiled, mysterious, and patted the black box. 'You know who I am, boy?'

'Yessir.'

'No, you don't. I'm a professor. Up at Harvard College. Or was, anyway. Glad to be in the army now, though. Pack of fools up there, most of them; can't see past the ends of their noses. Well, tonight, boy, we may win the war.'

'Yessir,' I said. Most officers higher than captain were a little queer in the head, I'd noticed, majors especially. That's how it was then, anyway, and I don't reckon it's changed any, even in the Air Force.

We stopped near the White House at the edge of the lawn and sat looking at it – a great big old house, silvery white in the moonlight, the light over the front door shining out through the porch columns onto the driveway. There was a light in an east window on the ground floor, and I kept hoping I'd see the President, but I didn't. The major opened his box. 'Know what this is, boy?'

'Nosir?'

'It's my own invention, based on my own theories, nobody else's. They think I'm a crackpot up at the School, but I think it'll work. Win the war, boy.' He moved a little lever inside the box. 'Don't want to send us too far ahead, son, or technical progress will be beyond us. Say ninety years or so from now, approximately; think that ought to be about right?'

'Yessir.'

'All right.' The major jammed his thumb down on a little button in the box; it made a humming sound that kept rising higher and higher till my ears began to hurt; then he lifted his hand. 'Well,' he said, smiling and nodding, the little pointy beard going up and down, 'it is now some ninety-odd years later.' He nodded at the White House. 'Glad to see it's still standing.'

I looked up at the White House again. It was just the same, the light still shining out between the big white columns, but I didn't say anything.

The major twitched his reins and turned. 'Well, boy, we've

got work ahead; come on.' And he set off at a trot along Pennsylvania Avenue with me beside him.

Pretty soon we turned south, and the major twisted around in his saddle and said, 'Now, the question is, what do they have in the future?' He held up his finger like a teacher in school, and I believed the part about him being a professor. 'We don't know,' the major went on, 'but we know where to find it. In a museum. We're going to the Smithsonian Institution, if it's still standing. For us it should be a veritable storehouse of the future.'

It had been standing last week, I knew, and after a while, off across the grass to the east, there it was, a stone building with towers like a castle, looking just the same as always, the windows now black and white in the moonlight. 'Still standing, sir,' I said.

'Good,' said the major. 'Reconnaissance approach, now,' and we went on to a cross-street and turned into it. Up ahead were several buildings I'd never noticed before, and we went up to them and swung down off our horses. 'Walk between these buildings,' the major said, leading his horse. 'Quiet, now; we're reconnoitring.'

We crept on, quiet as could be, in the shadows between the two buildings. The one to the right looked just like the Smithsonian to me, and I knew it must be a part of it; another building I'd never seen before. The major was all excited now, and kept whispering. 'Some new kind of weapon that will destroy the whole Rebel Army is what we're looking for. Let me know if you see any such thing, boy.'

'Yessir,' I said, and I almost bumped into something sitting out there in the open in front of the building at the left. It was big and made entirely out of heavy metal, and instead of wheels it rested on two movable belts made of metal; big flat plates linked together.

'Looks like a tank,' said the major, 'though I don't know what they keep in it. Keep moving, boy; this thing is obviously no use on a battlefield.'

We walked on just a step, and there on the pavement in front of us was a tremendous cannon, three times bigger than any I'd ever seen before in my life. It had an immense long barrel, wheels high as my chest, and it was painted kind of funny, in wavy stripes and splotches, so that you could hardly see it at first in the moonlight that got down between the buildings. 'Look at that thing!' the major said softly. 'It would pulverize Lee in an hour, but I don't know how we'd carry it. No,' he said, shaking his head, 'this isn't it. I wonder what they've got inside, though.' He stepped up to the doors and peered in through the glass, shading his eyes with his hand. Then he gasped and turned to me.

I went up beside him and looked through the glass. It was a long, big building, the moonlight slanting in through the windows all along one side; and all over the floor, and even hanging from the ceiling, were the weirdest-looking things I ever saw. They were each big as a wagon, some bigger, and they had wheels, but only two wheels, near the front; and I was trying to figure that out when the major got his voice back.

'Aircraft, by God!' he said. 'They've got aircraft! Win the war!'

'Air what, sir?'

'*Aircraft.* Flying machines. They fly through the air. Don't you see the wings, boy?'

Each of the machines I could see inside had two things sticking out at each side like oversize ironing boards, but they looked stiff to me, and I didn't see how they could flap like wings. I didn't know what else the major could be talking about, though. 'Yessir,' I said.

But the major was shaking his head again. 'Much too advanced,' he said. 'We could never master them. What we need is an earlier type, and I don't see any in here. Come on, boy; don't straggle.'

We walked on, leading the horses, towards the front of the other building. At the doors we peeked in, and there on the floor, with tools and empty crates lying around as though they'd just unpacked it, was another of the things, a flying machine. Only this was far smaller, and was nothing but a framework of wood like a big box kite, with little canvas wings, as the major called them. It didn't have wheels, either, just a couple of runners like a sled. Lying propped against a wall, as though they were just ready to put it up, was a sign. The moonlight didn't quite reach it, and I couldn't read all the words, but I could make out a few. 'World's first,' it said in one place, and farther down it said, 'Kitty Hawk'.

The major just stood there for maybe a minute, staring like a man in a trance. Then he murmured to himself, 'Very like sketches of da Vinci's model; only apparently this one worked.' He grinned suddenly, all excited. 'This is it, boy,' he said. 'This is why we came.'

I knew what he had in mind, and I didn't like it. 'You'll never break in there, sir,' I said. 'Those doors look mighty solid, and I'll bet this place is guarded like the mint.'

The major just smiled, mysterious again. 'Of course it is, son; it's the treasure house of a nation. No one could possibly get in with any hope of removing anything, let alone this aircraft – under ordinary circumstances. But don't worry about that, boy; just leave it to me. Right now we need fuel.' Turning on his heel, he walked back to his horse, took the reins, and led him off; and I followed with mine.

Off some distance, under some trees, near a big open space like a park, the major set the lever inside his black box, and pressed the button. 'Back in eighteen sixty-four, now,' he said then, and sniffed. 'Air smells fresher. Now, I want you to take your horse, go to garrison headquarters, and bring back all the petrol you can carry. They've got some for cleaning uniforms. Tell them I'll take full responsibility. Understand?'

'Yessir.'

'Then off with you. When you come back, this is where I want you to meet me.' The major turned and began walking away with his horse.

At headquarters the guard woke a private, who woke a corporal, who woke a sergeant, who woke a lieutenant, who woke a captain, who swore a little and then woke up the private again and told him to give me what I wanted. The private went away, murmuring softly to himself, and came back pretty soon with six five-gallon jugs; and I tied them to my saddle, signed six sets of receipts in triplicate, and led my horse back through the moonlit streets of Washington, taking a nip of applejack now and then.

I went by the White House again, on purpose; and this time someone was standing silhouetted against the lighted east window – a big man, tall and thin, his shoulders bowed, his head down on his chest – and I couldn't help but get the impression of a weary strength and purpose and a tremendous dignity. I felt sure it was him, but I can't rightly claim I saw the President, because I've always been one to stick to the facts and never stretch the truth even a little bit.

The major was waiting under the trees, and my jaw nearly dropped off, because the flying machine was sitting beside him. 'Sir,' I said, 'how did you –'

The major interrupted, smiling and stroking his little beard: 'Very simple. I merely stood at the front door' – he patted the black box at the saddle near his shoulder – 'and moved back in time to a moment when even the Smithsonian didn't exist. Then I stepped a few paces ahead with the box under my arm, adjusted the lever again, moved forward to the proper moment, and there I was, standing beside the flying machine. I took myself and the machine out by the same method, and my mount pulled it here on its skids.'

'Yessir,' I said. I figured I could keep up this foolishness as long as he could, though I did wonder how he had got the flying machine out.

The major pointed ahead. 'I've been exploring the ground, and it's pretty rocky and rough.' He turned to the black box, adjusted the dial, and pressed the button. 'Now, it's a park,' he said, 'sometime in the nineteen forties.'

'Yessir.' I said.

The major nodded at a little spout in the flying machine. 'Fill her up,' he said, and I untied one of the jugs, uncorked it, and began to pour. The tank sounded dry when the petrol hit it, and a cloud of dust puffed up from the spout. It didn't hold very much, only a few quarts, and the major began untying the other jugs. 'Lash these down in the machine,' he said, and while I was doing that, the major began pacing up and down, muttering to himself. 'To start the engine, I should imagine you simply turn the propellers. But the machine will need help in getting into the air.' He kept walking up and down, pulling his beard; then he nodded his head. 'Yes,' he said, 'that should do it, I think.' He stopped and looked at me. 'Nerves in good shape, boy? Hands steady and reliable?'

'Yessir.'

'All right, son, this thing should be easy to fly – mostly a matter of balance, I imagine.' He pointed to a sort of saddle at the front of the machine. 'I believe you simply lie on your stomach with your hips in this saddle; it connects with the rudder and wings by cables. By merely moving from side to side, you control the machine's balance and direction.' The major pointed to a lever. 'Work this with your hand,' he said, 'to go up or down. That's all there is to it, so far as I can see, and if I'm wrong in any details, you can correct them in the air with a little experimenting. Think you can fly it, boy?'

'Yessir.'

'Good,' he said, and grabbed one of the propellers at the back and began turning it. I worked on the other propeller, but nothing happened; they just creaked, stiff and rusty-like. But we kept turning, yanking harder and harder, and pretty soon the little engine coughed.

'Now, *heave*, boy!' the major said, and we laid into it hard, and every time, now, the engine would cough a little. Finally, we yanked so hard, both together, our feet nearly came off the ground, and the motor coughed and kept on coughing and like to choked to death. Then it sort of cleared its throat and started to stutter but didn't stop, and then it was running smooth, the propellers just whirling, flashing and shining in the moonlight till you could hardly see them, and the flying machine shaking like a wet dog, with little clouds of dust pouring up out of every part of it.

'Excellent,' said the major, and he sneezed from the dust. Then he began unfastening the horses' bridles, strapping them together again to make a single long rein. He posed the horses in front of the machine and said, 'Get in, boy. We've got a busy night ahead.' I lay down in the saddle, and he climbed up on the top wing and lay down on his stomach. 'You take the lever, and I'll take the rein. Ready, boy?'

'Yessir.'

'*Gee up!*' said the major, snapping the rein hard, and the horses started off, heads down, hoofs digging in.

The flying machine sort of bumped along over the grass on its skids, but it soon smoothed out and began sliding along, level as a sled on packed snow, and the horses' heads came up and they began to trot, the motor just chugging away.

'Sound *forward!*' said the major, and I unslung my trumpet and blew forward; the horses buckled into it, and we were skimming along, must have been fifteen, maybe twenty miles an hour or even faster.

'Now, *charge!*' yelled the major, and I blew charge, and the hoofs began drumming the turf, the horses whinnying and snorting, the engine chugging faster and faster, the propellers whining in back of us, and all of a sudden the grass was a good five feet below, and the reins were hanging straight down. Then – for a second it scared me – we were passing the horses. We were right over their backs; then they began slipping away under the machine, and the major dropped the reins and yelled, 'Pull back the lever!' I yanked back hard, and we shot up into the air like a rocket.

I remembered what the major had said about experimenting and tried easing back on the lever, and the flying machine sort of levelled out, and there we were, chugging along faster than I'd ever gone in my life. It was wonderful fun, and I glanced down and there was Washington spread out below, a lot bigger than I'd thought it was and with more lights than I'd known there were in the world. They were *bright*, too; didn't look like candles and kerosene lamps at all. Way off, towards the centre of town, some of the lights were red and green, and so bright they lighted up the sky.

'Watch out!' yelled the major, and just ahead, rushing straight at us, was a tremendous monument or something, a big tall stone needle.

I don't know why, but I twisted hard to the left in the little saddle and yanked back on the lever, and a wing heaved up and the flying machine shot off to one side, the wing tip nearly grazing the monument. Then I lay straight again, holding the lever steady. The machine levelled off, and it was like the first time I drove a team. I could feel in my bones that I was a natural-born flying-machine driver.

'Back to headquarters,' said the major. 'Can you find the way?'

'Yessir,' I said, and headed south.

The major fiddled with the dial in his black box and pressed the bottom, and down below now, in the moonlight, I could see the dirt road leading out of Washington back to headquarters. I turned for a last look at the city, but there were only a few lights now, not looking nearly as bright as before; the red and green lights were gone.

But the road was bright in the moonlight, and we tore along over it when it went straight, cut across bends when it curved, flying it must have been close to forty miles an hour. The wind streamed back cold, and I pulled out the white knit muffler my grandma gave me and looped it around my throat. One end streamed back, flapping and waving in the wind. I thought my forage cap might blow off, so I reversed it on my head, the peak at the back, and I felt that now I looked the way a flying-machine driver ought to, and wished the girls back home could have seen me.

For a while I practised with the lever and hip saddle, soaring up till the engine started coughing, and turning and dipping down, seeing how close I could shave the road. But finally the major yelled and made me quit. Every now and then we'd see a light flare up in a farmhouse and when we'd look back we'd see the light wobbling across the yard and know some farmer was out there with his lamp, staring up at the noise in the sky.

Several times, on the way, we had to fill the tank again, and pretty soon, maybe less than two hours, camp fires began sliding under our wings, and the major was leaning from side to side, looking down at the ground. Then he pointed ahead. 'That field down there, boy; can you land this thing with the engine off?'

'Yessir,' I said, and I stopped the engine, and the machine

began sliding down like a toboggan, and I kept easing the lever back and forth, watching the field come up to meet us, growing bigger and bigger every second. We didn't make a sound now, except for the wind sighing through the wires, and we came in like a ghost, the moonlight white on our wings. Our downward path and the edge of the field met exactly, and the instant before we hit, my arm eased the lever back and the skids touched the grass like a whisper. Then we bumped a little, stopped, and sat there a moment not saying a word. Off in the weeds the crickets began chirping again.

The major said there was a cliff at the side of the field and we found it, and slid the machine over to the edge of it, and then we started walking around the field, in opposite directions looking for a path or sentry. I found the sentry right away, guarding the path lying down with his eyes closed. My applejack was gone, so I shook him awake and explained my problem.

'How much you got?' he said; I told him a dollar, and he went off into the woods and came back with a jug. 'Good whisky,' he said, 'the best. And exactly a dollar's worth; the jug's nearly full.' So I tasted the whisky – it *was* good – paid him, took the jug back and tied it down in the machine. Then I went back to the path and called the major, and he came over, cutting across the field. Then the sentry led us down the path towards the general's tent.

It was a square tent with a gabled roof, a lantern burning inside, and the front flap open. The sentry saluted. 'Major of Cavalry here, sir.' He pronounced the word like an ignorant infantryman. 'Says it's secret and urgent.'

'Send the *calvary* in,' said a voice, pronouncing it just that way, and I knew the general was a horse soldier at heart.

We stepped forward, saluting. The general was sitting on a kitchen chair, his feet, in old army shoes with the laces untied, propped on a big wooden keg with a spigot. He wore a black slouch hat, his vest and uniform blouse were unbuttoned, and I saw three silver stars embroidered on a shoulder strap. The general's eyes were blue, hard, and tough, and he wore a full beard. 'At ease,' he said. 'Well?'

'Sir,' said the major, 'we have a flying machine and propose, with your permission, to use it against the rebs.'

'Well,' said the general, leaning back on the hind legs of his chair, you've come in the nick of time. Lee's men are massed at Cold Harbor, and I've been sitting here all night dri— thinking, They've got to be crushed before ... A *flying* machine, did you say?'

'Yessir,' said the major.

'H'mm,' said the general. 'Where'd you get it?'

'Well, sir, that's a long story.'

'I'll bet it is,' said the general. He picked up a stub of cigar from the table beside him and chewed it thoughtfully. 'If I hadn't been thinking hard and steadily all night, I wouldn't believe a word of this. What do you propose to do with your flying machines?'

'Load it with grenades!' The major's eyes began to sparkle. 'Drop them spang on rebel headquarters! Force immediate surrender –'

The general shook his head. 'No,' he said, 'I don't think so. Air power isn't enough, son, and will never replace the foot soldier, mark my words. Has its place, though, and you've done good work.' He glanced at me. 'You the driver, son?'

'Yessir.'

He turned to the major again. 'I want you to go up with a map. Locate Lee's positions. Mark them on the map and return. Do that, major, and tomorrow, June third, after the Battle of Cold Harbor, I'll personally pin silver leaves on your straps. Because I'm going to take Richmond like – well, I don't know what. As for you, son' – he glanced at my stripe – 'you'll make corporal. Might even design new badges for you; pair of wings on the chest or something like that.'

'Yessir,' I said.

'Where's the machine?' said the general. 'Believe I'll walk down and look at it. Lead the way.' The major and me saluted, turned and walked out, and the general said, 'Go ahead; I'll catch up.'

At the field the general caught up, shoving something into

his hip pocket – a handkerchief, maybe. 'Here's your map,' he said, and he handed a folded paper to the major.

The major took it, saluted, and said, 'For the Union, sir! For the cause of –'

'Save the speeches,' said the general, 'till you're running for office.'

'Yessir,' said the major, and he turned to me. 'Fill her up!'

I filled the tank, we spun the propellers, and this time the engine started right up. We climbed in, and I reversed my forage cap and tied on my scarf.

'Good,' said the general approvingly. 'Style; real calvary style.'

We shoved off and dropped over the cliff like a dead weight, the ground rushing up fast. Then the wings bit into the air, I pulled back my lever, and we shot up, the engine snorting, fighting for altitude, and I swung out wide and circled the field, once at fifty feet, then at a hundred. The first time, the general just stood there, head back, mouth open, staring up at us, and I could see his brass buttons gleam in the moonlight. The second time around he still had his head back, but I don't think he was looking at us. He had a hand to his mouth, and he was drinking a glass of water – I could tell because just as we straightened and headed south, he threw it off into the bushes hard as he could, and I could see the glass flash in the moonlight. Then he started back to headquarters at a dead run, in a hurry. I guess, to get back to his thinking.

The machine was snorting at the front end, kicking up at the hindquarters, high-spirited, and I had all I could do to keep her from shying, and I wished she'd had reins. Down below, cold and sparkly in the moonlight, I could see the James River, stretching east and west, and the lights of Richmond, but it was no time for sight-seeing. The machine was frisky, trembling in the flanks, and before I knew it she took the bit in her mouth and headed straight down, the wind screaming through her wires, the ripples on the water rushing up at us.

But I'd handled runaways before, and I heaved back on the lever, forcing her head up, and she curved back into the air fast as a calvary mount at a barrier. But this time she didn't cough at the top of the curve. She snorted through her nostrils, wild with power, and I barely had time to yell, 'Hang on!' to the major before she went clear over on her back and shot down towards the river again. The major yelled, but the applejack was bubbling inside me and I'd never had such a thrill, and I yelled, too, laughing and screaming. Then I pulled back hard, yelling, 'Whoa!' but up and over we went again, the wings creaking like saddle leather on a galloping horse. At the top of the climb, I leaned hard to the left, and we shot off in a wide, beautiful curve, and I never had such fun in my life.

Then she quieted down a little. She wasn't broken, I knew, but she could feel a real rider in the saddle, so she waited, figuring out what to try next. The major got his breath and used it for cursing. He didn't call me anything I'd ever heard before, and I'd been in the calvary since I joined the Army. It was a beautiful job and I admired it. 'Yessir,' I said when his breath ran out again.

He still had plenty to say, I think, but campfires were sliding under our wings, and he had to get out his map and go to work. We flew back and forth, parallel with the river, the major busy with his pencil and map. It was dull and monotonous for both me and the machine, and I kept wondering if the rebs could see or hear us. So I kept sneaking closer and closer to the ground, and pretty soon, directly ahead in a clearing, I saw a campfire with men around it. I don't rightly know if it was me or the machine had the idea, but I barely touched the lever and she dipped her nose and shot right down, aiming smack at the fire.

They saw us then, all right, and heard us, too. They scattered, yelling and cursing, with me leaning over screaming at them and laughing like mad. I hauled back on the lever maybe five feet from the ground, and the fire singed our tail as we curved back up. But this time, at the top of the climb, the engine got the hiccups, and I had to turn and come down in a slow glide to ease the strain off the engine till she got her breath, and now the men below had muskets out, and they were mad. They fired kneeling, following up with their sights the way you lead ducks, the musket balls whistling past us.

'Come on!' I yelled. I slapped the flying machine on her side, unslung my trumpet, and blew charge. Down we went, the engine neighing and whinnying like crazy, and the men tossed their muskets aside and dived in all directions, and we fanned the flames with our wings and went up like a bullet, the engine screaming in triumph. At the top of the curve I turned, and we shot off over the treetops, the wing tip pointing straight at the moon. 'Sorry, sir,' I said, before the major could get his breath. 'She's wild – feeling her oats. But I think I've got her under control.'

'Then get back to headquarters before you kill us,' he said coldly. 'We'll discuss this later.'

'Yessir,' I said. I spotted the river off to one side and flew over it, and when the major got us oriented he navigated us back to the field.

'Wait here,' he said when we landed, and he trotted down the path towards the general's tent. I was just as glad; I felt like a drink, and besides I loved that machine now and wanted to take care of her. I wiped her down with my muffler, and wished I could feed her something.

Then I felt around inside the machine, and then I was cussing that sentry, beating the major's record, I think, because my whisky was gone, and I knew what that sentry had done: sneaked back to my machine and got it soon as he had me and the major in the general's tent, and now he was back at the guardhouse, probably, lapping it up and laughing at me.

The major came down the path fast. 'Back to Washington, and hurry,' he said. 'Got to get this where it belongs before daylight or the space-time continuum will be broken and no telling what might happen then.'

So we filled the tank and flew on back to Washington. I was tired and so was the flying machine, I guess, because now she just chugged along, heading for home and the stable.

We landed near the trees again, and climbed out, stiff and tired. And after creaking and sighing a little, the flying machine just sat there on the ground, dead tired, too. There were a couple of musket-ball holes in her wings and some soot on her tail, but otherwise she looked just the same.

'Look alive, boy!' the major said. 'You go hunt for the horses, and I'll get the machine back,' and he got behind the flying machine and began pushing it along over the grass.

I found the horses grazing not far off, brought them back, and tethered them to the trees. When the major returned we started back, just as dawn was breaking.

Well, I never did get my promotion. Or my wings either. . . .

It got hot, and pretty soon I fell asleep.

After a while I heard the major call, 'Boy! Boy!' and I woke up saying, 'Yessir!' but he didn't mean me. A paper boy was running over with a newspaper, and when the major paid for it, I drew alongside and we both looked at it, sitting there in our saddles near the outskirts of Washington. BATTLE AT COLD HARBOR, it said, and underneath were a lot of smaller head-lines one after the other. *Disaster for Union Forces! Surprise Attack at Daybreak Fails! Repulsed in Eight Minutes! Know-ledge of Rebel Positions Faulty! Confederate Losses Small, Ours Large! Grant Offers No Explanation; Inquiry Urged!* There was a news story, too, but we didn't read it. The major flung the paper to the gutter and touched his spurs to his horse, and I followed.

By noon the next day we were back in our lines, but we didn't look for the general. We didn't feel any need to, because we felt sure he was looking for us. He never found us, though; possibly because I grew a beard, and the major shaved his off. And we never had told him our names.

Well, Grant finally took Richmond – he was a great general – but he had to take it by siege.

I only saw him one more time, and that was years later when he wasn't a general any more. It was a New Year's Day, and I was in Washington and saw a long line of people waiting to get into the White House, and knew it must be the public reception the Presidents used to hold every New Year's. So I stood in line, and an hour later I reached the President. 'Re-member me, General?' I said.

He stared at me, narrowing his eyes; then his face got red

and his eyes flashed. But he took a deep breath remembering I was a voter, forced a smile, and nodded at a door behind him. 'Wait in there,' he said.

Soon afterward the reception ended, and the general sat facing me, behind his big desk, biting the end off a short cigar. 'Well,' he said, without any preliminaries, 'what went wrong?'

So I told him; I'd figured it out long since, of course. I told him how the flying machine went crazy, looping till we could hardly see straight, so that we flew north again and mapped our own lines.

'I found that out,' said the general, 'immediately after ordering the attack.'

Then I told him about the sentry who'd stole me the whisky, and how I thought he'd stolen it back again, when he hadn't.

The general nodded. 'Poured that whisky into the machine, didn't you? Mistook it for a jug of gasoline.'

'Yessir,' I said.

He nodded again. 'Naturally the flying machine went crazy. That was my own private brand of whisky, the same whisky Lincoln spoke of so highly. That damned sentry of mine was stealing it all through the war.' He leaned back in his chair, puffing his cigar. 'Well,' he said, 'I guess it's just as well you didn't succeed; Lee thought so, too. We discussed it at Appomattox before the formal surrender, just the two of us chatting in the farmhouse. Never have told anyone what we talked about there, and everybody's been wondering and guessing ever since. Well, we talked about air power, son, and Lee was opposed to it, and so was I. Wars are meant for the ground, boy, and if they ever take to the air they'll start dropping bombshells, mark my words, and if they ever do that, there'll be hell to pay. So Lee and I decided to keep our mouths shut about air power, and we have – you won't find a word about it in my memoirs or his. Anyway, son, as Billy Sherman said, "War is hell, and there's no sense starting people thinking up ways to make it worse." So I want you to keep quiet about Cold Harbor. Don't say a word if you live to be a hundred.'

'Yessir,' I said, and I never have. But I'm way past a hundred now, son, and if the general wanted me to keep quiet after that he'd have said so. Now, take those hands out of the air, boy! Wait'll the world's *first* pilot gets through talking!

J. G. Ballard

Build-up

Noon talk on Millionth Street:

'Sorry, these are the West millions. You want 9775335d East.'

'Dollar five a cubic foot? Sell!'

'Take a westbound express to 495th Avenue, cross over to a Redline elevator and go up a thousand levels to Plaza Terminal. Carry on south from there and you'll find it between 568th Avenue and 422nd Street.'

'There's a cave-in down at KEN county! Fifty blocks by twenty by thirty levels.'

'Listen to this – "PYROS STAGE MASS BREAK-OUT! FIRE POLICE CORDON BAY COUNTY!"'

'It's a beautiful counter. Detects up to .005 per cent monoxide. Cost me $300.'

'Have you seen those new intercity sleepers? Takes only ten minutes to up 3,000 levels!'

'Ninety cents a foot? Buy!'

'You say the idea came to you in a dream?' the voice jabbed out. 'You're sure no one else gave it to you.'

'No,' M. said flatly. A couple of feet away from him a spotlamp threw a cone of dirty yellow light into his face. He dropped his eyes from the glare and waited as the sergeant paced over to his desk, tapped his fingers on the edge and swung round on him again.

'You talked it over with your friends?'

'Only the first theory,' M. explained quietly. 'About the possibility of flight.'

'But you told me the other theory was more important. Why keep it quiet from them?'

124

M. hesitated. Outside somewhere a trolley shunted and clanged along the elevated. 'I was afraid they wouldn't understand what I meant.'

The sergeant laughed sourly. 'You mean they would have thought you really were crazy?'

M. shifted uncomfortably on the stool. Its seat was only six inches off the floor and his thighs and lumbar muscles felt like slabs of inflamed rubber. After three hours of cross-questioning logic had faded and he groped helplessly. 'The concept was a little abstract. There weren't any words for it.'

The sergeant snorted. 'I'm glad to hear you say it.' He sat down on the desk, watched M. for a moment and then went over to him.

'Now look,' he said confidentially. 'It's getting late. Do you still think both theories are reasonable?'

M. looked up. 'Aren't they?'

The sergeant turned angrily to the man watching in the shadows by the window.

'We're wasting our time,' he snapped. 'I'll hand him over to Psycho. You've seen enough, haven't you, Doc?'

The surgeon stared thoughtfully at his hands. He was a tall heavy-shouldered man, built like a wrestler, with thick coarsely-lined features.

He ambled forward, knocking back one of the chairs with his knee.

'There's something I want to check,' he said curtly. 'Leave me alone with him for half an hour.'

The sergeant shrugged. 'All right,' he said, going over to the door. 'But be careful with him.'

When the sergeant had gone the surgeon sat down behind the desk and stared vacantly out of the window, listening to the dull hum of air through the huge ninety-foot ventilator shaft which rose out of the street below the station. A few roof lights were still burning and 200 yards away a single policeman slowly patrolled the iron catwalk running above the street, his boots ringing across the darkness.

M. sat on the stool, elbows between his knees, trying to edge a little life back into his legs.

Eventually the surgeon glanced down at the charge sheet.

Name ....Franz M.
Age ....20.
Occupation.......................Student.
Address ....3599719 West 783rd Str., Level
                                  549-7705-45 KN1 (Local).
Charge..............................Vagrancy.

'Tell me about this dream,' he said slowly, idly flexing a steel rule between his hands as he looked across at M.

'I think you've heard everything, sir,' M. said.

'In detail.'

M. shifted uneasily. 'There wasn't much to it, and what I do remember isn't too clear now.'

The surgeon yawned. M. waited and then started to recite what he'd already repeated twenty times.

'I was suspended in the air above a flat stretch of open ground, something like the floor of an enormous arena. My arms were out at my sides, and I was looking down, floating —'

'Hold on,' the surgeon interrupted. 'Are you sure you weren't swimming?'

'No,' M. said. 'I'm certain I wasn't. All around me there was free space. That was the most important part about it. There were no walls. Nothing but emptiness. That's all I remember.'

The surgeon ran his finger along the edge of the rule.

'Go on.'

'Well, the dream gave me the idea of building a flying machine. One of my friends helped me construct it.'

The surgeon nodded. Almost absently he picked up the charge sheet, crushed it with a single motion of his hand and flicked it into the waste basket.

'Don't be crazy, Franz!' Gregson remonstrated. They took their places in the chemistry cafeteria queue. 'It's against the laws of hydrodynamics. Where would you get your buoyancy?'

'Suppose you had a rigid fabric vane,' Franz explained as they shuffled past the hatchways. 'Say ten feet across, like one of those composition wall sections, with hand-grips on the ventral surface. And then you jump down from the gallery at the Coliseum Stadium. What would happen?'

'You'd make a hole in the floor. Why?'

'No, seriously.'

'If it was large enough and held together you'd swoop down like a paper dart.'

'Glide,' Franz said. 'Right.' Thirty levels above them one of the intercity expresses roared over, rattling the tables and cutlery in the cafeteria. Franz waited until they reached a table and sat forward, his food forgotten.

'And say you attached a propulsive unit, such as a battery-driven ventilator fan, or one of those rockets they use on the Sleepers. With enough thrust to overcome your weight. What then?'

Gregson shrugged. 'If you could control the thing, you'd, you'd ...' He frowned at Franz. 'What's the word? You're always using it.'

'Fly.'

'Basically, Matteson, the machine is simple,' Sanger, the physics lector, commented as they entered the Science Library. 'An elementary application of the Venturi Principle. But what's the point of it? A trapeze would serve its purpose equally well, and be far less dangerous. In the first place consider the enormous clearances it would require. I hardly think the traffic authorities will look upon it with any favour.'

'I know it wouldn't be practical here,' Franz admitted. 'But in a large open area it should be.'

'Allowed. I suggest you immediately negotiate with the Arena Garden on Level 347-25,' the lector said whimsically. 'I'm sure they'll be glad to hear about your scheme.'

Franz smiled politely. 'That wouldn't be large enough. I was really thinking of an area of totally free space. In three dimensions, as it were.'

Sanger looked at Franz curiously. 'Free space? Isn't that a contradiction in terms? Space is a dollar a cubic foot.' He scratched his nose. 'Have you begun to construct this machine yet?'

'No,' Franz said.

'In that event I should try to forget all about it. Remember, Matteson, the task of science is to consolidate existing knowledge, to systematize and reinterpret the discoveries of the past, not to chase wild dreams into the future.'

He nodded and disappeared among the dusty shelves.

Gregson was waiting on the steps.

'Well?' he asked.

'Let's try it out this afternoon,' Franz said. 'We'll cut Text 5 Pharmacology. I know those Fleming readings backwards. I'll ask Dr McGhee for a couple of passes.'

They left the library and walked down the narrow, dimly-lit alley which ran behind the huge new Civil Engineering laboratories. Over 75 per cent of the student enrolment was in the architectural and engineering faculties, a meagre 2 per cent in pure sciences. Consequently the physics and chemistry libraries were housed in the oldest quarter of the University, in two virtually condemned galvanized hutments which once contained the now closed Philosophy School.

At the end of the alley they entered the university plaza and started to climb the iron stairway leading to the next level a hundred feet above. Half-way up a white-helmeted F.P. checked them cursorily with his detector and waved them past.

'What did Sanger think?' Gregson asked as they stepped up into 637th Street and walked across to the Suburban Elevator station.

'He's no use at all,' Franz said. 'He didn't even begin to understand what I was talking about.'

Gregson laughed ruefully. 'I don't know whether I do.'

Franz took a ticket from the automat and mounted the Down platform. An elevator dropped slowly towards him, its bell jangling.

'Wait until this afternoon,' he called back. 'You're really going to see something.'

The floor manager at the Coliseum initialled the two passes.

'Students, eh? All right.' He jerked a thumb at the long

package Franz and Gregson were carrying. 'What have you got there?'

'It's a device for measuring air velocities,' Franz told him.

The manager grunted and released the stile.

Out in the centre of the empty arena Franz undid the package and they assembled the model. It had a broad fan-like wing of wire and paper, a narrow strutted fusilage and a high curving tail.

Franz picked it up and launched it into the air. The model glided for twenty feet and then slithered to a stop across the sawdust.

'Seems to be stable,' Franz said. 'We'll tow it first.'

He pulled a reel of twine from his pocket and tied one end to the nose.

As they ran forward the model lifted gracefully into the air and followed them round the stadium, ten feet off the floor.

'Let's try the rockets now,' Franz said.

He adjusted the wing and tail settings and fitted three firework display rockets into a wire bracket mounted above the wing.

The stadium was four hundred feet in diameter and had a roof two hundred and fifty high. They carried the model over to one side and Franz lit the tapers.

There was a burst of flame and the model accelerated off across the floor, two feet in the air, a bright trail of coloured smoke spitting out behind it. Its wings rocked gently from side to side. Suddenly the tail burst into flames. The model lifted steeply and looped up towards the roof, stalled just before it hit one of the pilot lights and dived down into the sawdust.

They ran across to it and stamped out the glowing cinders. 'Franz!' Gregson shouted. 'It's incredible! It actually works.'

Franz kicked the shattered fuselage.

'Of course it works,' he said impatiently, walking away. 'But as Sanger said, what's the point of it?'

'The point? It flies! Isn't that enough?'

'No. I want one big enough to hold me.'

'Franz, slow down. Be reasonable. Where could you fly it?'

'I don't know,' Franz said fiercely. 'But there must be somewhere. Somewhere!'

The floor manager and two assistants, carrying fire extinguishers, ran across the stadium to them.

'Did you hide that match?' Franz asked quickly. 'They'll lynch us if they think we're pyros.'

Three afternoons later Franz took the elevator up 150 levels to 677-98, where the Precinct Estate Office had its bureau.

'There's a big development between 493 and 554 in the next sector,' one of the clerks told him. 'I don't know whether that's any good to you. Sixty blocks by twenty by fifteen levels.'

'Nothing bigger?' Franz queried.

The clerk looked up. 'Bigger? No. *What* are you looking for? A slight case of agoraphobia?'

Franz straightened the maps spread across the counter.

'I wanted to find an area of more or less continuous development. Two or three hundred blocks long.'

The clerk shook his head and went back to his ledger. 'Didn't you go to Engineering School?' he asked scornfully. 'The City won't take it. One hundred blocks is the maximum.'

Franz thanked him and left.

A south-bound express took him to the development in two hours. He left the car at the detour point and walked the 300 yards to the end of the level.

The street, a seedy but busy thoroughfare of garment shops and small business premises running through the huge ten mile thick BIR Industrial Cube, ended abruptly in a tangle of ripped girders and concrete. A steel rail had been erected along the edge and Franz looked down over it into the cavity, three miles long, a mile wide and 1,200 feet deep, which thousands of engineers and demolition workers were tearing out of the matrix of the City.

Eight hundred feet below him unending lines of trucks and railcars carried away the rubble and debris, and clouds of dust swirled up into the arc-lights blazing down from the roof.

As he watched a chain of explosions ripped along the wall on his left and the whole face suddenly slipped and fell slowly towards the floor, revealing a perfect cross-section through fifteen levels of the City.

Franz had seen big developments before, and his own parents had died in the historic QUA County cave-in ten years earlier, when three master-pillars had sheared and two hundred levels of the City had abruptly sunk 10,000 feet, squashing half a million people like flies in a concertina, but the enormous gulf of emptiness still made his imagination gape.

All around him, standing and sitting on the jutting terraces of girders, a silent throng stared down.

'They say they're going to build gardens and parks for us,' an elderly man at Franz's elbow remarked in a slow patient voice. 'I even heard they might be able to get a tree. It'll be the only tree in the whole County.'

A man in a frayed sweat-shirt spat over the rail. 'That's what they always say. At a dollar a foot promises are all they can waste space on.'

Below them a woman who had been looking out into the air started to simper nervously. Two bystanders took her by the arms and tried to lead her away. The woman began to thresh about and an F.P. came over and dragged her away roughly.

'Poor fool,' the man in the sweat-shirt commented. 'She probably lived out there somewhere. They gave her ninety cents a foot when they took it away from her. She doesn't know yet she'll have to pay a dollar ten to get it back. Now they're going to start charging five cents an hour just to sit up here and watch.'

Franz looked out over the railing for a couple of hours and then bought a postcard from one of the vendors and walked back thoughtfully to the elevator.

He called in to see Gregson before returning to the student dormitory.

The Gregsons lived up in the west million on 985th Avenue, in a top three-room flat right under the roof. Franz had known them since his parents' death, but Gregson's mother still regarded him with a mixture of sympathy and suspicion, and as she let him in with her customary smile of welcome he noticed her glancing quickly at the detector mounted in the hall.

Gregson was in his room, happily cutting out frames of paper and pasting them on to a great rickety construction that vaguely resembled Franz's model.

'Hullo, Franz. What was it like?'

Franz shrugged. 'Just a development. Worth seeing.'

Gregson pointed to his construction. 'Do you think we can try it out there?'

'We could do.' Franz sat down on the bed, picked up a paper dart lying beside him and tossed it out of the window. It swam out into the street, lazed down in a wide spiral and vanished into the open mouth of a ventilator shaft.

'When are you going to build another model?' Gregson asked.

'I'm not.'

Gregson swung round. 'Why? You've proved your theory.'

'That's not what I'm after.'

'I don't get you, Franz. What are you after?'

'Free space.'

'Free?' Gregson repeated.

Franz nodded. 'In both senses.'

Gregson shook his head sadly and snipped out another paper panel.

'Franz, you're crazy.'

Franz stood up. 'Take this room,' he said. 'It's twenty feet by fifteen by ten. Extend its dimensions infinitely. What do you find?'

'A development.'

'*Infinitely!*'

'Non-functional space.'

'Well?' Franz asked patiently.

'The concept's absurd.'

'Why?'

'Because it couldn't exist.'

Franz pounded his forehead in despair. '*Why* couldn't it?'

Gregson gestured with the scissors. 'It's self-contradictory. Like the statement "I am lying". Just a verbal freak. Interesting theoretically, but it's pointless to press it for meaning.' He tossed the scissors on to the table. 'And anyway, do you know how much free space would cost?'

Franz went over to the bookshelf and pulled out one of the volumes.

'Let's have a look at your street atlas.'

He turned to the index. 'This gives a thousand levels. KNI County, one hundred thousand cubic miles, population 30 million.'

Gregson nodded.

Franz closed the atlas. 'Two hundred and fifty counties, including KNI, together form the 493rd Sector, and an association of 1,500 adjacent sectors comprise the 298th Local Union.'

He broke off and looked at Gregson. 'As a matter of interest, ever heard of it?'

Gregson shook his head. 'No. How did –'

Franz slapped the atlas onto the table. 'Roughly 4×10^{15} cubic Great-Miles.' He leaned on the window ledge. 'Now tell me: what lies beyond the 298th Local Union?'

'Other Unions, I suppose,' Gregson said. 'I don't see your difficulty.'

'And beyond those?'

'Farther ones. Why not?'

'Forever?' Franz pressed.

'Well, as far as forever is.'

The great street directory in the old Treasury Library on 247th Street is the largest in the County,' Franz said. 'I went down there this morning. It occupies three complete levels. Millions of volumes. But it doesn't extend beyond the 598th Local Union. No one there had any idea what lay further out. Why not?'

'Why should they?' Gregson asked. 'Franz, what are you driving at?'

Franz walked across to the door. 'Come down to the Bio-History Museum. I'll show you.'

The birds perched on humps of rock or waddled about the sandy paths between the water pools.

'"Archaeopteryx," Franz read off one of the cage indicators. The bird, lean and mildewed, uttered a painful croak when he fed a handful of beans to it.

'Some of these birds have the remnants of a pectoral girdle,' Franz said. 'Minute fragments of bone embedded in the tissues around their rib cages.'

'Wings?'

'Dr McGhee thinks so.'

They walked out between the lines of cages.

'When does he think they were flying?'

'Before the Foundation,' Franz said. 'Three hundred billion years ago.'

When they got outside the Museum they started down 859th Avenue. Half-way down the street a dense crowd had gathered and people were packed into the windows and balconies above the Elevated, watching a squad of Fire Police break their way into a house.

The bulkheads at either end of the block had been closed and heavy steel traps sealed off the stairways from the levels above and below. The ventilator and exhaust shafts were silent and already the air was stale and soupy.

'Pyros,' Gregson murmured. 'We should have brought our masks.'

'It's only a scare,' Franz said. He pointed to the monoxide detectors which were out everywhere, their long snouts sucking at the air. The dial needles stood safely at zero.

'Let's wait in the restaurant opposite.'

They edged their way over to the restaurant, sat down in the window and ordered coffee. This, like everything else on the menu, was cold. All cooking appliances were thermostated to a maximum 95°F., and only in the more expensive restaurants and hotels was it possible to obtain food that was at most tepid.

Below them in the street a lot of shouting went up. The F.P.s seemed unable to penetrate beyond the ground floor of the house and had started to baton back the crowd. An electric winch was wheeled up and bolted to the girders running below the kerb, and half a dozen heavy steel grabs were carried into the house and hooked round the walls.

Gregson laughed. 'The owners are going to be surprised when they get home.'

Franz was watching the house. It was a narrow shabby dwelling sandwiched between a large wholesale furniture store and a new supermarket. An old sign running across the front had been painted over and evidently the ownership had recently changed. The present tenants had made a half-hearted attempt to convert the ground floor room into a cheap stand-up diner.

The F.P.S appeared to be doing their best to wreck everything, and pies and smashed crockery were strewn all over the pavement.

'Crowd's pretty ugly,' Franz said. 'Do you want to move?'

'Hold on.'

The noise died away and everyone waited as the winch began to revolve. Slowly the hawsers wound in and tautened, and the front wall of the house bulged and staggered outwards in rigid jerky movements.

Suddenly there was a yell from the crowd.

Franz raised his arm.

'Up there! Look!'

On the fourth floor a man and woman had come to the window and were looking down frantically. The man helped the woman out onto the ledge and she crawled out and clung to one of the waste pipes.

The crowd roared: 'Pyros! You bloody pyros!'

Bottles were lobbed up at them and bounced down among the police. A wide crack split the house from top to bottom and the floor on which the man was standing dropped and catapulted him backwards out of sight.

Then one of the lintels in the first floor snapped and the entire house tipped over and collapsed.

Franz and Gregson stood up involuntarily, almost knocking over the table.

The crowd surged forward through the cordon. When the

dust had settled there was nothing left but a heap of masonry and twisted beams. Embedded in this was the battered figure of the man. Almost smothered by the dust he moved slowly, painfully trying to free himself with one hand and the crowd started roaring again as one of the grabs wound in and dragged him down under the rubble.

The manager of the restaurant pushed past Franz and leant out of the window, his eyes fixed on the dial of a portable detector.

Its needle, like all the others, pointed to zero.

A dozen hoses were playing on the remains of the house and after a couple of minutes the crowd shifted and began to thin out.

The manager switched off the detector and left the window, nodding to Franz.

'Damn Pyros. You can relax now, boys.'

Franz pointed at the detector.

'Your dial was dead. There wasn't a trace of monoxide anywhere here. How do you know they were Pyros?'

'Don't worry, we knew.' He smiled obliquely. 'We don't want that sort of element in this neighbourhood.'

Franz shrugged and sat down. 'I suppose that's one way of getting rid of them.'

The manager eyed Franz unpleasantly. 'That's right, boy. This is a good five-dollar neighbourhood.' He smirked to himself. 'Maybe a six-dollar now everybody knows about our safety record.'

'Careful, Franz,' Gregson warned him when the manager had gone. 'He may be right. Pyros do take over small cafés and food bars.'

Franz stirred his coffee. 'Dr McGhee estimates that at least 15 per cent of the City's population are submerged Pyros. He's convinced the number's growing and that eventually the whole City will flame-out.'

He pushed away his coffee. 'How much money have you got?'

'On me?'

'Altogether.'

'About thirty dollars.'

'I've saved fifteen,' Franz said thoughtfully. 'Forty-five dollars; that should be enough for three or four weeks.'

'Where?' Gregson asked.

'On a Supersleeper.'

'Super – !' Gregson broke off, alarmed. 'Three or four weeks! What do you mean?'

'There's only one way to find out,' Franz explained calmly. 'I can't just sit here thinking. Somewhere there's free space and I'll ride the Sleeper until I find it. Will you lend me your thirty dollars?'

'But Franz –'

'If I don't find anything within a couple of weeks I'll change tracks and come back.'

'But the ticket will . . .' Gregson searched ' . . . billions. Forty-five dollars won't even get you out of the Sector.'

'That's just for coffee and sandwiches,' Franz said. 'The ticket will be free.' He looked up from the table. 'You know . . .'

Gregson shook his head doubtfully. 'Can you try that on the Supersleepers?'

'Why not? If they query it I'll say I'm going back the long way round. Greg, will you?'

'I don't know if I should.' Gregson played helplessly with his coffee. 'Franz, how can there be free space? How?'

'That's what I'm going to find out,' Franz said. 'Think of it as my first physics practical.'

Passenger distances on the transport system were measured point to point by the application of $a = \sqrt{b^2 + c^2 + d^2}$. The actual itinerary taken was the passenger's responsibility, and as long as he remained within the system he could choose any route he liked.

Tickets were checked only at the station exits, where necessary surcharges were collected by an inspector. If the passenger was unable to pay the surcharge – 10 cents a mile – he was sent back to his original destination.

Franz and Gregson entered the station on 984th Street and

went over to the large console where tickets were automatically dispensed.

Franz put in a penny and pressed the destination button marked 984. The machine rumbled, coughed out a ticket, and the change slot gave him back his coin.

'Well, Greg, good-bye,' Franz said as they moved towards the barrier. 'I'll see you in about two weeks. They're covering me down at the dormitory. Tell Sanger I'm on Fire Duty.'

'What if you don't get back, Franz?' Gregson asked. 'Suppose they take you off the Sleeper?'

'How can they? I've got my ticket.'

'And if you do find free space? Will you come back then?'

'If I can.'

Franz patted Gregson on the shoulder reassuringly, waved and disappeared among the commuters.

He took the local Suburban Green to the district junction in the next county. The Green Line train travelled at an interrupted 70 m.p.h. and the ride took two and a half hours.

At the Junction he changed to an express elevator which got him up out of the Sector in ninety minutes, at 400 m.p.h.

Another fifty minutes in a Through-Sector Special brought him to the Mainline Terminus which served the Union.

There he bought a coffee and gathered his determination together. Supersleepers ran east and west, halting at this and every tenth station. The next arrived in seventy-two hours time, Westbound.

The Mainline Terminus was the largest station Franz had seen, a vast mile-long cavern tiered up through thirty levels. Hundreds of elevator shafts sank into the station and the maze of platforms, escalators, restaurants, hotels, and theatres seemed like an exaggerated replica of the City itself.

Getting his bearings from one of the information booths Franz made his way up an escalator to Tier 15, where the Supersleepers berthed. Running the length of the station were two gigantic steel vacuum tunnels, each two hundred feet in diameter, supported at thirty-foot intervals by massive concrete buttresses.

Franz walked slowly along the platform and stopped by

the telescopic gangway that plunged into one of the airlocks.

Two-seventy feet true, he thought, all the way, gazing up at the curving underbelly of the tunnel. It must come out somewhere. He had forty-five dollars in his pocket, sufficient coffee and sandwich money to last him three weeks, six if he needed it, time anyway to find the City's end.

He passed the next three days nursing coffees in any of the thirty cafeterias in the station, reading discarded newspapers and sleeping in the local Red trains which ran four hour journeys round the nearest sector.

When at last the Supersleeper came in he joined the small group of fire police and municipal officials waiting by the gangway, and followed them into the train. There were two cars; a sleeper which no one used, and a day coach.

Franz took an inconspicuous corner seat near one of the indicator panels in the day coach, pulled out his notebook and got ready to make his first entry.

1st Day: West 270 feet. Union 4,350.

'Coming out for a drink?' a Fire Captain across the aisle asked. 'We have a ten-minute break here.'

'No thanks,' Franz said. 'I'll hold your seat for you.'

Dollar five a cubic foot. Free space, he knew, would bring the price down. There was no need to leave the train or make too many inquiries. All he had to do was borrow a paper and watch the market averages.

2nd Day: West 270 feet. Union 7,550.

'They're slowly cutting down on these Sleepers,' someone told him. 'Everyone sits in the day coach. Look at this one. Seats sixty, and only four people in it. There's no need to move around. People are staying where they are. In a few years there'll be nothing left but the suburban services.'

97 cents.

At an average of a dollar a cubic foot, Franz calculated idly, it's so far worth about 4×10^{27}.

'Going on to the next stop, are you? Well, good-bye young fellow.'

Few of the passengers stayed on the Sleeper for more than three or four hours. By the end of the second day Franz's back and neck ached from the constant acceleration. He got a little exercise walking up and down the narrow corridor in the deserted sleeping coach, but had to spend most of his time strapped to his seat as the train began its long braking runs into the next station.

3rd Day: West 270 feet. Federation 657.

'Interesting, but how could you demonstrate it?'

'It's just an odd idea of mine,' Franz said, screwing up the sketch and dropping it in the disposal chute. 'Hasn't any real application.'

'Curious, but it rings a bell somewhere.'

Franz sat up. 'Do you mean you've seen machines like this? In a newspaper or a book?'

'No, no. In a dream.'

Every half day's run the pilot signed the log, the crew handed over to their opposites on an Eastbound sleeper, crossed the platform and started back for home.

125 cents.

8×10^{33}.

4th Day: West 270 feet. Federation 1,225.

'Dollar a cubic foot. You in the estate business?'

'Starting up,' Franz said easily. 'I'm hoping to open a new office on my own.'

He played cards, bought coffee and rolls from the dispenser in the washroom, watched the indicator panel and listened to the talk around him.

'Believe me, a time will come when each union, each sector, almost I might say, each street and avenue will have achieved complete local independence. Equipped with its own power services, aerators, reservoirs, farm laboratories ...'

The car bore.

6×10^{75}.

5th Day: West 270. 17th Greater Federation.

At a kiosk on the station Franz bought a clip of razor blades and glanced at the brochure put out by the local chamber of commerce.

"12,00 levels, 98 cents a foot, unique Elm Drive, fire safety records unequalled . . ."

He went back to the train, shaved, and counted the thirty dollars left. He was now ninety-five million Great-Miles from the suburban station on 984th Street and he knew he couldn't delay his return much longer. Next time he'd save up a couple of thousand.

7×10^{127}.

7th Day: West 270. 212th Metropolitan Empire.

Franz peered at the indicator.

'Aren't we stopping here?' he asked a man three seats away. 'I wanted to find out the market average.'

'Varies. Anything from fifty cents a –'

'Fifty!' Franz shot back, jumping up. 'When's the next stop? I've got to get off!'

'Not here, son.' He put out a restraining hand. 'This is Night Town. You in real estate?'

Franz nodded, holding himself back. 'I thought . . .'

'Relax.' He came and sat opposite Franz. 'It's just one big slum. Dead areas. In places it goes as low as five cents. There are no services, no power.'

It took them two days to pass through.

'City Authority are starting to seal it off,' the man told him. 'Huge blocks. It's the only thing they can do. What happens to the people inside I hate to think.'

He chewed on a sandwich. 'Strange, but there are a lot of these black areas. You don't hear about them, but they're growing. Starts in a back street in some ordinary dollar neighbourhood; a bottleneck in the sewage disposal system, not enough ash cans, and before you know it – a million cubic miles have gone back to jungle. They try a relief scheme, pump in a little cyanide, and then – brick it up. Once they do that they're closed for good.

Franz nodded, listening to the dull humming air.

'Eventually there'll be nothing left but these black areas. The City will be one huge cemetery. What a thought!'

10th Day: East 90 feet. 755th Greater Metropolitan –

'Wait!' Franz leapt out of his seat and stared at the indicator panel.

'What's the matter?' someone opposite asked.

'East!' Franz shouted. He banged the panel sharply with his hand but the lights held. 'Has this train changed direction?'

'No, it's eastbound,' another of the passengers told him. 'Are you on the wrong train?'

'It should be heading west,' Franz insisted. 'It has been for the last ten days.'

'Ten days!' the man exclaimed. 'Have you been on this sleeper for ten days? Where the hell are you going?'

Franz went forward and grabbed the car attendant.

'Which way is this train going? West?'

The attendant shook his head. 'East, sir. It's always been going east.'

'You're crazy,' Franz snapped. 'I want to see the pilot's log.'

'I'm afraid that isn't possible. May I see your ticket, sir?'

'Listen,' Franz said weakly, all the accumulated frustration of the last twenty years mounting inside him. 'I've been on this ...'

He stopped and went back to his seat.

The five other passengers watched him carefully.

'Ten days,' one of them was still repeating in an awed voice.

Two minutes later someone came and asked Franz for his ticket.

'And of course it was completely in order,' the police surgeon commented.

He walked over to M. and swung the spot out of his eyes.

'Strangely enough there's no regulation to prevent anyone else doing the same thing. I used to go for free rides myself when I was younger, though I never tried anything like your journey.'

He went back to the desk.

'We'll drop the charge,' he said. 'You're not a vagrant in any indictable sense, and the Transport authorities can do nothing against you. How this curvature was built into the system they can't explain. Now about yourself. Are you going to continue this search?'

'I want to build a flying machine,' M. said carefully. 'There must be free space somewhere. I don't know ... perhaps on the lower levels.'

The surgeon stood up. 'I'll see the sergeant and get him to hand you over to one of our psychiatrists. He'll be able to help you with that dream.'

The surgeon hesitated before opening the door. 'Look,' he began to explain sympathetically, 'you can't get out of time, can you? Subjectively it's a plastic dimension, but whatever you do to yourself you'll never be able to stop that clock –' he pointed to the one on the desk '– or make it run backwards. In exactly the same way you can't get out of the City.'

'The analogy doesn't hold,' M. said. He gestured at the walls around them and the lights in the street outside. 'All this was built by us. The question nobody can answer is: what was here before we built it?'

'It's always been here,' the surgeon said. 'Not these particular bricks and girders, but others before them. You accept that time has no beginning and no end. The City is as old as time and continuous with it.'

'The first bricks were laid by someone,' M. insisted. 'There was the Foundation.'

'A myth. Only the scientists believe in that, and even they don't try to make too much of it. Most of them privately admit that the Foundation Stone is nothing more than a superstition. We pay it lip service out of convenience, and because it gives us a sense of tradition. Obviously there can't have been a first brick. If there was, how can you explain who laid it, and even more difficult, where they came from?'

'There must be free space somewhere,' M. said doggedly. 'The City must have bounds.'

'*Why?*' the surgeon asked. 'It can't be floating in the middle of nowhere. Or is that what you're trying to believe?'

M. sank back limply. 'No.'

The surgeon watched M. silently for a few minutes and paced back to the desk. 'This peculiar fixation of yours puzzles me. You're caught between what the psychiatrists call paradoxical faces. I suppose you haven't misinterpreted something you've heard about the wall?'

M. looked up. 'Which wall?'

The surgeon nodded to himself. 'Some advanced opinion maintains that there's a wall around the City, through which it's impossible to penetrate. I don't pretend to understand the theory myself. It's far too abstract and sophisticated. Anyway I suspect they've confused this wall with the bricked-up black areas you passed through on the Sleeper. I prefer the accepted view that the City stretches out in all directions without limits.'

He went over to the door. 'Wait here, and I'll see about getting you a probationary release. Don't worry, the psychiatrists will straighten everything out for you.'

When the surgeon had left M. stared emptily at the floor, too exhausted to feel relieved. He stood up and stretched himself, walking unsteadily round the room.

Outside the last pilot lights were going out and the patrolman on the catwalk under the roof was using his torch. A police car roared down one of the avenues crossing the street, its rails screaming. Three lights snapped on along the street and then one by one went off again.

M. wondered why Gregson hadn't come down to the station.

Then the calendar on the desk riveted his attention.

The date exposed on the fly leaf was 12 August.

That was the day he had started off on his journey.

Exactly three weeks ago.

Today!

Take a west-bound Green to 298th Street, cross over at the

intersection and get a Red elevator up to Level 237. Walk down to the station on Route 175, change to a 438 suburban and go down to 795th Street. Take a Blue line to the Plaza, get off at 4th and 275th, turn left at the roundabout and

You're back where you first started from. $HELL × 10.

Isaac Asimov

The Fun They Had

Margie even wrote about it that night in her diary. On the page headed 17 May, 2155, she wrote, 'Today Tommy found a real book!'

It was a very old book. Margie's grandfather once said that when he was a little boy *his* grandfather told him that there was a time when all stories were printed on paper.

They turned the pages, which were yellow and crinkly, and it was awfully funny to read words that stood still instead of moving the way they were supposed to – on a screen, you know. And then, when they turned back to the page before, it had the same words on it that it had had when they read it the first time.

'Gee,' said Tommy, 'what a waste. When you're through with the book, you just throw it away, I guess. Our television screen must have had a million books on it and it's good for plenty more. I wouldn't throw *it* away.'

'Same with mine,' said Margie. She was eleven and hadn't seen as many telebooks as Tommy had. He was thirteen.

She said, 'Where did you find it?'

'In my house.' He pointed without looking, because he was busy reading. 'In the attic.'

'What's it about?'

'School.'

Margie was scornful. 'School? What's there to write about school? I hate school.' Margie always hated school, but now she hated it more than ever. The mechanical teacher had been giving her test after test in geography and she had been doing worse and worse until her mother had shaken her head sorrowfully and sent for the County Inspector.

He was a round little man with a red face and a whole box of tools with dials and wires. He smiled at her and gave her an apple, then took the teacher apart. Margie had hoped he wouldn't know how to put it together again, but he knew how all right and after an hour or so, there it was again, large and black and ugly with a big screen on which all the lessons were shown and the questions were asked. That wasn't so bad. The part she hated most was the slot where she had to put homework and test papers. She always had to write them out in a punch code they made her learn when she was six years old, and the mechanical teacher calculated the mark in no time.

The Inspector had smiled after he was finished and patted her head. He said to her mother, 'It's not the little girl's fault, Mrs Jones. I think the geography sector was geared a little too quick. Those things happen sometimes. I've slowed it up to an average ten-year level. Actually, the overall pattern of her progress is quite satisfactory.' And he patted Margie's head again.

Margie was disappointed. She had been hoping they would take the teacher away altogether. They had once taken Tommy's teacher away for nearly a month because the history sector had blanked out completely.

So she said to Tommy, 'Why would anyone write about school?'

Tommy looked at her with very superior eyes. 'Because it's not our kind of school, stupid. This is the old kind of school that they had hundreds and hundreds of years ago.' He added loftily, pronouncing the word carefully, '*Centuries* ago.'

Margie was hurt. 'Well, I don't know what kind of school they had all that time ago.' She read the book over his shoulder for a while, then said, 'Anyway, they had a teacher.'

'Sure they had a teacher, but it wasn't a *regular* teacher. It was a man.'

'A man? How could a man be a teacher?'

'Well, he just told the boys and girls things and gave them homework and asked them questions.'

'A man isn't smart enough.'

'Sure he is. My father knows as much as my teacher.'

'He can't. A man can't know as much as a teacher.'

'He knows almost as much I betcha.'

Margie wasn't prepared to dispute that. She said, 'I wouldn't want a strange man in my house to teach me.'

Tommy screamed with laughter, 'You don't know much, Margie. The teachers didn't live in the house. They had a special building and all the kids went there.'

'And all the kids learned the same thing?'

'Sure, if they were the same age.'

'But my mother says a teacher has to be adjusted to fit the mind of each boy and girl it teaches and that each kid has to be taught differently.'

'Just the same they didn't do it that way then. If you don't like it, you don't have to read the book.'

'I didn't say I didn't like it,' Margie said quickly. She wanted to read about those funny schools.

They weren't even half finished when Margie's mother called, 'Margie! School!'

Margie looked up. 'Not yet, mamma.'

'Now,' said Mrs. Jones. 'And it's probably time for Tommy, too.'

Margie said to Tommy, 'Can I read the book some more with you after school?'

'Maybe,' he said, nonchalantly. He walked away whistling, the dusty old book tucked beneath his arm.

Margie went into the schoolroom. It was right next to her bedroom, and the mechanical teacher was on and waiting for her. It was always on at the same time every day except Saturday and Sunday, because her mother said little girls learned better if they learned at regular hours.

The screen was lit up, and it said: 'Today's arithmetic lesson is on the addition of proper fractions. Please insert yesterday's homework in the proper slot.'

Margie did so with a sigh. She was thinking about the old schools they had when her grandfather's grandfather was a little boy. All the kids from the whole neighbourhood came, laughing and shouting in the school-yard, sitting together in the school-room, going home together at the end of the day. They learned the same things so they could help one another on the home-work and talk about it.

And the teachers were people . . .

The mechanical teacher was flashing on the screen: 'When we add the fractions ½ and ¼ –'

Margie was thinking about how the kids must have loved it in the old days. She was thinking about the fun they had.

Eric Frank Russell

Diabologic

He made one circumnavigation to put the matter beyond doubt. That was standard space-scout technique; look once on the approach, look again all the way round. It often happened that second and closer impressions contradicted first and more distant ones. Some perverse factor in the probability sequence frequently caused the laugh to appear on the other side of a planetary face.

Not this time, though. What he'd observed coming in remained visible right around the belly. This world was occupied by intelligent life of a high order. The unmistakable markings were there in the form of dockyards, railroad marshalling grids, power stations, space-ports, quarries, factories, mines, housing projects, bridges, canals, a hundred and one other signs of life that spawns fast and vigorously.

The space-ports in particular were highly significant. He counted three of them. None held a flightworthy ship at the moment he flamed high above them but in one was a tubeless vessel undergoing repair. A long, black, snouty thing about the size and shape of an Earth-Mars tramp. Certainly not as big and racy-looking as a Sol-Sirius liner.

As he gazed down through his tiny control-cabin's armour-glass he knew that this was to be contact with a vengeance. During long, long centuries of human expansion more than seven hundred inhabitable worlds had been found, charted, explored and in some cases exploited. All contained life. A minority held intelligent life. But up to this moment nobody had found one other life form sufficiently advanced to cavort among the stars.

Of course, such a discovery had been theorized. Human

adventuring created an exploratory sphere that swelled into the cosmos. Sooner or later, it was assumed, that sphere must touch another one at some point within the heavenly host. What would happen then was anybody's guess. Perhaps they'd fuse, making a bigger, shinier biform bubble. Or perhaps both bubbles would burst. Anyway, by the looks of it the touching-time was now.

If he'd been within reach of a frontier listening-post he'd have beamed a signal detailing this find. Even now it wasn't too late to drive back for seventeen weeks and get within receptive range. But that would mean seeking a refuelling dump while he was at it. The ship just hadn't enough for such a double run plus the return trip home. Down there they had fuel. Maybe they'd give him some and maybe it would suit his engines. And just as possibly it would prove useless.

Right now he had adequate power reserves to land here and eventually get back to base. A bird in the hand is worth two in the bush. So he tilted the vessel and plunged into the alien atmosphere, heading for the largest space-port of the three.

What might be awaiting him at ground level did not bother him at all. The Terrans of today were not the nervy, apprehensive Terrans of the earthbound and lurid past. They had become space-sophisticated. They had learned to lounge around with a carefree smile and let the other life forms do the worrying. It lent an air of authority and always worked. Nothing is more intimidating than an idiotic grin worn by a manifest non-idiot.

Quite a useful weapon in the diabological armoury was the knowing smirk.

His landing created a most satisfactory sensation. The planet's point-nine Earth-mass permitted a little extra dexterity in handling the ship. He swooped it down, curved it up, dropped tail-first, stood straddle-legged on the tail-fins, cut the braking blast and would not have missed centring on a spread handkerchief by more than ten inches.

They seemed to spring out of the ground the way people do when cars collide on a deserted road. Dozens of them, hundreds.

They were on the short side, the tallest not exceeding five feet. Otherwise they differed from his own pink faced, blue eyed type no more than would a Chinese covered in fine grey fur.

Massing in a circle beyond range of his jet-rebound, they stared at the ship, gabbled, gesticulated, nudged each other, argued, shrugged shoulders, and generally behaved in the manner of a curious mob that has discovered a deep, dark hole with strange noises issuing therefrom. The noteworthy feature about their behaviour was that none were scared, none attempted to get out of reach either openly or surreptitiously. The only thing about which they were wary was the chance of a sudden blast from the silent jets.

He did not emerge at once. That would have been an error – and blunderers are not chosen to pilot scout-vessels. Pre-exit rule number one is that air must be tested. What suited that crowd outside would not necessarily agree with him. Anyway, he'd have checked air even if his own mother had been smoking a cigar in the front rank of the audience.

The Schrieber analyser required four minutes in which to suck a sample through the pilot-tube, take it apart, sneer at the bits, make a bacteria-count and say whether its lord and master could condescend to breathe the stuff.

While it made up its mind, he sat in patience. Finally the needle on its half-red, half-white dial crawled reluctantly to mid-white. A fast shift would have pronounced the atmosphere socially acceptable. Slowness was the Schrieber's way of saying that his lungs were about to go slumming. The analyser was and always had been a robotic snob that graded alien atmospheres on the caste system. The best and cleanest air was Brahmin, pure Brahmin. The worst was untouchable.

Switching it off, he opened the inner and outer airlock doors, sat in the rim with his feet dangling eighty yards above ground-level. From this vantage-point he calmly surveyed the mob, his expression that of one who can spit but not be spat upon. The sixth diabolical law states that the higher, the fewer. Proof: the seagull's tactical advantage over man.

Being intelligent, those placed by unfortunate circumstances eighty yards deeper in the gravitational field soon appreciated their state of vertical disadvantage. Short of toppling the ship or climbing a polished surface they were impotent to get at him. Not that they wanted to in any inimical way. But desires grow strongest when least possible of satisfaction. So they wanted him down there, face to face, merely because he was out of reach.

To make matters worse, he turned sideways and lay within the rim, one leg hitched up and hands linked around the knee, then continued looking at them in obvious comfort. They had to stand. And they had to stare upward at the cost of a crick in the neck. Alternatively they could adjust their heads and eyes to a crickless level and endure being looked at while not looking. Altogether, it was a hell of a situation.

The longer it lasted the less pleasing it became. Some of them shouted at him in squeaky voices. Upon those he bestowed a benign smile. Others gesticulated. He gestured back and the sharpest among them weren't happy about it. For some strange reason no scientist had bothered to investigate why certain digital motions stimulate especial glands in any part of the cosmos. Basic diabological training included a course in what was known as signal-deflation whereby the yolk could be removed from an alien ego with one wave of the hand.

For a while the crowd surged restlessly around nibbling the grey fur on the backs of their fingers, muttering to each other and occasionally throwing sour looks upward. They still kept clear of the danger zone, apparently assuming that the specimen reclining in the lock-rim might have a companion at the controls. Next, they became moody, content to do no more than scowl futilely at the tail-fins.

That state of affairs lasted until a convoy of heavy vehicles arrived and unloaded troops. The newcomers bore riot-sticks, hand-guns, and wore uniforms the colour of stuff hogs roll in. Forming themselves into three ranks, they turned right at a barked command, marched forward. The crowd opened to make way.

Expertly they stationed themselves in an armed circle separating the ship from the horde of onlookers. A trio of officers paraded around and examined the tail-fins without going nearer than was necessary. Then they backed off, stared up at the airlock-rim. The subject of their attention gazed back with academic interest.

The senior of the three officers patted his midriff where his heart was located, bent and patted the ground, forced pacific innocence into his face as again he stared at the arrival high above. The tilt of his head made his hat fall off and in turning to pick it up he trod on it.

This petty incident seemed to gratify the one eighty yards higher because he chuckled, let go the leg he was nursing, leaned out for a better look at the victim. Red-faced under his fur complexion, the officer once more performed the belly and ground massage. The other understood this time. He gave a nod of gracious assent, disappeared into the lock. A few seconds later a nylon ladder snaked down the ship's side and the invader descended with monkey-like agility.

Three things struck the troops and the audience immediately he stood before them, namely, the nakedness of his face and hands, his great size and weight, and the fact that he carried no visible weapons. Strangeness of shape and form was to be expected. After all, they had done some space-roaming themselves and knew of life-forms more outlandish. But what sort of creature has the brains to build a ship and not the sense to carry means of defence?

They were essentially a logical people.

The poor saps.

The officers made no attempt to converse with this specimen from the great unknown. They were not telepathic and space-experience had taught them that mere mouth-noises are useless until one side or the other has learned the meanings thereof. So by signs they conveyed to him their wish to take him to town where he would meet others of their kind more competent to establish contact. They were pretty good at explaining with their hands, as was natural for the only other lifeform that had found new worlds.

He agreed to this with the same air of a lord consorting with the lower orders that had been apparent from the start. Perhaps he had been unduly influenced by the Schrieber. Again the crowd made way while the guard conducted him to the trucks. He passed through under a thousand eyes, favoured them with deflatory gesture number seventeen, this being a nod that acknowledged their existence and tolerated their vulgar interest in him.

The trucks trundled away leaving the ship with airlock open, ladder dangling, and the rest of the troops still standing guard around the fins. Nobody failed to notice that touch, either. He hadn't bothered to prevent access to the vessel. There was nothing to prevent experts looking through it and stealing ideas from another space-going race.

Nobody of that calibre could be so criminally careless. Therefore it could not be carelessness. Pure logic said the ship's designs were not worth protecting from the stranger's viewpoint because they were long out of date. Or else they were unstealable because beyond the comprehension of a lesser people. Who the heck did he think they were? By the Black World of Khas, they'd show him!

A junior officer climbed the ladder, explored the ship's interior, came down, reported no more aliens within, not even a pet *lansim*, not a pretzel. The stranger had come alone. This item of information circulated through the crowd. They did not care for it overmuch. A visit by a fleet of battleships bearing ten thousand they could understand. It would be a show of force worthy of their stature. But the casual arrival of one and only one smacked somewhat of the dumping of a missionary among the heathens of the twin worlds of Morantia.

Meanwhile the trucks rolled clear of the space-port, speeded up through twenty miles of country, entered a city. Here the leading vehicle parted company from the rest, made for the western suburbs, arrived at a fortress surrounded by huge walls. The stranger dismounted and promptly got tossed into clink.

The result of that was odd, too. He should have resented incarceration seeing that nobody had yet explained the purpose of it. But he didn't. Treating the well-clothed bed in his cell as if it were a luxury provided as recognition of his rights, he sprawled on it full length, boots and all, gave a sigh of deep satisfaction and went to sleep. His watch hung close by his ear and compensated for the constant ticking of the auto-pilot without which slumber in space was never complete.

During the next few hours guards came frequently to look at him and make sure that he wasn't finagling the locks or disintegrating the bars by means of some alien technique. They had not searched him and accordingly were cautious. But he snored on, dead to the world, oblivious to the ripples of alarm spreading through a spatial empire.

He was still asleep when Parmith arrived bearing a load of picture-books. Parmith, elderly and myopic, sat by the bedside and waited until his own eyes became heavy in sympathy and he found himself considering the comfort of the carpet. At that point he decided he must either get to work or lie flat. He prodded the other into wakefulness.

They started on the books. Ah is for ahmud that plays in the grass. Ay is for aysid that's kept under glass. Oom is for oom-tuk that's found in the moon. Uhm is for uhmlak, a clown or buffoon. And so on.

Stopping only for meals they were at it the full day and progress was fast. Parmith was a first-class tutor, the other an excellent pupil able to pick up with remarkable speed and forget nothing. At the end of the first long session they were able to indulge a brief and simple conversation.

'I am called Parmith. What are you called?'

'Wayne Hillder.'

'Two callings?'

'Yes.'

'What are many of you called?'

'Terrans.'

'We are called Vards.'

Talk ceased for lack of enough words and Parmith left. Within nine hours he was back accompanied by Gerka, a younger specimen who specialized in reciting words and phrases again and again until the listener could echo them to perfection. They carried on another four days, working into late evening.

'You are not a prisoner.'

'I know,' said Wayne Hillder, blandly self-assured.

Parmith looked uncertain. 'How do you know?'

'You would not dare to make me one.'

'Why not?'

'You do not know enough. Therefore you seek common speech. You must learn from me – and quickly.'

This being too obvious to contradict, Parmith let it go by and said, 'I estimated it would take about ninety days to make you fluent. It looks as if twenty will be sufficient.'

'I wouldn't be here if my kind weren't smart,' Hillder pointed out.

Gerka registered uneasiness, Parmith was disconcerted.

'No Vard is being taught by us,' he added for good measure. 'Not having got to us yet.'

Parmith said hurriedly, 'We must get on with this task. An important commission is waiting to interview you as soon as you can converse with ease and clarity. We'll try again this fth-prefix that you haven't got quite right. Here's a tongue-twister to practise on. Listen to Gerka.'

'Fthon deas fthleman fthangafth,' recited Gerka, punishing his bottom lip.

'Futhong deas –'

'Fthon,' corrected Gerka. 'Fthon deas fthleman fthangafth.'

'It's better in a civilized tongue. Wet evenings are gnatless Futhong –'

'Fthon!' insisted Gerka, playing catapults with his mouth.

The commission sat in an ornate hall containing semi-circular rows of seats rising in ten tiers. There were four hundred present. The way in which attendants and minor officials fawned around them showed that this was an assembly of great importance.

It was, too. The four hundred represented the political and military power of a world that had created a space-empire extending through a score of solar systems and controlling twice as many planets. Up to a short time ago they had been to the best of their knowledge and belief the lords of creation. Now there was some doubt about it. They had a serious problem to settle, one that a later Terran historian irreverently described as 'a moot point'.

They ceased talking among themselves when a pair of guards arrived in charge of Hillder, led him to a seat facing the tiers. Four hundred pairs of eyes examined the stranger, some curiously, some doubtfully, some challengingly, many with unconcealed antagonism.

Sitting down, Hillder looked them over much as one looks into one of the more odorous cages at the zoo. That is to say, with faint distaste. Gently he rubbed the side of his nose with a forefinger and sniffed. Deflatory gesture twenty-two, suitable for use in the presence of massed authority. It brought its carefully calculated reward. Half a dozen of the most bellicose characters glared at him.

A furry-faced oldster stood up frowning, spoke to Hillder as if reciting a well rehearsed speech. 'None but a highly intelligent and completely logical species can conquer space. It being self-evident that you are of such a kind, you will appreciate our position. Your very presence compels us to consider the ultimate alternatives of cooperation or competition, peace or war.'

'There are no two alternatives to anything,' Hillder asserted. 'There is black and white and a thousand intermediate shades. There is yes and no and a thousand ifs, buts, or maybes. For example: you could move farther out of reach.'

Being tidy-minded, they didn't enjoy watching the thread of their logic being tangled. Neither did they like the resultant knot in the shape of the final suggestion. The oldster's frown grew deeper, his voice sharper.

'You should also appreciate your own position. You are one among countless millions. Regardless of whatever may be the strength of your kind you, personally, are helpless. Therefore it is for us to question and for you to answer. If our respective positions were reversed the contrary would be true. That is logical. Are you ready to answer our questions?'

'I am ready.'

Some showed surprise at that. Others looked resigned, taking it for granted that he would give all the information he saw fit and suppress the rest.

Resuming his seat, the oldster signed to the Vard on his left who stood up and asked, 'Where is your base-world?'

'At the moment I don't know.'

'You don't know?' His expression showed that he had expected awkwardness from the start. 'How can you return to it if you don't know where it is?'

'When within its radio-sweep I pick up its beacon. I follow that.'

'Aren't your space-charts sufficient to enable you to find it?'

'No.'

'Why not?'

'Because,' said Hillder, 'it isn't tied to a primary. It wanders around.'

Registering incredulity, the other said, 'Do you mean that it is a planet broken loose from a solar system?'

'Not at all. It's a scout-base. Surely you know what that is?'

'I do not,' snapped the interrogator. 'What is it?'

'A tiny, compact world equipped with all the necessary contraptions. An artificial sphere that functions as a frontier outpost.'

There was a deal of fidgeting and murmuring among the audience as individuals tried to weigh the implications of this news.

Hiding his thoughts, the questioner continued, 'You define it as a frontier outpost. That does not tell us where your home-world is located.'

'You did not ask about my home-world. You asked about my base-world. I heard you with my own two ears.'

'Then where is your home-world?'

'I cannot show you without a chart. Do you have charts of unknown regions?'

'Yes.' The other smiled like a satisfied cat. With a dramatic flourish he produced them, unrolled them. 'We obtained them from your ship.'

'That was thoughtful of you,' said Hillder, disappointingly pleased. Leaving his seat he placed a fingertip on the topmost chart and said, 'There! Good old Earth!' Then he returned and sat down.

The Vard stared at the designated point, glanced around at his fellows as if about to make a remark, changed his mind and said nothing. Producing a pen he marked the chart, rolled it up with the others.

'This world you call Earth is the origin and centre of your empire?'

'Yes.'

'The mother-planet of your species?'

'Yes.'

'Now,' he went on, firmly, 'how many of your kind are there?'

'Nobody knows.'

'Don't you check your own numbers?'

'We did once upon a time. These days we're too scattered around.' Hillder pondered a moment, added helpfully, 'I can tell you that there are four billions of us spread over three planets in our own solar system. Outside of those the number is a guess. We can be divided into the rooted and the rootless and the latter can't be counted. They won't let themselves be counted because somebody might want to tax them. Take the grand total as four billions plus.'

'That tells us nothing,' the other objected. 'We don't know the size of the plus.'

'Neither do we,' said Hillder, visibly awed at the thought of it. 'Sometimes it frightens us.' He surveyed the audience. 'If nobody's ever been scared by a plus now's the time.'

Scowling, the questioner tried to get at it another way. 'You say you are scattered. Over how many worlds?'

'Seven-hundred-fourteen at last report. That's already out of date. Every report is eight to ten planets behind the times.'

'And you have mastery of that huge number?'

'Whoever mastered a planet? Why, we haven't yet dug into the heart of our own and I doubt that we ever shall.' He shrugged, finished, 'No, we just amble around and maul them a bit. Same as you do.'

'You mean you exploit them?'

'Put it that way if it makes you happy.'

'Have you encountered no opposition at any time?'

'Feeble, friend, feeble,' said Hillder.

'What did you do about it?'

'That depended upon circumstances. Some folk we ignored, some we smacked, some we led towards the light.'

'What light?' asked the other, baffled.

'That of seeing things our way.'

It was too much for a paunchy specimen in the third row. Coming to his feet he spoke in acidulated tones. 'Do you expect *us* to see things your way?'

'Not immediately,' Hillder said.

'Perhaps you consider us incapable of . . .'

The oldster who had first spoken now arose and interjected, 'We must proceed with this inquisition logically or not at all. That means one line of questioning at a time and one questioner at a time.' He gestured authoritatively towards the Vard with the charts. 'Carry on, Thormin.'

Thormin carried on for two solid hours. Apparently he was an astronomical expert for all his questions bore more or less on that subject. He wanted details of distances, velocities, solar classifications, planetary conditions and a host of similar items. Willingly Hillder answered all that he could, pleaded ignorance with regard to the rest.

Eventually Thormin sat down and concentrated on his notes in the manner of one absorbed in fundamental truth. He was succeeded by a hard-eyed individual named Grasud who for the last half-hour had been fidgeting with impatience.

'Is your vessel the most recent example of its type?'

'No.'

'There are better models?'

'Yes,' agreed Hillder.

'Very much better?'

'I wouldn't know, not having been assigned one yet.'

'Strange, is it not,' said Grasud pointedly, 'that an old-type ship should discover us while superior ones have failed to do so?'

'Not at all. It was sheer luck. I happened to head this way. Other scouts, in old or new ships, boosted other ways. How many directions are there in deep space? How many radii can be extended from a sphere?'

'Not being a mathematician, I –'

'If you were a mathematician,' Hillder interrupted, 'you would know that the number works out at 2^n.' He glanced over the audience, added in tutorial manner. 'The factor of two being determined by the demonstrable fact that a radius is half a diameter and 2^n being defined as the smallest number that makes one boggle.'

Grasud boggled as he tried to conceive it, gave it up, said, 'Therefore the total number of your exploring vessels is of equal magnitude?'

'No. We don't have to probe in every direction. It is necessary only to make for visible stars.'

'Well, aren't there stars in every direction?'

'If distance is disregarded, yes. But one does not disregard distance. One makes for the nearest yet-unexplored solar systems and thus cuts down repeated jaunts to a reasonable number.'

'You are evading the issue,' said Grasud. 'How many ships of your type are in actual operation?'

'Twenty.'

'Twenty?' He made it sound an anti-climax. 'Is that all?'

'It's enough, isn't it? How long do you expect us to keep antiquated models in service?'

'I am not asking about out-of-date vessels. How many scout-ships of all types are functioning?'

'Really I don't know. I doubt whether anyone knows. In addition to Earth's fleets some of the most advanced colonies are running expeditions of their own. What's more, a couple of allied life-forms have learned things from us, caught the fever and started poking around. We can no more take a complete census of ships than we can of people.'

Accepting that without argument, Grasud went on, 'Your vessel is not large by our standards. Doubtless you have others of greater mass.' He leaned forward, gazed fixedly. 'What is the comparative size of your biggest ship?'

'The largest I've seen was the battleship *Lance*. Forty times the mass of my boat.'

'How many people does it carry?'

'It has a crew numbering more than six hundred but at a pinch it can transport three times that.'

'So you know of at least one ship with an emergency capacity of about two thousand?'

'Yes.'

More murmurings and fidgetings among the audience. Disregarding them, Grasud carried on with the air of one determined to learn the worst.

'You have other battleships of equal size?'

'Yes.'

'How many?'

'I don't know. If I did, I'd tell you. Sorry.'

'You may have some even bigger?'

'That is quite possible,' Hillder conceded. 'If so, I haven't seen one yet. But that means nothing. One can go through a lifetime and not see everything. If you calculate the number of seeable things in existence, deduct the number already viewed, the remainder represents the number yet to be seen. And if you study them at the rate of one per second it would require . . .'

'I am not interested,' snapped Grasud, refusing to be bollixed by alien argument.

'You should be,' said Hillder. 'Because infinity minus umpteen millions leaves infinity. Which means that you can take the part from the whole and leave the whole still intact. You can eat your cake and have it. Can't you?'

Grasud flopped into his seat, spoke moodily to the oldster. 'I seek information, not a blatant denial of logic. His talk confuses me. Let Shahding have him.'

Coming up warily, Shahding started on the subject of weapons, their design, mode of operation, range and effectiveness. He stuck with determination to this single line of inquiry and avoided all temptations to be side-tracked. His questions were astute and penetrating. Hillder answered all he could, freely, without hesitation.

'So,' commented Shahding, towards the finish, 'it seems that you put your trust in force-fields, certain rays that paralyse the nervous system, bacteriological techniques, demonstrations of number and strength, and a good deal of persuasiveness. Your science of ballistics cannot be advanced after so much neglect.'

'It could never advance,' said Hillder. 'That's why we abandoned it. We dropped fiddling around with bows and arrows for the same reason. No initial thrust can outpace a continuous and prolonged one. Thus far and no farther shalt thou go.' Then he added by way of speculative afterthought, 'Anyway, it can be shown that no bullet can overtake a running man.'

'Nonsense!' exclaimed Shahding, having once ducked a couple of slugs himself.

'By the time the bullet has reached the man's point of departure the man has retreated,' said Hillder. 'The bullet then has to cover that extra distance but finds the man has retreated farther. It covers that too, only to find that again the man is not there. And so on and so on.'

'The lead is reduced each successive time until it ceases to exist,' Shahding scoffed.

'Each successive advance occupies a finite length of time no matter how small,' Hillder pointed out. 'You cannot divide and subdivide a fraction to produce zero. The series is infinite. An infinite series of finite time-periods totals an infinite time. Work it out for yourself. The bullet does not hit the man because it cannot get to him.'

The reaction showed that the audience had never encountered this argument before or concocted anything like it of their own accord. None were stupid enough to accept it as serious assertion of fact. All were sufficiently intelligent to recognize it as logical or pseudo-logical denial of something self-evident and demonstrably true.

Forthwith they started hunting for the flaw in this alien reasoning, discussing it between themselves so noisily that perforce Shahding stood in silence waiting for a break. He posed like a dummy for ten minutes while the row rose to a crescendo. A group in the front semi-circle left their seats, kneeled and commenced drawing diagrams on the floor while arguing vociferously and with some heat. A couple of Vards in the back tier showed signs of coming to blows.

Finally the oldster, Shahding, and two others bellowed a united, 'Quiet!'

The investigatory commission settled down with reluctance, still muttering, gesturing, showing each other sketches on pieces of paper. Shahding fixed ireful attention on Hillder, opened his mouth in readiness to resume.

Beating him to it, Hillder said casually, 'It sounds silly, doesn't it? But anything is possible, anything at all. A man can marry his widow's sister.'

'Impossible,' declared Shahding, able to dispose of that without abstruse calculations. 'He must be dead for her to have the status of a widow.'

'A man married a woman who died. He then married her sister. He died. Wasn't his first wife his widow's sister?'

Shahding shouted, 'I am not here to be tricked by the tortuous squirmings of an alien mind.' He sat down hard, fumed a bit, said to his neighbour, 'All right, Kadina, you can have him and welcome.'

Confident and self-assured, Kadina stood up, gazed authoritatively around. He was tall for a Vard, wore well-cut uniform with crimson epaulettes and crimson-banded sleeves. For the first time in a while there was silence. Satisfied with the effect he had produced, he faced Hillder, spoke in tones deeper, less squeaky than any heard so far.

'Apart from the petty problems with which it has amused you to baffle my compatriots,' he began in oily manner, 'you have given candid, unhesitating answers to our questions. You have provided much information that is useful from the military viewpoint.'

'I am glad you appreciate it,' said Hillder.

'We do. Very much so,' Kadina bestowed a craggy smile that looked sinister. 'However, there is one matter that needs clarifying.'

'What is that?'

'If the present situation were reversed, if a lone Vard-scout was subject to intensive cross-examination by an assembly of your life-form, and if he surrendered information as willingly as you have done ...' He let it die out while his eyes hardened, then growled, 'We would consider him a traitor to his kind. The penalty would be death.'

'How fortunate I am not to be a Vard,' said Hillder.

'Do not congratulate yourself too early,' Kadina retorted. 'A death sentence is meaningless only to those already under such a sentence.'

'What are you getting at?'

'I am wondering whether you are a major criminal seeking sanctuary among us. There may be some other reason. Whatever it is, you do not hesitate to betray your own kind.' He put on the same smile again. 'It would be nice to know *why* you have been so cooperative.'

'That's an easy one,' Hillder said, smiling back in a way that Kadina did not like. 'I am a consistent liar.'

With that, he left his seat and walked boldly to the exit. The guards led him to his cell.

He was there three days, eating regular meals and enjoying them with irritating gusto, amusing himself writing figures in a little pocketbook, as happy as a legendary space-scout named Larry. At the end of that time a ruminative Vard paid a visit.

'I am Bulak. Perhaps you remember me. I was seated at the end of the second row when you were before the commission.'

'Four hundred were there,' Hillder reminded. 'I cannot recall all of them. Only the ones who suffered.' He pushed forward a chair. 'But never mind. Sit down and put your feet up – if you do have feet inside those funny-looking boots. What can I do for you?'

'I don't know.'

'You must have come for some reason, surely?'

Bulak looked mournful. 'I'm a refugee from the fog.'

'What fog?'

'The one you've spread all over the place.' He rubbed a fur-coated ear, examined his fingers, stared at the wall. 'The commission's main purpose was to determine relative standards of intelligence, to settle the prime question of whether your kind's cleverness is less than, greater than or equal to our own. Upon that and that alone depends our reaction to contact with another space-conqueror.'

'I did my best to help, didn't I?'

'Help?' echoed Bulak as if it were a new and strange word. 'Help? Do you call it that? The true test should be that of whether your logic has been extended farther than has ours, whether your premises have been developed to more advanced conclusions.'

'Well?'

'You ended up by trampling all over the laws of logic. A bullet cannot kill anybody. After three days fifty of them are still arguing about it and this morning one of them proved that a person cannot climb a ladder. Friends have fallen out, relatives are starting to hate the sight of each other. The remaining three-hundred-fifty are in little better state.'

'What's troubling them?' inquired Hillder with interest.

'They are debating veracity with everything but brickbats,' Bulak informed, somewhat as if compelled to mention an obscene subject. 'You are a consistent liar. Therefore the statement itself must be a lie. Therefore you are not a consistent liar. The conclusion is that you can be a consistent liar only by not being a consistent liar. Yet you cannot be a consistent liar without being consistent.'

'That's bad,' Hillder sympathized.

'It's worse,' Bulak gave back. 'Because if you really are a consistent liar – which logically is a self-contradiction – none of your evidence is worth a sack of rotten muna-seeds. If you have told us the truth all the way through then your final claim to be a liar must also be true. But if you are a consistent liar then none of it is true.'

'Take a deep breath,' advised Hillder.

'But,' continued Bulak, taking a deep breath, 'since that final statement must be untrue all the rest may be true.' A wild look came into his eyes and he started waving his arms around.

'But the claim to consistency makes it impossible for any statement to be assessed as either true or untrue because, on analysis, there is an unresolvable contradiction that . . .'

'Now, now,' said Hillder, patting his shoulder. 'It is only natural that the lower should be confused by the higher. The trouble is that you've not yet advanced far enough. Your thinking remains a little primitive.' He hesitated, added with the air of making a daring guess, 'In fact it wouldn't surprise me if you still think *logically.*'

'In the name of the Big Sun,' exclaimed Bulak, 'how *else* can we think?'

'Like us,' said Hillder. 'When you're mentally developed.' He strolled twice around the cell, said by way of musing afterthought, 'Right now you couldn't cope with the problem of why a mouse when it spins.'

'Why a mouse when it spins?' parroted Bulak, letting his jaw hang down.

'Or let's try an easier one, a problem any Earth-child could tackle.'

'Such as what?'

'By definition an island is a body of land entirely surrounded by water?'

'Yes, that is correct.'

'Then let us suppose that the whole of this planet's northern hemisphere is land and all the southern hemisphere is water. Is the northern half an island? Or is the southern half a lake?'

Bulak gave it five minutes' thought. Then he drew a circle on a sheet of paper, divided it, shaded the top half and contemplated the result. In the end he pocketed the paper and got to his feet.

'Some of them would gladly cut your throat but for the possibility that your kind may have a shrewd idea where you are and be capable of retribution. Others would send you home with honours but for the risk of bowing to inferiors.'

'They'll have to make up their minds some day,' Hillder commented, refusing to show concern about which way it went.

'Meanwhile,' Bulak continued morbidly, 'we've had a look over your ship which may be old or new according to whether or not you have lied about it. We can see everything but the engines and remote controls, everything but the things that matter. To determine whether they're superior to ours we'd have to pull the vessel apart, ruining it and making you a prisoner.'

'Well, what's stopping you?'

'The fact that you may be bait. If your kind has great power and is looking for trouble they'll need a pretext. Our victimization of you would provide it. The spark that fires the powder-barrel.' He made a gesture of futility. 'What can one do when working utterly in the dark?'

'One could try settling the question of whether a green leaf remains a green leaf in complete absence of light.'

'I have had enough,' declared Bulak, making for the door. 'I have had more than enough. An island or a lake? Who cares? I am going to see Mordafa.'

With that he departed, working his fingers around while the fur quivered on his face. A couple of guards peered through the bars in the uneasy manner of those deputed to keep watch upon a dangerous maniac.

Mordafa turned up next day in the mid-afternoon. He was a thin, elderly, and somewhat wizened specimen with incongruously youthful eyes. Accepting a seat, he studied Hillder, spoke with smooth deliberation.

'From what I have heard, from all that I have been told, I deduce a basic rule applying to life-forms deemed intelligent.'

'You deduce it?'

'I have to. There is no choice about the matter. All the life-forms we have discovered so far have not been truly intelligent. Some have been superficially so but not genuinely so. It is obvious that you have had experiences that may come to us sooner or later but have not arrived yet. In that respect we may have been fortunate seeing that the results of such contact are highly speculative. There's just no way of telling.'

'And what is this rule?'

'That the governing body of any life-form such as ours will be composed of power-lovers rather than of specialists.'

'Well, isn't it?'

'Unfortunately, it is. Government falls into the hands of those with desire for authority and escapes those with other interests.' He paused, went on, 'That is not to say that those who govern us are stupid. They are quite clever in their own particular field of mass-organization. But by the same token they are pathetically ignorant of other fields. Knowing this, your tactic is to take advantage of their ignorance. The weakness of authority is that it cannot be diminished and retain strength. To play upon ignorance is to dull the voice of command.'

'Hm!' Hillder surveyed him with mounting respect. 'You're the first one I've encountered who can see beyond the end of his nose.'

'Thank you,' said Mordafa. 'Now the very fact that you have taken the risk of landing here alone, and followed it up by confusing our leaders, proves that your kind has developed a technique for a given set of conditions and, in all probability, a series of techniques for various conditions.'

'Go on,' urged Hillder.

'Such techniques must be created empirically rather than theoretically,' Mordafa continued. 'In other words, they result from many experiences, the correcting of many errors, the search for workability, the effort to gain maximum results from minimum output.' He glanced at the other. 'Am I correct so far?'

'You're doing fine.'

'To date we have established foot-hold on forty-two planets without ever having to combat other than primitive life. We may find foes worthy of our strength on the forty-third world whenever that is discovered. Who knows? Let us assume for the sake of argument that intelligent life exists on one in every forty-three inhabitable planets.'

'Where does that get us?' Hillder prompted.

'I would imagine,' said Mordafa thoughtfully, 'that the experience of making contact with at least six intelligent life-forms would be necessary to enable you to evolve techniques for dealing with their like elsewhere. Therefore your kind must have discovered and explored not less than two-hundred-fifty worlds. That is an estimate in minimum terms. The correct figure may well be that stated by you.'

'And I am not a consistent liar?' asked Hillder, grinning.

'That is beside the point if only our leaders would hold on to sanity long enough to see it. You may have distorted or exaggerated for purposes of your own. If so, there is nothing we can do about it. The prime fact holds fast, namely, that your space-venturings must be far more extensive than ours. Hence you must be older, more advanced, and numerically stronger.'

'That's logical enough,' conceded Hillder, broadening his grin.

'Now don't start on me,' pleaded Mordafa. 'If you fool me with an intriguing fallacy I won't rest until I get it straight. And that will do either of us no good.'

'Ah, so your intention is to do me good?'

'Somebody has to make a decision seeing that the top brass is no longer capable of it. I am going to suggest that they set you free with our best wishes and assurances of friendship.'

'Think they'll take any notice?'

'You know quite well they will. You've been counting on it all along.' Mordafa eyed him shrewdly. 'They'll grab at the advice to restore their self-esteem. If it works, they'll take the credit. If it doesn't, I'll get the blame.' He brooded a few seconds, asked with open curiosity, 'Do you find it the same elsewhere, among other peoples?'

'Exactly the same,' Hillder assured. 'And there is always a Mordafa to settle the issue in the same way. Power and scapegoats go together like husband and wife.'

'I'd like to meet my alien counterparts some day.' Getting up, he moved to the door. 'If I had not come along how long would you have waited for your psychological mixture to congeal?'

'Until another of your type chipped in. If one doesn't arrive of his own accord the powers-that-be lose patience and drag one in. The catalyst mined from its own kind. Authority lives by eating its vitals.'

'That is putting it paradoxically,' Mordafa observed, making it sound a mild reproof. He went away.

Hillder stood behind the door and gazed through the bars in its top half. The pair of guards leaned against the opposite wall and stared back.

With amiable pleasantness, he said to them, 'No cat has eight tails. Every cat has one tail more than no cat. Therefore every cat has nine tails.'

They screwed up their eyes and scowled.

Quite an impressive deputation took him back to the ship. All the four hundred were there, about a quarter of them resplendent in uniforms, the rest in their Sunday best. An armed guard juggled guns at barked command. Kadina made an unctuous speech full of brotherly love and the glorious shape of things to come. Somebody presented a bouquet of evil-smelling weeds and Hillder made mental note of the difference in olfactory senses.

Climbing eighty yards to the lock, Hillder looked down. Kadina waved an officious farewell. The crowd chanted, 'Hurrah!' in conducted rhythm. He blew his nose on a handkerchief, that being deflatory gesture number nine, closed the lock, sat at the control-board.

Tubes fired into a low roar. A cloud of vapour climbed around and sprinkled ground-dirt over the mob. That touch was involuntary and not recorded in the book. A pity, he thought. Everything ought to be listed. We should be systematic about such things. The showering of dirt should be duly noted under the heading of the spaceman's farewell.

The ship snored into the sky, left the Vard-world far behind. He remained at the controls until free of the entire system's gravitational field. Then he headed for the beacon-area and locked the auto-pilot on that course.

For a while he sat gazing meditatively into star-spangled darkness. After a while he sighed, made notes in his log-book.

'Cube K49, Sector 10, solar-grade D7, third planet. Name Vard. Life-form named Vards, cosmic intelligence rating BB, space-going, forty-two colonies. Comment: softened up.'

He glanced over his tiny library fastened to a steel bulkhead. Two tomes were missing. They had swiped the two that were replete with diagrams and illustrations. They had left the rest, having no Rosetta Stone with which to translate cold print. They hadn't touched the nearest volume titled: *Diabologic, the Science of Driving People Nuts.*

Sighing again, he took paper from a drawer, commenced his hundredth, two-hundredth, or maybe three-hundredth try at concocting an Aleph number higher than A, but lower than C. He mauled his hair until it stuck out in spikes and although he didn't know it he did not look especially well-balanced himself.

J. T. McIntosh

Made in U.S.A.

I

Not a soul watched as Roderick Liffcom carried his bride across the threshold. They were just a couple of nice, good-looking kids – Roderick a psychologist and Alison an ex-copywriter. They weren't news yet. There was nothing to hint that in a few days the name of Liffcom would be known to almost everyone in the world, the tag on a case which interested everybody. Not everyone would follow a murder case, a graft case, or an espionage case. But everyone would follow the Liffcom case.

Let's have a good look at them while we have the chance, before the mobs surround them. Roderick was big and strong enough to treat his wife's 115 pounds with contempt, but there was no contempt in the way he held her. He carried her as if she were a million dollars in small bills and there was a strong wind blowing. He looked down at her with his heart in his eyes. He had black hair and brown eyes and one could see at a glance that he could have carried any girl he liked over the threshold.

Alison nestled in his arms like a kitten, eyes half-closed with rapture, arms about his neck. She was blonde and had fantastically beautiful eyes, not to mention the considerable claims to notice of her other features. But even at first glance one would know that there was more to Alison than beauty. It might be brains, or courage, or hard, bitter experience that had tempered her keen as steel. One could see at a glance that she could have been carried over the threshold by any man she liked.

As they went in, it was the end of a story. But let's be different and call it the beginning.

In the morning, when they were at breakfast on the terrace,

174

the picture hadn't changed radically. That is, Roderick was rather different, blue-chinned and sleepy-eyed and in a brown flannel bathrobe, and Alison was more spectacularly different in a pale green negligée that wasn't so much worn as wafted about. But the way they looked at each other hadn't changed remotely – then.

'There's something' remarked Alison casually; tracing patterns on the damask tablecloth with one slim finger, 'that perhaps I ought to tell you.'

Two minutes later they were fighting for the phone.

'I want to call my lawyer,' Roderick bellowed.

'I want to call my lawyer,' Alison retorted.

He paused, the number half dialled. 'You can't,' he told her roughly. 'It's the same lawyer.'

She recovered herself first, as she always had. She smiled sunnily. 'Shall we toss a coin for him?' she suggested.

'No,' said Roderick brutally. Where, oh, where was his great blinding love? 'He's mine. I pay him more than you ever could.'

'Right,' agreed Alison. 'I'll fight the case myself.'

'So will I,' Roderick exclaimed and slammed the receiver down. Instantly he picked it up again. 'No, we'll need him to get things moving.'

'Collusion?' asked Alison sweetly.

'It was a low, mean, stinking, dirty, cattish, obscene, disgusting, filthy-minded thing to wait until . . .'

'Until what?' Alison asked with more innocence than one would have thought there was in the world.

'Android!' he spat viciously at her.

Despite herself, her eyes flashed with anger.

2

The newspapers not only mentioned it, they said it at the top of their voices: HUMAN SUES ANDROID FOR DIVORCE. It wasn't much of a headline, for one naturally wondered why a human suing an android for divorce should rate a front-page story. After all, half the population of the world was android.

Every day humans divorced humans, humans androids, androids humans, and androids androids. The natural reaction to a headline like that was: 'So what? Who cares?'

But it didn't need particular intelligence to realize that there must be something rather special about this case.

The report ran:

Everton, Tuesday. History is made today in the first human *vs.* android divorce case since the recent grant of full legal equality to androids. It is also the first case of a divorce sought on the grounds that one contracting party did not know the other was an android. This became possible only because the equality law made it no longer obligatory to disclose android origin in any contract.

Recognizing the importance of this test case, certain to affect millions in the future, *Twenty-four Hours* will cover the case, which opens on Friday, in meticulous detail. Ace reporters Anona Grier and Walter Hallsmith will bring to our readers the whole story of this historic trial. Grier is human and Hallsmith android ...

The report went on to give such details as the names of the people in this important test case, and remarked incidentally that although the Liffcom marriage had lasted only ten hours and thirteen minutes before the divorce plea was entered, there had been even briefer marriages recorded.

Twenty-four Hours thus adroitly obviated thousands of letters asking breathlessly: 'Is this a record?

3

Alison, back at her bachelor flat, stretched herself on a divan, focused her eyes past the ceiling on infinity, and thought and thought and thought.

She wasn't particularly unhappy. Not for Alison were misery and resentment and wild, impossible hope. She met the tragedy of her life with placid resignation and even humour.

'Let's face it,' she told herself firmly. 'I'm hurt. I hoped he'd say, "It doesn't matter. What difference could that make? It's you I love" – the sort of thing men say in love stories. But what did he say? *Dirty android.*'

Oh, well. Life wasn't like love stories or they wouldn't just be stories.

She might as well admit for a start that she still loved him. That would clarify her feelings.

She should have told him earlier that she was an android. Perhaps he had some excuse for believing she merely waited until non-consummation was no longer grounds for divorce, and then triumphantly threw the fact that she was an android in his lap. (But what good was that supposed to do her?)

It wasn't like that at all, of course. She hadn't told him because they had to get to know each other before the question arose. One didn't say the moment one was introduced to a person: 'I'm married,' or 'I once served five years for theft,' or 'I'm an android. Are you?'

If in the first few weeks she had known Roderick, some remark had been made about androids, she'd have remarked that she was one herself. But it never had.

When he asked her to marry him, she honestly didn't think of saying she was an android. There were times when it mattered and times when it didn't; this seemed to be one of the latter. Roderick was so intelligent, so liberal-minded, and so easy-going (except when he lost his temper) that she didn't think he would care.

It never did occur to her that he might care. She just mentioned it, as one might say: 'I hope you don't mind my drinking iced coffee every morning.' Well, almost. She just mentioned . . .

And happiness was over.

Now an idea was growing in the sad ripple of her thoughts. Did Roderick really want this divorce case, after all, or was he only trying to prove something? Because if he was, she was ready to admit cheerfully that it was proved.

She wanted Roderick. She didn't quite understand what had happened – perhaps he would take her back on condition that he could trample on her face first. If so, that was all right. She was prepared to let him swear at her and rage at androids and work off any prejudice and hate he might have accumulated somehow, somewhere – as long as he took her back.

She reached behind her, picked up the telephone and dialled Roderick's number.

'Hello, Roderick,' she said cheerfully. 'This is Alison. No, don't hang up. Tell me, why do you hate androids?'

There was such a long silence that she knew he was considering everything, including the advisability of hanging up without a word. It could be said of Roderick that he thought things through very carefully before going off half-cocked.

'I don't hate androids,' he barked at last.

'You've got something against android girls, then?'

'No!' he shouted. 'I'm a psychologist. I think comparatively straight. I'm not fouled up with race hatred and prejudice and megalomania and –'

'Then,' said Alison very quietly, 'it's just one particular android girl you hate.'

Roderick's voice was suddenly quiet, too. 'No, Alison. It has nothing to do with that. It's just . . . children.'

So that was it. Alison's eyes filled with tears. That was the one thing she could do nothing about, the thing she had refused even to consider.

'You really mean it?' she asked. 'That's not just the case you're going to make out?'

'It's the case I'm going to make out,' he replied, 'and I mean it. Trouble is, Alison, you hit something you couldn't have figured on. Most people want children, but are resigned to the fact that they're not likely to get them. I was one of a family of eight. The youngest. You'd have thought, wouldn't you, that that line was pretty safe?

'Well, all the others are married. Some have been for a long time. One brother and two sisters have been married twice. That makes a total of seventeen human beings, not counting me. And their net achievement in the way of reproduction is zero.

'It's a question of family continuity, don't you see? I don't think we'd mind if there was *one* child among the lot of us – *one* extension into the future. But there isn't, and there's only this chance left.'

Alison dropped as close to misery as she ever did. She understood every word Roderick said and what was behind every word. If she ever had a chance of having children, she wouldn't give it up for one individual or love of one individual, either.

But then, of course, she never had it.

In the silence, Roderick hung up. Alison looked down at her own beautiful body and for once couldn't draw a shadow of complacency or content from looking at it. Instead, it irritated her, for it would never produce a child. What was the use of all the appearance, all the mechanism of sex, without its one real function?

But it never occurred to her to give up, to let the suit go undefended. There must be something she could do, some line she could take. Winning the case was nothing, except that that might be a tiny, unimportant part of winning back Roderick.

4

The judge was a little pompous, and it was obvious from the start that under the very considerable power he had under the contract-court system, he meant to run this case in his own way and enjoy it.

He clasped his hands on the bench and looked around the packed courtroom happily. He made his introductory remarks with obvious intense satisfaction that at least fifty reporters were writing down every word.

'This has been called an important case,' he said, 'and it is. I could tell you why it is important, but that would not be justice. Our starting point must be this.' He wagged his head in solemn glee at the jury. 'We know nothing.'

He liked that. He said it again. '*We know nothing*. We don't know the factors involved. We have never heard of androids. All this and more, we have to be told. We can call on anyone anywhere for evidence. And we must make up our minds *here* and *now*, on what we are told *here* and *now*, on the rights and wrongs of this case – and on nothing else.'

He had stated his theme and he developed it. He swooped and soared; he shot away out of sight and returned like a swift raven to cast pearls before swine. For, of course, his audience was composed of swine. He didn't say so or drop the smallest hint to that effect, but it wasn't necessary. Only on Roderick and Alison did he cast a fatherly, friendly eye. They had given him his hour of glory. They weren't swine.

But Judge Collier was no fool. Before he had lost the interest he had created, he was back in the courtroom, getting things moving.

'I understand,' he said, glancing from Alison to Roderick and then back at Alison, which was understandable, 'that you are conducting your own cases. That will be a factor tending towards informality, which is all to the good. First of all, will you look at the jury?'

Everyone in court looked at the jury. The jury looked at each other. In accordance with contract-court procedure, Roderick and Alison faced each other across the room, with the jury behind Alison so that they could see Roderick full-face and Alison in profile, and would know when they were lying.

'Alison Liffcom,' said the judge, 'have you any objection to any member of the jury?'

Alison studied them. They were people, no more, no less. Careful police surveys produced juries that were as near genuine random groups as could reasonably be found.

'No,' she said.

'Roderick Liffcom. Have you any objection –'

'Yes,' said Roderick belligerently. 'I want to know how many of them are androids.'

There was a stir of interest in the court.

So it was really to be a human-android battle.

Judge Collier's expression did not change. 'Out of order,' he said. 'Humans and androids are equal at law, and you cannot object to any juror because he is an android.'

'But this case concerns the rights of humans and androids,' Roderick protested.

'It concerns nothing of the kind,' replied the judge sternly, 'and if your plea is along those lines, we may as well forget the whole thing and go home. You cannot divorce your wife because she is an android.'

'But she didn't tell me –'

'Nor because she didn't tell you. No android now is obliged, ever, to disclose –'

'I know all that,' said Roderick, exasperated. 'Must I state the obvious? I never had much to do with the law, but I do know this – the fact that A equals B may cut no ice, while the fact that B equals A may sew the whole case up. Okay, I'll state the obvious. I seek divorce on the grounds that Alison concealed from me until after our marriage her inability to have a child.'

It was the obvious plea, but it was still a surprise to some people. There was a murmur of interest. Now things could move. There was something to argue about.

Alison watched Roderick and smiled at the thought that she knew him much better than anyone else in the courtroom did. Calm, he was dangerous, and he was fighting to be calm. And as she looked steadily at him, part of her was wondering how she could upset him and put him off stroke, while the other part was praying that he would be able to control himself and show up well.

She was asked to take the stand and she did it absently, still thinking about Roderick. Yes, she contested the divorce. No, she didn't deny that the facts were as stated. On what grounds did she contest the case, then?

She brought her attention back to the matter in hand. 'Oh, that's very simple. I can put it in –' she counted on her fingers – 'nine words. How do we know I can't have a child?'

Reporters wrote down the word 'sensation'. It wouldn't have lasted, but Alison knew that. She piled on more fuel.

'I'm not stating my whole case,' she said. 'All I'm saying at the moment is ...' She blushed. She felt it on her face and was pleased with herself. She hadn't been sure she could do it. 'I don't like to speak of such things, but I suppose I must. When I married Roderick, I was a virgin. How could I possibly know then that I couldn't have a baby?'

It took a long time to get things back to normal after that. The judge had to exhaust himself hammering with his gavel and threatening to clear the court. But Alison caught Roderick's eye, and he grinned and shook his head slowly. Roderick was two people, at least. He was the hot-head, quick to anger, impulsive, emotional. But he was also, though it was hard to believe sometimes, a psychologist, able to sift and weigh and classify things and decide what they meant.

She knew what he meant as he shook his head at her. She had made a purely artificial point, effective only for the moment. She knew she was an android and that androids didn't have children. The rest was irrelevant.

'We have now established,' the judge was saying, breathless from shouting and banging with his gavel, 'what the case is about and some of the facts. Alison Liffcom admits that she concealed the fact that she was an android, as she was perfectly entitled to do –' He frowned down at Roderick, who had risen. 'Well?'

Roderick, at the moment, was the psychologist. 'You mentioned the word "android", Judge. Have you forgotten that none of us knows what an android is? You said, I believe: "We have never heard of androids." '

Judge Collier clearly preferred the other Roderick, whom he could squash when he liked. 'Precisely,' he said without enthusiasm. 'Do you propose to tell us?'

'I propose to have you told,' said Roderick.

Dr Geller took the stand. Roderick faced him, looking calm and competent. Most of the audience were women. He knew how to make the most of himself, and he did. Dr Geller, silver-haired, dignified, was as impassive as a statue.

'Who are you, Doctor?' asked Roderick coolly.

'I am director of the Everton Crèche, where the androids for the entire state are made.'

'You know quite a bit about androids?'

'I do.'

'Just incidentally, in case anyone would like to know, do you mind telling us whether you are human or android?'

'Not at all. I am an android.'

'I see. Now perhaps you'll tell us what androids are, when they were first made, and why?'

'Androids are just people. No different from humans except that they're made instead of born. I take it you don't want me to tell you the full details of the process. Basically, one starts with a few living cells – that's always necessary – and gradually forms a complete human body. There is no difference. I must stress that. An android is a man or a woman, not in any sense a robot or automaton.'

There was a stir again, and the judge smiled faintly. Roderick's witness looked like something of a burden to Roderick. But Roderick merely nodded. Everything, apparently, was under control.

'About two hundred years ago,' the doctor went on, 'it was shown beyond reasonable doubt that the human race was headed for extinction fairly soon. The population was halving itself every generation. Even if human life continued, civilization could not be maintained . . .'

It was dull for everybody. Even Dr Geller didn't seem very interested in what he was saying. This was the part that everyone knew already. But the judge didn't interfere. It was all strictly relevant.

At first the androids had only been an experiment, interesting because they were from the first an astonishingly successful experiment. There was little failure, and a lot of startling success. Once the secret was discovered, one could, by artificial means, manufacture creatures who were men and women to the last decimal point. There was only one tiny flaw. They couldn't reproduce, either among themselves or with human partners. Everything was normal except that conception never took place.

But as the human population dropped, and as the public services slowed, became inefficient, or closed down, it was natural that the bright idea should occur to someone: Why shouldn't the androids do it?

So androids were made and trained as public servants. At first they were lower than the beasts. But that, to do humanity justice, lasted only until it became clear that androids were people. Then androids ascended the social scale to the exalted level of slaves. The curious thing, however, was that there was only one way to make androids, and that was to make them as babies and let them grow up. It wasn't possible to make only stupid, imperfect, adult androids. They turned out like humans, good, bad, and indifferent.

And then came the transformation. Human births took an upsurge. It was renaissance. There was even unemployment for a while again. It would have been inhuman, of course, to kill off the androids, but on the other hand, if anyone was going to starve, they might as well.

They did.

No more androids were made. Human births subsided. Androids were manufactured again. Human births rose.

It became obvious at last. The human race had not so much been extinguishing itself with birth control as actually failing to reproduce. Most people, men and women, were barren these days. But a certain proportion of this barrenness was psychological. The androids were a challenge. They stimulated a stubborn strain deep in humans.

So a balance was reached. Androids were made for two reasons only – to have that challenging effect that kept the human race holding its ground, almost replacing its losses, and to do all the dirty work of keeping a juggernaut of an economic system functioning smoothly for a decimated population.

Even in the early days, the androids had champions. Curiously enough, it wasn't a matter of the androids fighting for and winning equality, but of humans fighting among each other and gradually giving the androids equality.

The humans who fought most were those who couldn't have children. All these people could do if they were to have a family was adopt baby androids. Naturally they lavished on them all the affection and care that their own children would have had. They came to look on them as their own children. They therefore were very strongly in favour of any move to remove restrictions on androids. One's own son or daughter shouldn't be treated as an inferior being.

That was some of the story, as Dr Geller sketched it. The court was restive, the judge looked at the ceiling, the jury looked at Alison. Only Roderick was politely attentive to Dr Geller.

6

Everyone knew at once when the lull was over. If anyone missed Roderick's question, no one missed the doctor's answer: '— reasonably established that androids cannot reproduce. At first there was actually some fear that they might. It was thought that the offspring of android and human would be some kind of monster. But reproduction did not occur.'

'Just one more point, Doctor,' said Roderick easily. 'There is, I understand, some method of identification — some means of telling human from android, and vice versa?'

'There are two,' replied the doctor. Some of the people in court looked up, interested. Others made their indifference obvious to show that they knew what was coming. 'The first is the fingerprint system. It is just as applicable to androids as to humans, and every android at every crèche is finger-printed. If for any reason it becomes necessary to identify a person who may or may not be android, prints are taken. Once these have been sent to every main android centre in the world — a process which takes only two weeks — the person is either positively identified as android or by elimination is known to be human.'

'There is no possibility of error?'

'There is always the possibility of error. The system is perfect, but to err is human — and, if I may be permitted the pleasantry, android as well.'

'Quite,' said Roderick. 'But may we take it that the possibility of error in this case is small?'

'You may. As for the other method of identification: this is a relic of the early days of android manufacture and many of us feel – but that is not germane.'

For the first time, however, he looked somewhat uncomfortable as he went on: 'Androids, of course, are not born. There is no umbilical cord. The navel is small, even, and symmetrical, and faintly but quite clearly marked inside it are the words – in this country, at any rate – "Made in U.S.A."'

A wave of sniggers ran round the court. The doctor flushed faintly. There were jokes about the little stamp that all androids carried. Once there had been political cartoons with the label as the motif. The point of one allegedly funny story came when it was discovered that a legend which was expected to be 'Made in U.S.A.' turned out to be 'Fabriqué en France' instead.

It had always been something humans could jibe about, the stamp that every android would carry on his body to his grave. Twenty years ago, all persecution of androids was over, supposedly, and androids were free and accepted and had all but the same rights as humans. Yet twenty years ago, women's evening dress invariably revealed the navel, whatever else was chastely concealed. Human girls flaunted the fact that they were human. Android girls either meekly showed the proof or, by hiding it, admitted they were android.

'There is under review,' said the doctor, 'a proposal to discontinue what some people feel must always be a badge of subservience –'

'That is *sub judice*,' interrupted the judge, 'and no part of the matter in question. We are concerned with things as they are.' He looked inquiringly at Roderick. 'Have you finished with the witness?'

'Not only the witness,' said Roderick, 'but my case.' He looked so pleased with himself that Alison who was difficult to anger, wanted to hit him. 'You have heard Dr Geller's evidence. I demand that Alison submit herself to the two tests he mentioned. When it is established that she is an android, it will also be established that she cannot have a child. And that she therefore, by concealing her android status from me, also concealed the fact that she could not have a child.'

The judge nodded somewhat reluctantly. He looked over his glasses at Alison without much hope. It would be a pity if such a promising case were allowed to fizzle out so soon and so trivially. But he personally could see nothing significant that Alison could offer in rebuttal.

'Your witness,' said Roderick, with a gesture that called for a kick in the teeth, or so Alison thought.

'Thank you,' she said sweetly. She rose from her seat and crossed the floor. She wore a plain grey suit with a vivid yellow blouse, only a little of it visible, supplying the necessary touch of colour. She had never looked better in her life and she knew it.

Roderick looked as though he were losing the iron control which he had held for so long against all her expectations, and she did what she could to help by wriggling her skirt straight in the way he had always found so attractive.

'Stop that!' he hissed at her. 'This is serious.'

She merely showed him twenty-eight of her perfect teeth, and then turned to Dr Geller.

7

'I was most interested in a phrase you used, Doctor,' said Alison. 'You said it was "reasonably established" that androids could not reproduce. Now I take it I have the facts correct. You are director of the Everton Crèche?'

'Yes.'

'And your professional experience is therefore confined to androids up to the age of ten?'

'Yes.'

'Is it usual for even humans,' asked Alison, 'to reproduce before the age of ten?'

There was stunned silence, then a laugh, then applause. 'This is not a radio show,' shouted the judge. 'Proceed, if you please, Mrs Liffcom.'

Alison did. Dr Geller was the right man to come to for all

matters relating to *young* androids, she said apologetically, but for matters relating to adult androids (no offence to Dr Geller intended, of course), she proposed to call Dr Smith.

Roderick interrupted. He was perfectly prepared to hear Alison's case, but hadn't they better conclude his first? Was Alison prepared to submit herself to the two tests mentioned?

'It's unnecessary,' said Alison. 'I am an android. I am not denying it.'

'Nevertheless –' said Roderick.

'I don't quite understand, Mr Liffcom,' the judge put in. 'If there were any doubt, yes. But Mrs Liffcom is not claiming that she is not an android.'

'I want to *know*.'

'Do you think there is any doubt?'

'I only wish there were.'

It was 'sensation' again.

'And yet it's all perfectly natural, when you consider it,' said Roderick, when he could be heard. 'I want a divorce because Alison is an android and can't have a child. If she's been mistaken, or has been playing some game, or whatever it might be, I don't want a divorce. I want Alison, the girl I married. Surely that's easy enough to understand?'

'All right,' said Alison emotionlessly. 'It'll take some time to check my fingerprints, but the other test can be made now. What do I do, Judge, peel here in front of everybody?'

'Great Scott, no!'

Five minutes later, in the jury room, the judge, the jury, and Roderick examined the proof. Alison surrendered none of her dignity or self-possession while showing it to them.

There was no doubt. The mark of the android was perfectly clear.

Roderick was last to look. When he had examined the brand, his eyes met Alison's, and she had to fight back the tears. For he wasn't satisfied or angry, only sorry.

Back in court, Roderick said he waived the fingerprint test. And Alison called Dr Smith. He was older than Dr Geller, but bright-eyed and alert. There was something about him –

people leaned forward as he took the stand, knowing somehow that what he had to say was going to be worth hearing.

'Following the precedent of my learned friend,' said Alison, 'may I ask you if you are human or android, Dr Smith?'

'You may. I am human. However, most of my patients have been android.'

'Why is that?'

'Because I realized long ago that androids represented the future. Humans are losing the fight. That being so, I wanted to find out what the differences between humans and androids were, or if there were any at all. If there were none, so much the better – the human race wasn't going to die out, after all.'

'But of course,' said Alison casually, yet somehow everyone hung on her words, 'there was one essential difference. Humanity was becoming sterile, but androids couldn't reproduce.'

'There was no difference,' said Dr Smith.

Sometimes an unexpected statement produces silence, sometimes bedlam. Dr Smith got both in turn. There was the stillness of shock as he elaborated and put his meaning beyond doubt.

'*Androids can have and have had children.*'

Then the rest was drowned in a wave of gasps, whispers and exclamations that swelled in a few seconds to a roar. The judge hammered and shouted in vain.

There was anger in the shouts. There was excitement, anxiety, incredulity, fear. Either the doctor was lying or he wasn't. If he was lying, he would suffer for it. People tricked by such a hoax are angry, vengeful, people.

If he wasn't lying, everyone must re-evaluate his whole view of life. Everyone – human and android. The old religious questions would come up again. The question would be decided of whether Man, himself becoming extinct, had actually conquered life, instead of merely reaching a compromise with it. It would cease to matter whether any person was born or made.

There would be no more androids, only human beings. And Man would be master of creation.

8

The court sat again after a brief adjournment. The judge peered at Alison and at Dr Smith, who was again on the stand.

'Mrs Liffcom,' he said, 'would you care to take up your examination at the same point?'

'Certainly,' said Alison. She addressed herself to Dr Smith. 'You say that androids can have children?'

This time there was silence except for the doctor's quiet voice. 'Yes. There is, as may well be imagined, conflicting evidence on this. The evidence I propose to bring forward has frequently been discredited. The reaction when I first made this statement shows why. It is an important question on which everyone must have reached some conclusion. Possibly one merely believes what one is told.'

As he went on, Alison cast a glance at Roderick. At first he was indifferent. He didn't believe it. Then he showed mild interest in what the doctor was saying. Eventually he became so excited that he could hardly sit still.

And Alison began to hope again.

'There is a psychologist in court,' remarked the doctor mildly, 'who may soon be asking me questions. I am not a psychologist any more than any other general practitioner, but before I mention particular cases, I must make this point. Every android grows up knowing he or she cannot have children. That is accepted in our civilization.

'I don't think it should be accepted. I'll tell you why.'

No one interrupted him. He wasn't spectacular, but he wasted no time.

He mentioned the case of Betty Gordon Holbein, 178 years before. No one had heard of Betty Gordon Holbein. She was human, said the doctor. Prostrate with shock, she testified she had been raped by an android. The android concerned was lynched. In due course, Betty Holbein had a normal child.

'The records are available to everyone,' said the doctor. 'There was a lot of interest and indignation when the girl was raped, very little when she had her child. The suggestion that she had conceived after the incident was denied, without much publicity, or belief, for even then it was known that androids were barren.'

Roderick was on his feet. He looked at the judge, who nodded.

'Look, are you twisting this to make a legal case,' he demanded, 'or did this girl –'

'You cannot ask the witness if he is perjuring himself,' remarked the judge reprovingly.

'I don't give a damn about perjury!' Roderick exclaimed. 'I just want to know if this is true!'

It was all very irregular; but Alison knew he might explode any moment and swear at the doctor and the judge. She didn't want that. So her eyes met his and she said levelly: 'It's true, Roderick.'

Roderick sat down.

'Now to get a true picture,' the doctor continued, 'we must remember that millions of androids were being tested, and mating among themselves, and even having irregular liaisons with humans – and no conception took place. Or did it?

'A little over a century ago, an android girl had been found in a wood, alive, but only just. Around her there were marks of many feet. She had been mutilated. Though she lived, she was never quite sane after that.

'But she also had a child.'

Roderick rose again, frowning. 'I don't understand,' he said. 'If this is true, why is it not known?'

The judge was going to intervene, but Roderick went on quickly, 'The doctor and I are professional men. I can ask him for a professional opinion, surely? Well, Doctor?'

'Because it has always been possible to disbelieve what one has decided to disbelieve. In this case, that nameless woman was mutilated so that the navel mark would be removed. There was a record of her fingerprints as those of an android. But it was authoritatively stated that there must have been a mistake and that, by having a child, the woman had thus been proved to be human.

'A century and a half ago, Winnie – androids had begun to

have at least a first name by this time – had a child and it was again decided that this girl, who had been a laundry maid, must have been mixed up with an android while a baby and was in fact human.

'A little dead baby was found buried in a garden and an android couple was actually in court over the matter. But since they were androids, it could obviously not be their child, and they were discharged.'

Roderick jumped up again. 'If you knew this,' he asked Dr Smith, 'why keep it secret until now?'

'Five years ago,' said the doctor, 'I wrote an article on the subject. I sent it to all the medical journals. Eventually one of the smaller publications printed it. I had half a dozen letters from people who were interested. Then nothing more.

'One must admit,' he added, 'that not one of the cases I have mentioned – as reported at the time – would be accepted as positive scientific proof that androids can reproduce. The facts were recorded for posterity by people who didn't believe them. But . . . '

'But,' said Alison, a few minutes later, when the doctor had finished giving his evidence, 'in view of this, it can hardly be stated that I *know* I cannot have a child. It may be unlikely; shall I call more medical evidence to show how unlikely conception is for the average human woman?'

Judge Collier said nothing, so she continued: 'The present position, as anyone concerned with childbirth would tell you, is that few marriages produce children, but those that do produce a lot. People who *can* have children go on doing it, these days.

'Now I want to introduce a new point. It is not grounds for divorce among humans if the woman is barren and is not aware of it. It *is*, on the other hand, if she has had an operation which makes it impossible for her to have children and she conceals the fact.'

'I see what you are getting at,' said the judge, 'and it is most ingenious. Finish it, please.'

'Having had no such operation,' said Alison, 'and being

able to prove it, I understand that I can't be held, legally, to
have known that I could never have children.'

'To save reference to case histories,' said the judge content-
edly, 'I can say here and now that the lady is right. It is for the
jury to decide on the merits of the case, but Mrs Liffcom may be
said to have established –'

'I demand an adjournment,' said Roderick.

There was a low murmur that gradually died out. Roderick
and Alison were both on their feet, staring at each other across
ten yards of space. The intensity of their feeling could be felt
by everyone in the courtroom.

'Court adjourned until tomorrow,' said the judge hastily.

9

Almost every newspaper which mentioned the Liffcom case
committed contempt of court. Perhaps the feeling was that no
action could be taken against so many. All the newspapers went
into the rights and wrongs of the affair as if they were giving
evidence, too. Very little of the material was pro- or anti-
android. It was, rather, for or against the evidence brought up.

Anyone could see, remarked one newspaper bluntly, that
Alison Liffcom was nobody's fool. If a woman like that went
to the trouble of defending a suit of any kind, she would dig up
something good and play it to the limit. This was no aspersion
on the morals or integrity of Mrs Liffcom, for whom the newspaper had the keenest admiration. All she had to do was cast the
faintest doubt on the truism that androids could not reproduce.
She had done that.

But that, of course, said the paper decisively, didn't mean
that androids *could*.

Another newspaper took it from there. Just as good a case,
it remarked, could have been made out for spiritualism, tele-
pathy, possession, the existence of werewolves ... Dr Smith,
who was undoubtedly sincere, had been misled by a few mistakes. Obviously, when androids were human in all respects
save one, *some* humans would be passed off or mistaken for
androids and vice versa. Equally obviously; the mistake would

only be discovered if and when conception occurred, as in the cases quoted by Dr Smith.

A third paper even offered Alison a point to make in court if she liked. True enough Dr Smith had shown that such mistakes could occur. It was only necessary for Alison then to quote these cases and stress the possibility that the same thing might have happened to her. If the proof of android origin was not proof, the case would collapse.

Other papers, however, took the view that there might be something in the possibility that androids could reproduce. Why not? asked one. Androids weren't bloodless, inferior beings. One could keep things warm by holding them against the human body – or by building a fire. In the same way, children could be nurtured in a human body or in culture tanks. The results were identical. They must be identical if one could take them forty years later, give them rigorous tests, and tell one from the other only because the android was stamped 'Made in U.S.A.' and because his fingerprints were on file.

People had believed androids could not have children because they had been told androids never had. Now they were told androids *had* reproduced. Where was the difficulty? You believed you had finished your cigarettes until you took out the pack and saw there was one left. What did you do then – say you had finished them, therefore that what looked like a cigarette wasn't, and throw it away?

And almost all the newspapers, whatever their general view, asked the real, fundamental question as well.

That artificially made humans could conceive was credible, in theory. That they could not was also credible, in theory.

But why one in a million, one in five million, one in ten million? Even present-day humans could average one fertile marriage in six.

10

'If you have no objections,' said Roderick politely – determined to be on his best behaviour, thought Alison – 'let's turn this into a court of inquiry. Let's say, if you like, that Alison has successfully defended the case on the grounds that she can't legally be said to have known she couldn't have a child. Forget the divorce. That's not the point.'

'I thought it was,' the judge objected, dazed.

'Anyone can see that what matters now,' said Roderick impatiently, 'is what Dr Smith brought up. Let's get down to the question of whether there's any prospect of Alison having a baby.'

'A courtroom is hardly the place to settle that,' murmured Alison. But she felt the first warm breath of a glow of happiness she had thought she would never be able to experience again.

'Women always go from the general to the particular,' Roderick retorted. 'I don't mean the question of whether you *will* have children. I mean the question of whether it's really possible that you might.'

The judge rapped decisively. 'I have been too lenient. I insist on having a certain amount of order in my own court. Roderick Liffcom, do you withdraw your suit?'

'What does it matter? Anyway, if you must follow that line, we'd have to have a few straight questions and answers like whether Alison still loves me.'

The judge gasped.

'Do you?' demanded Roderick, glaring at Alison.

Alison felt as if her heart was going to explode. 'If you want a straight answer,' she said, 'yes.'

'Good,' said Roderick with satisfaction. 'Now we can go on from there.'

He turned to glower at Judge Collier, who was trying to interrupt.

'Look here,' Roderick demanded, 'are you interested in getting at the truth?'

'Certainly, but –'

'So am I. Be quiet, then. I meant to keep my temper with you, but you're constantly getting in my hair. Alison, would you mind taking the stand?'

There was no doubt that Roderick had personality.

With Alison on the stand, he turned to the jury. 'I'll tell you what I have in mind,' he told them in friendly fashion. 'We all wonder why, if this thing's possible, it's happened so seldom. Unfortunately, to date there hasn't been any real admission that it is possible, so I didn't know. I never had a chance to work on it. Now I have. What I want to know is, if androids can have children, what prevents them from doing so.'

He reached out absently, without looking around, and squeezed Alison's shoulder. 'We've got Alison here,' Roderick went on. 'Let's find out if we can, shall we, what would stop her from having children?'

Alison was glad she was sitting down. Her knees felt so weak that she knew they wouldn't support her. Did she have Roderick back or didn't she? Could she really have a baby? *Roderick's* baby? The court swam dizzily in front of her eyes.

Only gradually did she become aware of Roderick's voice asking anxiously if she was all right, Roderick bending over her, Roderick's arm behind her back, supporting her.

'Yes,' she said faintly. 'I'm sorry. Roderick, I'll help you all I can, but do you think there's really very much chance?'

'I'm a psychologist,' he reminded her quietly, 'and since you've never seen me at work, there's no harm in telling you I'm pretty good. Maybe we won't work this out here in half an hour, but we'll get through it in the next sixty years.'

Alison didn't forget where she was, but everything was so crazy that a little more wouldn't hurt. She reached up and drew his lips down to hers.

II

'What I'm looking for must be in the life of every android, male and female,' said Roderick. 'I don't expect to find it right away. Just tell us, Alison, about any times when you were aware of distinction – when you were made aware that you were an android, not a human. Start as early as you like.

'And,' he added with a sudden, unexpected grin, 'please address your remarks to the judge. Let's keep this as impersonal as we can.'

Alison composed her mind for the job. She didn't really want to look back. She wanted to look into the new, marvellous future. But she forced herself to begin.

'I grew up in the New York Android Crèche,' she said. 'There was no distinction there. Some of the children thought there was. Sometimes I heard older children talking about how much better off they would be if they were humans. But twice when there was overcrowding in the crèche and plenty of room at the orphanage for human children, I was moved to the orphanage. And there was absolutely no difference.

'In a crèche, it's far more important to be able to sell yourself than it ever can be later. If you're attractive or appealing enough, someone looking for a child to adopt will notice you and you'll have a home and security and affection. I wasn't attractive or appealing. I stayed in the crèche until I was nine. I saw so many couples looking for children, always taking away some child but never me, that I was sure I would stay there until I was too old to be adopted and then have to earn my living, always on my own.

'Then, one day, one of the sisters at the crèche found me crying – I forget what I was crying about – and told me there was no need for me to cry about anything because I had brains and I was going to be a beauty, and what more could any girl want? I looked in the mirror, but I still seemed the same as ever. She must have known what she was talking about, though, for just a week later, a couple came and looked around the crèche and picked me.'

Alison took a deep breath, and there was no acting about the tears in her eyes.

'Nobody who's never experienced it can appreciate what it is to have a home for the first time at the age of nine,' she said. 'To say I'd have died for my new parents doesn't tell half of it. Maybe this is something that misled Roderick. He knew that twice a month, at least, I go and see my folks. He must have thought they were my real parents, so he didn't ask if I was android.'

She looked at Roderick for the first time since she started the story. He nodded.

'Go on, Alison,' he said quietly. 'You're doing fine.'

'This isn't a hard world for androids,' Alison insisted. 'It's only very occasionally . . .'

She stopped, and Roderick had to prompt her. 'Only very occasionally that what?'

But Alison wasn't with him. She was eleven years back in the past.

12

Alison had known all about that awkward period when she would cease to be a child and become a woman. But she had never quite realized how rapid it would be, and how it would seem even more rapid, so that it was over before she was ready for it to start.

She wasn't sleeping well, but she was so healthy and had such reserves of strength that it didn't show, and for once her adopted parents failed her. Though Alison would never admit that, it would have been so much easier if Susan had talked with her, and Roger, without saying a word, had indicated in his manner that he knew what was going on.

One day she was out walking, trying to tire herself for sleep later, and ran into a group of youths of her own age in the woods. She knew one of them slightly, Bob Thompson, and she knew that their apparent leader, as tall as a man at fifteen, was Harry Hewitt. She didn't know whether any of them were androids or not – the question had never occurred to her. And it didn't seem of any immediate interest or importance that she was an android, either, as she passed through them and some of them whistled, and involuntarily, completely aware of their eyes on her, she reddened.

She saw Bob Thompson whisper to Harry Hewitt and Hewitt burst out: 'Android, eh? *Android!* That's fine!' He stepped in front of her and barred her path. 'What a pretty android,' he said loudly, playing to his gallery. 'I've seen you before, but I thought you were just a girl. Take off your blouse, android.'

There was a startled movement in the group, and someone nudged Hewitt.

'It's all right,' he said. 'She's an android. No real parents, only people who have taken her in to pretend they can have kids.'

Alison looked from side to side like a cornered animal.

'Humans can do anything they like with androids,' Hewitt told his more timorous companions. 'Don't you know that?' He turned back to Alison. 'But we must be sure she is an android. Hold her, Butch.'

Alison was grasped firmly by the hips, which had so recently stopped being boyish and swelled alarmingly. She kicked and struggled, her heart threatening to burst, but Butch, whoever he was, was strong. Two other boys held her arms. Carefully, to a chorus of nervous, excited sniggers, Hewitt parted her blouse and skirt a narrow slit and peered at her navel.

'Made in U.S.A.,' he said with satisfaction. 'It's all right then.'

In contrast to his previous cautious, decorous manner, he tore the blouse out of her waistband and ripped it off. Alison's knees sagged as someone behind her began to fumble with her brassiere.

'No, no!' Hewitt exclaimed in mock horror. 'Mustn't do that until she says you can. Even androids have rights. Or at least, if they haven't, we should be polite and pretend they have. Android, say we can do whatever we like with you.'

'No!' cried Alison.

'That's too bad. Shift your grip a bit, Butch.'

The rough hands went up around her ribs, rasping her soft skin.

Alison struggled and twisted wildly.

'Keep still,' said Hewitt. He spoke very quietly, but there was savage joy in his face. Slowly and carefully, he loosened Alison's belt and eased her skirt and the white trunks under it down to the pit of her stomach. Then he took out a heavy clasp knife, opened it and set the point neatly in the centre of her belly. Alison drew in her stomach; the knife point followed, indenting the flesh.

'Say we can do whatever we like with you, android.'

The knife pricked deeper. A tiny drop of crimson came from under it and ran slowly down to Alison's skirt. Her nerve broke.

'You can do whatever you like with me!' she screamed.

Her brassiere came loose and fluttered to the ground. Hewitt's knife cut her belt and her skirt began to slip over her hips. Butch's hands went down to her waist again, biting into it cruelly. From behind, a hand tentatively touched her breast and another clutched her shoulder. One at a time, her feet were raised and the shoes taken off them and thrown in the bushes.

But someone else had heard Alison's scream. Long after she had thought no one would come, someone did.

'Hell,' said Hewitt as one of his companions shouted and pointed, 'something always spoils everything. Beat it, boys.'

They were gone. Alison clutched her skirt and looked behind her thankfully. A man and a woman were only a few yards from her. The woman was young and heavy with child. Humans, both of them. She opened her mouth to thank them, to explain, to weep.

But they were looking at her as if she were a crushed beetle of some kind.

'Android, of course,' said the man disgustedly. 'Dirty little beast.'

'Hardly more than child,' the woman said, 'and already at this.'

'I think I'll give her a good hiding,' the man went on. 'Won't do any good, I suppose, but . . .'

Alison burst into tears and darted among the bushes. She didn't wait to see whether the man started after her. Branches and thorns tore her skin. Her skirt dropped and tripped her. She flew headlong, flinched away from a thorny bush, slammed hard into a tree-trunk, and waited on the ground, sick and breathless, for the man to beat her.

Her legs and arms and shoulders were covered with long scratches and a wiry branch had lashed her ribs like a whip, leaving a long weal. But that didn't matter. A twisted root was digging into her side – that, too, didn't matter. Nothing mattered. Why had no one told her she was an inferior being? Somehow she had known; she had always known. But no one had *ever* shown her before.

She realized afterward why the man and the woman, who must have seen or guessed what had really happened, had spoken as they did. They had, or were going to have, children.

They hated all androids. Androids were unnecessary, their enemies, and the enemies of their children.

But at the time she merely waited helpless, incapable of thought. The man would come and beat her, Susan and Roger would turn her away again, and she would never know happiness again.

13

'My parents never knew about that,' said Alison. 'I hid in the bushes until it was dark, and then went straight home. I climbed into my bedroom from the outhouse and pretended later I'd been there for hours.'

'Why didn't you tell anyone?' Roderick asked.

Alison shrugged. 'It was a small incident that concerned me alone. I knew, once I'd had time to think, that my adopted parents would be upset and angry, but not at me. I thought I'd better keep it to myself. I wasn't hurt and none of it matters when you look back on it, does it?'

'How about the man who was going to give you a good hiding?'

'I never saw him again. It was two years later when I got my first punishment.'

'Just a minute,' said Roderick. 'You said that even then you knew you were an inferior being – you had always known, but this was the first time anyone showed you. How had you known? Who or what had told you? When? Where?'

Alison tried. They could see her try. But she had to say: 'I don't know.'

'All right,' said Roderick, as if it weren't important. 'What was this that happened two years later?'

'Perhaps I am giving too much significance to these incidents,' Alison remarked apologetically. 'Certainly they happened. But when I say "two years passed," perhaps I'm not making it clear that in those two years hardly anything happened, hardly anything was said or done, to remind me I was an android and not a human being.

'When I was about sixteen or seventeen, I suddenly developed a talent for tennis. I had played since I was quite young, but just as front-rank players run in and out of form, I improved quite unexpectedly. I joined a new club. I was picked for an important match. I was in singles, mixed and women's doubles. I did well, but that's not the point.

'After the match, my doubles partner told me I was wanted in the locker room. There was something strange about the way she told me, but I couldn't place it. I wondered if I'd broken some rule, failed to check with someone, played in the wrong match, or forgotten to bow three times to the east – you know what these clubs are like.'

'No, we don't,' said Judge Collier. 'We know nothing remember? Tell us.'

Unexpectedly, he got an approving nod from the unpredictable Roderick.

14

Alison smiled uncertainly as she followed Veronica. She wasn't nervous or sensitive as a rule; she seldom felt apprehension. She was curious, naturally, and even wilder possibilities suggested themselves. Had she been mistaken for someone else? Had someone stolen something and they thought she'd done it? Had someone inspected her racket and found it was an inch too wide?

The whole team was waiting in the locker room. It looked serious, especially when she saw their expressions. It still didn't occur to her that the fact that she was an android could have anything to do with it. Only once in her life had there been any real indication that in some way androids were inferior beings.

But that was what it was. Bob Walton, the captain of the team, said gravely that their opponents, well beaten, had accused them of recruiting star androids to help them.

Alison laughed. 'That's a new one. I've heard some peculiar excuses. Made them myself, too – the light was bad, the umpire was crazy, I had a stone in my shoe, people were moving about, the net was too high. But never "You fielded androids against us." Androids are just ordinary people – good and bad tennis players. The open singles champion is an android, but the number one woman is human. You know that as well as I do. Might as well complain because you're beaten by tall people, or short people, or people with long arms.'

Everyone had relaxed.

'Sorry, Alison,' said Walton. 'It's just that none of us knew you *weren't* an android.'

Alison frowned. 'What's all this? I'm an android, sure. I didn't say so only because nobody asked me.'

'We took it for granted,' said Walton stiffly, 'that you would know ... as, of course, you did. There are no androids competing in the Athenian League. We try to keep one group, at least, clean.'

He looked at the other two men in the team and inclined his head. Without a word they left the room, all three of them.

Alison, left with the other three girls, one of whom she had kept out of the team, looked exasperated.

'This is nonsense,' she said. 'If you like to run an all-human league, that's all right as far as I'm concerned, but you should put up notices to avoid misunderstanding. I didn't know you were –'

'Whether you knew or not is beside the point,' said Veronica coldly – the same Veronica who had laughed and talked and won a match with Alison only a few minutes before. 'We're going to make sure you never forget.'

They closed in on her. It was to be a fight, apparently. Alison didn't mind. She jabbed Veronica in the ribs and sent her gasping across the room. She expected them to tear her clothes, thinking it would be conventional in dealing with android girls. But it was quite different from the scene in the bushes. This was clean and sporting. The men had left, very properly, and instead of half a dozen youths with a knife against a terrified child, it was only three girls to one.

Alison fought hard, but fair. She guessed that, if she didn't fight clean, it would be ammunition for the android-haters. To do them justice, the other girls were clean, too. They didn't mind hurting her, but they didn't go for her face, use their nails or yank her hair.

Alison gave a good account of herself, but other things being equal, three will always overcome one. She was turned on her face on the floor. One of the girls sat on her legs and one on her shoulders while the third beat the seat of her shorts with a firmly swung racket.

It was no joke. Alison wouldn't have made a sound if it had been far worse, but when they let her go, she was feeling sorry for herself. They left her alone in the room.

She picked herself up and dusted herself off. The floor was clean and the mirror in one corner showed that she looked all right. In fact, she looked considerably better than the three girls who had beaten her.

Still angry, she was able to grin philosophically at the thought that she could beat them all in a beauty contest and at tennis. She could tell herself, if she liked, that they were jealous of her. It was probably at least partly true.

Her feelings were hurt, but there was no other damage. She could even see their point of view.

15

'What *was* their point of view?' asked Roderick.

'Well, they were human and they were snobs. They'd even have admitted they were snobs, if you put the question the right way. It was a private club –'

'And it was quite reasonable,' suggested Roderick softly, 'that they should exclude androids, who are inferior beings.'

'No, not quite that,' Alison protested, laughing. 'I don't really believe . . .'

She stopped.

'Just sometimes?' Roderick persisted. 'Or just one part of you, while the other knows quite well an android is as good as a human?'

Alison shivered suddenly. 'You know, I have a curious feeling, as if I were being trapped into something.'

'That's how people always feel,' said Roderick, 'just before they decide they needn't be terrified any more of spiders or whatever it was they feared.'

The court was very quiet. There was something about Roderick's professional competence and Alison's determination to cooperate that made any kind of interruption out of the question.

'There's very little more I can say about this,' said Alison. 'I took a job, not because I had to, but because I wanted to. It was with an advertising agency. They knew I was an android. They paid me exactly what they paid anyone else. When I did well, they gave me a rise.

'But then I noticed something – I never got any credit for anything. When I had an idea, somehow it was always possible to give the credit to someone else. Soon there was a very curious situation. I held a very junior position, I had little or no standing, but I did responsible work and I was paid well for it.

'I went to another agency and it was quite different. Again, they knew I was an android, but no one seemed remotely interested. When I did well, I was promoted. When I did badly on any job, my chief swore at me and called me a fool and an incompetent and an empty-headed glamour girl and a lot of things I'd rather not repeat here.

'But it never seemed to occur to him to call me a dirty android. I don't think he was an android himself, either.

'I joined a dramatic society, but again I chose the wrong club. They didn't mind at all that I was an android. They didn't keep me in small parts. But it was perfectly natural that the three human girls in the cast shouldn't want to use the same dressing-room as another android girl in the show and I did. When we were at small places, she and I had to change in the wings.

'There were scores of other little incidents of the same kind. They multiplied as I grew older – not because differentiation was getting worse, but because I was moving in higher society. In places where it's held against you that you didn't go to Harvard or Yale, naturally it's a disadvantage if you're an android, besides.

'Then a law was passed and it was no longer necessary to admit being an android. I don't know what the Athenian Tennis League did about that. I'd come to Everton then and hardly

205

anyone knew I was an android. And the plain fact, despite everything I've said, is that hardly anyone cared. There are so many androids, so many humans. You may find yourself the only android in a group – or the only human.

'Then I met Roderick.'

'There,' said Roderick, 'I think we can stop.' He turned to the judge. 'I'm withdrawing my suit, of course. I think I made that clear quite a while ago.'

He gave Alison his arm. 'Come on, sweetheart, let's go.'

The roar burst out again. It must have been both one of the noisiest and one of the quietest trials on record. The judge, dignity forgotten, was standing up, hopping from one foot to the other in impatience and vexation.

'You can't go like that!' he shrieked. 'We haven't finished ... we don't know ...'

'I've gone as far as I can here,' said Roderick. He hesitated as the roar grew. 'All right,' he went on, raising his voice. 'But you don't explain people to themselves. Any little quirks that make them do funny things, or not do normal things, you get them gradually to explain to you, and to themselves.'

He searched in his pockets and pulled out a key ring. 'Go and wait in the car, honey,' he said, and told Alison where it was. She went, dazed.

'I'll have to keep the papers from her for a day or two,' Roderick went on, almost to himself. 'After that, it won't matter.' He turned his attention to the court. 'All right, then, listen. If I'm right, I've found something that's been under everyone's nose for two hundred years and has never been seen before. I don't say I found it in five minutes. I've been working it out for the last twenty-four hours, with the help of quite a few records of android patients.

'Will you listen?' he yelled as the excited chatter increased. 'I don't want to tell you this. I want to go home with Alison. You've seen her. Wouldn't you want to?'

The court gradually settled.

'Let's consider human sterility for a moment,' said Roderick.

'As you might imagine, some of it's medical and some psychological. As a psychologist, I've cured people of so-called barrenness – and when I did, of course, it wasn't sterility at all, but a neurosis. These people didn't and don't have children because owing to some unconscious conclusion they've reached, they don't want them, feel they shouldn't have them, or are certain they can't have them.

'But that's only some. Others come to me and, in consultation with a specialist in that line, I find there's nothing psychological about it whatever.

'I have an idea, now, that *all* androids are psychologically sterile. Sterility has eaten into the cycle of human reproduction but how should it touch the androids? If one android can reproduce, they all can. Unless they, like these humans I've cured, have reached unconscious conclusions to the effect that androids can't or shouldn't or mustn't have children.

'And we know they nearly all have.'

His voice suddenly dropped, and when Roderick spoke quietly, he was emphasizing points and people listened. There was no murmuring now.

'I think if you were to run a survey and find who now is continuing to deny – passionately, honestly, sincerely – that androids can reproduce, you'd find the most passionate, honest, and sincere are androids. If you looked into the past, I think you'd find the same thing. Wasn't it significant that it had to be a *human* doctor who declared publicly that androids weren't sterile?

'Into every android is built the psychological axiom that an android must be inferior to a human to survive. That's the answer. Androids don't come to me to be cured of this because they don't *want* to be cured of it. They know it's essential to them. With the more aware part of their brains, they may know exactly the opposite, but that doesn't count when it comes to things like this.

'And long ago, without knowing it, androids picked on this. Androids could not be a menace if they couldn't reproduce. Androids would be duly inferior if they couldn't reproduce.

Androids would be allowed to exist if they couldn't reproduce. Androids could compete with humans in other things if they couldn't reproduce.'

He knew he was right as he looked around the court. For once, almost at a glance, it was possible to tell humans from androids. Half the people in court were interested, bored, amused, indifferent, thoughtful – the humans. The other half were angry, frightened, ashamed, apathetic, resentful, wildly excited or in tears ... for Roderick was tearing at the very foundation of their world.

'I have real hopes for Alison,' he remarked mildly, 'because she brought in Dr Smith. See what that means? Not one android in a thousand could have done it. She must love me a lot ... but that's none of your business.'

He went the way Alison had gone. No one tried to stop him this time. At the door, he paused.

'When the first acknowledged android children are born,' he observed, 'it'll mean that regardless of the trials or disasters mankind still has to face, the *human* race won't die out. Because ... I think we might all chew a little on this point ... the children of androids can't be android, can they?'

16

Roderick drove. Alison usually did when they were out in a car together, but there was an unspoken agreement that Roderick would have to take charge of almost everything for a while.

'We both won,' she said happily. 'At least, we will have when little Roderick arrives.'

'Do you believe he will?' asked Roderick, in his professional, neutral tone.

'Not quite. I wonder what you said in the court. I suppose I'm not to try to find out?'

'Find out if you like. But do it from yourself. From what's in you. I'll help.'

'I think,' Alison mused, 'it must be something to do with Dr Smith.'

'Oh? Why?'

'Because I had the most peculiar feeling when I remembered hearing about him and the idea that androids could have children. Like when Hewitt had his knife in my stomach, only as if . . .'

She laughed nervously, uncomfortably. 'As if I were holding it myself, and had to cut something out, but couldn't do it without killing myself. Yet I had a sort of idea I could cut it out, if I tried hard enough and long enough, and *not* kill myself.'

Roderick turned the corner into their street. 'This is a little unprofessional,' he said, the exhilaration in his voice ill-concealed, 'but I don't think it'll do any harm with you, Alison. There is going to be a little Roderick. I didn't decide it. *You* decided it. And it won't kill you. And – God, look at that!'

Cameras clicked like grasshoppers as Roderick Liffcom carried his bride across the threshold. The photographers hadn't had to follow them, for they knew where the Liffcoms were going. Scores of plates were exposed. The Liffcoms were news. The name of Liffcom was known to almost everyone.

Roderick was big and strong enough to treat his wife's 115 pounds with contempt, but there was no contempt in the way he held her. He carried her as if she were made of crystal which the faintest jar would shatter. One could see at a glance that he could have carried any girl he liked over the threshold.

Alison nestled in his arms like a kitten, eyes half-closed with rapture, arms about Roderick's neck. One could see at a glance she could have been carried over the threshold by any man she liked.

As they went in, it was the beginning of a story. But let's be different and call it the end.

Fredric Brown

The Waveries

Definitions from the school-abridged Webster-Hamlin Diction-
ary, 1998 edition:

> wavery (WA-věr-i) n. a vader – *slang* vader
> (VA-děr) n. inorgan of the class Radio
> inorgan (in-ÔR-gǎn) n. noncorporeal ens, a
> vader
> radio (RA-di-ō) n. n. class of inorgans 2.
> etheric frequency between light and elec-
> tricity 3. (obsolete) method of communica-
> tion used up to 1957

The opening guns of invasion were not at all loud, although
they were heard by millions of people. George Bailey was one of
the millions. I choose George Bailey because he was the only
one who came within a googol of light-years of guessing what
they were.

George Bailey was drunk and under the circumstances one
can't blame him for being so. He was listening to radio adver-
tisements of the most nauseous kind. Not because he wanted
to listen to them, I need hardly say, but because he'd been told
to listen to them by his boss, J. R. McGee of the MID network.

George Bailey wrote advertising for the radio. The only
thing he hated worse than advertising was radio. And here on
his own time he was listening to fulsome and disgusting commercials on a rival network.

'Bailey,' J. R. McGee had said, 'you should be more familiar
with what others are doing. Particularly, you should be
informed about those of our own accounts who use several
networks. I strongly suggest ...'

One doesn't quarrel with an employer's strong suggestions and keep a two hundred dollar a week job.

But one can drink whisky sours while listening. George Bailey did.

Also, between commercials, he was playing gin rummy with Maisie Hetterman, a cute little redheaded typist from the studio. It was Maisie's apartment and Maisie's radio (George himself, on principle, owned neither a radio or TV set) but George had brought the liquor.

'– only the very finest tobaccos,' said the radio, '*go dit-dit-dit* nation's favourite cigarette –'

George glanced at the radio. 'Marconi,' he said.

He meant Morse, naturally, but the whisky sours had muddled him a bit so his first guess was more nearly right than anyone else's. It *was* Marconi, in a way. In a very peculiar way.

'Marconi?' asked Maisie.

George, who hated to talk against a radio, leaned over and switched it off.

'I meant Morse,' he said. 'Morse, as in Boy Scouts or the Signal Corps. I used to be a Boy Scout once.'

'You've sure changed,' Maisie said.

George sighed. 'Somebody's going to catch hell, broadcasting code on that wave length.'

'What did it mean?'

'Mean? Oh, you mean what did it mean. Uh – S, the letter S. *Dit-dit-dit* is S. SOS is *dit-dit-dit dah-dah-dah dit-dit-dit*.'

'O is *dah-dah-dah*?'

George grinned. 'Say that again Maisie. I like it. And I think you are *dah-dah-dah* too.'

'George, maybe it's really an SOS message. Turn it back on.'

George turned it back on. The tobacco ad was still going. '– gentlemen of the most *dit-dit-dit* -ing taste prefer the finer taste of *dit-dit-dit* -arettes. In the new package that keeps them *dit-dit-dit* and ultra fresh –'

'It's not SOS. It's just S's.'

'Like a tea-kettle or – say, George, maybe it's just some advertising gag.'

George shook his head. 'Not when it can blank out the name of the product. Just a minute till I –'

He reached over and turned the dial of the radio a bit to the right and then a bit to the left, and an incredulous look came into his face. He turned the dial to the extreme left, as far as it would go. There wasn't any station there, not even the hum of a carrier wave. But:

'*Dit-dit-dit*,' said the radio, '*dit-dit-dit*.'

He turned the dial to the extreme right. '*Dit-dit-dit*.'

George switched it off and stared at Maisie without seeing her, which was hard to do.

'Something wrong, George?'

'I hope so,' said George Bailey. 'I certainly hope so.'

He started to reach for another drink and changed his mind. He had a sudden hunch that something big was happening and he wanted to sober up to appreciate it.

He didn't have the faintest idea *how* big it was.

'George, what do you mean?'

'I don't know what I mean. But Maisie, let's take a run down to the studio, huh? There ought to be some excitement.'

5 April, 1957; that was the night the waveries came.

It had started like an ordinary evening. It wasn't one, now.

George and Maisie waited for a cab but none came so they took the subway instead. Oh yes, the subways were still running in those days. It took them within a block of the MID Network Building.

The building was a madhouse. George, grinning, strolled through the lobby with Maisie on his arm, took the elevator to the fifth floor and for no reason at all gave the elevator boy a dollar. He'd never before in his life tipped an elevator operator.

The boy thanked him. 'Better stay away from the big shots, Mr Bailey,' he said. 'They're ready to chew the ears off anybody who even looks at 'em.'

'Wonderful,' said George.

From the elevator he headed straight for the office of J. R. McGee himself.

There were strident voices behind the glass door. George reached for the knob and Maisie tried to stop him. 'But George,' she whispered, 'you'll be fired!'

'There comes a time,' said George. 'Stand back away from the door, honey.'

Gently but firmly he moved her to a safe position.

'But George, what are you –'

'Watch,' he said.

The frantic voices stopped as he opened the door a foot. All eyes turned towards him as he stuck his head around the corner of the doorway into the room.

'*Dit-dit-dit*,' he said. '*Dit-dit-dit*.'

He ducked back and to the side just in time to escape the flying glass as a paperweight and an inkwell came through the pane of the door.

He grabbed Maisie and ran for the stairs.

'Now we get a drink,' he told her.

The bar across the street from the network building was crowded but it was a strangely silent crowd. In deference to the fact that most of its customers were radio people it didn't have a TV set but there was a big cabinet radio and most of the people were bunched around it.

'*Dit*,' said the radio. '*Dit-dah-d'dah-dit-dahditdah dit* –'

'Isn't it beautiful?' George whispered to Maisie.

Somebody fiddled with the dial. Somebody asked, 'What band is that?' and somebody said, 'Police.' Somebody said, 'Try the foreign band,' and somebody did. 'This ought to be Buenos Aires,' somebody said. '*Dit-d'dah-dit* –' said the radio.

Somebody ran fingers through his hair and said, 'Shut that damn thing off.' Somebody else turned it back on.

George grinned and led the way to a back booth where he'd spotted Pete Mulvaney sitting alone with a bottle in front of him. He and Maisie sat across from Pete.

'Hello,' he said gravely.

'Hell,' said Pete, who was head of the technical research staff of MID.

'A beautiful night, Mulvaney,' George said. 'Did you see the moon riding the fleecy clouds like a golden galleon tossed upon silver-crested whitecaps in a stormy –'

'Shut up,' said Pete. 'I'm thinking.'

'Whisky sours,' George told the waiter. He turned back to the man across the table. 'Think out loud, so we can hear. But first, how did you escape the booby hatch across the street?'

'I'm bounced, fired, discharged.'

'Shake hands. And then explain. Did you say *dit-dit-dit* to them?'

Pete looked at him with sudden admiration. 'Did you?'

'I've a witness. What *did* you do?'

'Told 'em what I thought it was and they think I'm crazy.'

'Are you?'

'Yes.'

'Good,' said George. 'Then we want to hear –' He snapped his fingers. 'What about TV?'

'Same thing. Same sound on audio and the pictures flicker and dim with every dot or dash. Just a blur by now.'

'Wonderful. And now tell me what's wrong. I don't care what it is, as long as it's nothing trivial, but I want to know.'

'I think it's space. Space is warped.'

'Good old space,' George Bailey said.

'George,' said Maisie, 'please shut up. I want to hear this.'

'Space,' said Pete, 'is also finite.' He poured himself another drink. 'You go far enough in any direction and get back where you started. Like an ant crawling around an apple.'

'Make it an orange,' George said.

'All right, an orange. Now suppose the first radio waves ever sent out have just made the round trip. In fifty-six years.'

'Fifty-six years? But I thought radio waves travelled at the same speed as light. If that's right, then in fifty-six years they could go only fifty-six light years, and *that* can't be around the universe because there are galaxies known to be millions or maybe billions of light-years away. I don't remember the figures, Pete, but our own galaxy alone is a hell of a lot bigger than fifty-six light-years.'

Pete Mulvaney sighed. 'That's why I say space must be warped. There's a short cut somewhere.'

'*That* short a short cut? Couldn't be.'

'But George, listen to that stuff that's coming in. Can you read code?'

'Not any more. Not that fast, anyway.'

'Well, I can,' Pete said. 'That's early American ham. Lingo and all. That's the kind of stuff the air was full of before regular broadcasting. It's the lingo, the abbreviations, the barnyard to attic chitchat of amateurs with keys, with Marconi coherers or Fessenden barreters – and you can listen for a violin solo pretty soon now. I'll tell you what it'll be.'

'What?'

'Handel's *Largo*. The first phonograph record ever broadcast. Sent out by Fessenden from Brant Rock in 1906. You'll hear his CQ-CQ any minute now. Bet you a drink.'

'Okay, but what was the *dit-dit-dit* that started this?'

Mulvaney grinned. 'Marconi, George. What was the most powerful signal ever broadcast and by whom and when?'

'Marconi? *Dit-dit-dit*? Fifty-six years ago?'

'Head of the class. The first transatlantic signal on 12 December 1901. For three hours Marconi's big station at Poldhu, with two-hundred-foot masts, sent out an intermittent S, *dit-dit-dit*, while Marconi and two assistants at St Johns in Newfoundland got a kite-born aerial four hundred feet in the air and finally got the signal. Across the Atlantic, George, with sparks jumping from the big Leyden jars at Poldhu and 20,000-volt juice jumping off the tremendous aerials –'

'Wait a minute, Pete, you're off the beam. If that was in 1901 and the first broadcast was about 1906 it'll be five years before the Fessenden stuff gets here on the same route. Even if there's a fifty-six light-year short cut across space and even if those signals didn't get so weak *en route* that we couldn't hear them – it's crazy.'

'I told you it was,' Pete said gloomily. 'Why, those signals after travelling that far would be so infinitesimal that for practical purposes they wouldn't exist. Furthermore they're all over the band on everything from microwave on up and equally strong on each. And, as you point out, we've already come almost five years in two hours, which isn't possible. I told you it was crazy.'

'But –'

'Ssshh. Listen,' said Pete.

A blurred, but unmistakably human voice was coming from the radio, mingling with the cracklings of code. And then music, faint and scratchy, but unmistakably a violin. Playing Handel's *Largo*.

Only suddenly it climbed in pitch as though modulating from key to key until it became so horribly shrill that it hurt the ear. And kept on going past the high limit of audibility until they could hear it no more.

Somebody said, 'Shut that God damn thing off.' Somebody did, and this time nobody turned it back on.

Pete said, 'I didn't really believe it myself. And there's another thing against it, George. Those signals affect TV too, and radio waves are the wrong length to do that.'

He shook his head slowly. 'There must be some other explanation, George. The more I think about it now the more I think I'm wrong.'

He was right: he was wrong.

'Preposterous,' said Mr Ogilvie. He took off his glasses, frowned fiercely, and put them back on again. He looked through them at the several sheets of copy paper in his hand and tossed them contemptuously to the top of his desk. They slid to rest against the triangular name plate that read:

B. R. OGILVIE
Editor-in-Chief

'Preposterous,' he said again.

Casey Blair, his best reporter, blew a smoke ring and poked his index finger through it. 'Why?' he asked.

'Because – why, it's *utterly* preposterous.'

Casey Blair said, 'It is now three o'clock in the morning. The interference has gone on for five hours and not a single programme is getting through on either TV or radio. Every major broadcasting and telecasting station in the world has gone off the air.

'For two reasons. One, they were just wasting current. Two the communications bureaux of their respective governments requested them to get off to aid their campaigns with the direction finders. For five hours now, since the start of the interference, they've been working with everything they've got. And what have they found out?'

'It's preposterous!' said the editor.

'Perfectly, but it's true. Greenwich at 11 p.m. New York time; I'm translating all these times into New York time – got a bearing in about the direction of Miami. It shifted northward until at two o'clock the direction was approximately that of Richmond, Virginia. San Francisco at eleven got a bearing in about the direction of Denver; three hours later it shifted southward towards Tucson. Southern hemisphere: bearings from Cape Town, South Africa, shifted from direction of Buenos Aires to that of Montevideo, a thousand miles north.

'New York at eleven had weak indications towards Madrid; but by two o'clock they could get no bearings at all.' He blew another smoke ring. 'Maybe because the loop antennae they use turn only on a horizontal plane?'

'Absurd.'

Casey said, 'I like "preposterous" better, Mr Ogilvie. Preposterous it is, but it's not absurd. I'm scared stiff. Those lines – and all other bearings I've heard about – run in the *same direction* if you take them as straight lines running as tangents off the Earth instead of curving them around the surface. I did it with a little globe and a star map. They converge on the constellation Leo.'

He leaned forward and tapped a forefinger on the top page of the story he'd just turned in. 'Stations that are directly under Leo in the sky get no bearings at all. Stations on what would be the perimeter of Earth relative to that point get the strongest bearings. Listen, have an astronomer check those figures if you want before you run the story, but get it done damn quick – unless you want to read about it in the other newspapers first.'

'But the heaviside layer, Casey – isn't that supposed to stop all radio waves and bounce them back.'

'Sure, it does. But maybe it leaks. Or maybe signals can get through it from the outside even though they can't get out from the inside. It isn't a solid wall.'

'But –'

'I know, it's preposterous. But there it is. And there's only an hour before press time. You'd better send this story through fast and have it being set up while you're having somebody check my facts and directions. Besides, there's something else you'll want to check.'

'What?'

'I didn't have the data for checking the positions of the planets. Leo's on the ecliptic; a planet could be in line between here and there. Mars, maybe.'

Mr Ogilvie's eyes brightened, then clouded again. He said, 'We'll be the laughing-stock of the world, Blair, if you're wrong.'

'And if I'm right?'

The editor picked up the phone and snapped an order.

6 April headline of the New York *Morning Messenger*, final (6 a.m.) edition:

RADIO INTERFERENCE COMES FROM SPACE, ORIGINATES IN LEO

May Be Attempt at Communication by Beings Outside Solar System

All television and radio broadcasting was suspended.

Radio and television stocks opened several points off the previous day and then dropped sharply until noon when a moderate buying rally brought them a few points back.

Public reaction was mixed; people who had no radios rushed out to buy them and there was a boom, especially in portable and table-top receivers. On the other hand, no TV sets were sold at all. With telecasting suspended there were no pictures on their screens, even blurred ones. Their audio circuits, when turned on, brought in the same jumble as radio receivers. Which, as Pete Mulvaney had pointed out to George Bailey, was impossible; radio waves cannot activate the audio circuits of TV sets. But these did, if they *were* radio waves.

In radio sets they seemed to be radio waves, but horribly hashed. No one could listen to them very long. Oh, there were flashes – times when, for several consecutive seconds, one could recognize the voice of Will Rogers or Geraldine Farrar or catch flashes of the Dempsey-Carpentier fight or the Pearl Harbour excitement. (Remember Pearl Harbour?) But things even remotely worth hearing were rare. Mostly it was a meaningless mixture of soap opera, advertising, and off-key snatches of what had once been music. It was utterly indiscriminate, and utterly unbearable for any length of time.

But curiosity is a powerful motive. There *was* a brief boom in radio sets for a few days.

There were other booms, less explicable, less capable of analysis. Reminiscent of the Wells-Welles Martian scare of 1938 was a sudden upswing in the sale of shotguns and side-arms. Bibles sold as fast as books on astronomy – and books on astronomy sold like hot cakes. One section of the country showed a sudden interest in lightning rods; builders were flooded with orders for immediate installation.

For some reason which has never been clearly ascertained there was a run on fish-hooks in Mobile, Alabama; every hardware and sporting goods store sold out of them within hours.

The public libraries and bookstores had a run on books on astrology and books on Mars. Yes, on Mars – despite the fact that Mars was at that moment on the other side of the sun and that every newspaper article on the subject stressed the fact that *no* planet was between Earth and the constellation Leo.

Something strange was happening – and no news of developments available except through the newspapers. People waited in mobs outside newspaper buildings for each new edition to appear. Circulation managers went quietly mad.

People also gathered in curious little knots around the silent broadcasting studios and stations, talking in hushed voices as though at a wake. MID network doors were locked, although there was a doorman on duty to admit technicians who were trying to find an answer to the problem. Some of the technicians who had been on duty the previous day had now spent over twenty-four hours without sleep.

George Bailey woke at noon, with only a slight headache. He shaved and showered, went out and drank a light breakfast and was himself again. He bought early editions of the afternoon papers, read them, grinned. His hunch had been right; whatever was wrong, it was nothing trivial.

But *what* was wrong?

The later editions of the afternoon papers had it.

EARTH INVADED, SAYS SCIENTIST

Thirty-six line type was the biggest they had; they used it. Not a home-edition copy of a newspaper was delivered that evening. Newsboys starting on their routes were practically mobbed. They sold papers instead of delivering them; the smart ones got a dollar apiece for them. The foolish and honest ones who didn't want to sell because they thought the papers should go to the regular customers on their routes lost them anyway. People grabbed them.

The final editions changed the heading only slightly – only slightly, that is, from a typographical viewpoint. Nevertheless, it was a tremendous change in meaning. It read:

EARTH INVADED, SAY SCIENTISTS

Funny what moving an S from the ending of a verb to the ending of a noun can do.

Carnegie Hall shattered precedent that evening with a lecture given at midnight. An unscheduled and unadvertised lecture. Professor Helmetz had stepped off the train at eleven-thirty and a mob of reporters had been waiting for him. Helmetz, of

Harvard, had been the scientist, singular, who had made that first headline.

Harvey Ambers, director of the board of Carnegie Hall, had pushed his way through the mob. He arrived minus glasses, hat, and breath, but got hold of Helmetz's arm and hung on until he could talk again. 'We want you to talk at Carnegie, Professor,' he shouted into Helmetz's ear. 'Five thousand dollars for a lecture on the "vaders".'

'Certainly. Tomorrow afternoon.'

'Now! I've a cab waiting. Come on.'

'But –'

'We'll get you an audience. Hurry!' He turned to the mob. 'Let us through. All of you can't hear the professor here. Come to Carnegie Hall and he'll talk to you. And spread the word on your way there.'

The word spread so well that Carnegie Hall was jammed by the time the professor began to speak. Shortly after, they'd rigged a loud-speaker system so the people outside could hear. By one o'clock in the morning the streets were jammed for blocks around.

There wasn't a sponsor on Earth with a million dollars to his name who wouldn't have given a million dollars gladly for the privilege of sponsoring that lecture on TV or radio, but it was not telecast or broadcast. Both lines were busy.

'Questions?' asked Professor Helmetz.

A reporter in the front row made it first. 'Professor,' he asked, 'have *all* direction-finding stations on Earth confirmed what you told us about the change this afternoon?'

'Yes, absolutely. At about noon all directional indications began to grow weaker. At 2.45 o'clock, Eastern Standard Time, they ceased completely. Until then the radio waves emanated from the sky, constantly changing direction with reference to the Earth's surface, but *constant* with reference to a point in the constellation Leo.'

'What star in Leo?'

'No star visible on our charts. Either they came from a point in space or from a star too faint for our telescopes.

'But at 2.45 p.m. today – yesterday rather, since it is now past midnight – all direction finders went dead. But the signals persisted, now coming from all sides equally. The invaders had all arrived.

'There is no other conclusion to be drawn. Earth is now surrounded, completely blanketed, by radio-type waves which have *no point of origin*, which travel ceaselessly around the Earth in all directions, changing shape at their will – which currently is still in imitation of the Earth-origin radio signals which attracted their attention and brought them here.'

'Do you think it was from a star we can't see, or could it have really been just a point in space?'

'Probably from a point in space. And why not? They are not creatures of matter. If they came here from a star, it must be a very dark star for it to be invisible to us, since it would be relatively near to us – only twenty-eight light-years away, which is quite close as stellar distances go.'

'How can you know the distance?'

'By assuming – and it is a quite reasonable assumption – that they started our way when they first discovered our radio signals – Marconi's S-S-S code broadcast of fifty-six years ago. Since that was the form taken by the first arrivals, we assume they started towards us when they encountered those signals. Marconi's signals, travelling at the speed of light, would have reached a point twenty-eight light-years away twenty-eight years ago; the invaders, also travelling at light-speed would require an equal time to reach us.

'As might be expected only the first arrivals took Morse code form. Later arrivals were in the form of other waves that they met and passed on – or perhaps absorbed – on their way to Earth. There are now wandering around the Earth, as it were, fragments of programmes broadcast as recently as a few days ago. Undoubtedly there are fragments of the very last programmes to be broadcast, but they have not yet been identified.'

'Professor, can you *describe* one of these invaders?'

'As well as and no better than I can describe a radio wave. In effect, they *are* radio waves, although they emanate from no broadcasting station. They are a form of life dependent on wave motion, as our form of life is dependent on the vibration of matter.'

'They are different sizes?'

'Yes, in two senses of the word size. Radio waves are measured from crest to crest, which measurement is known as the wave length. Since the invaders cover the entire dials of our radio sets and television sets it is obvious that either one of two things is true: Either they come in all crest-to-crest sizes or each one can change his crest-to-crest measurement to adapt himself to the tuning of any receiver.

'But that is only the crest-to-crest length. In a sense it may be said that a radio wave has an over-all length determined by its duration. If a broadcasting station sends out a programme that has a second's duration, a wave carrying that programme is one light-second long, roughly 187,000 miles. A continuous half-hour programme is, as it were, on a continuous wave one-half light-hour long, and so on.

'Taking that form of length, the individual invaders vary in length from a few thousand miles – a duration of only a small fraction of a second – to well over half a million miles long – a duration of several seconds. The longest continuous excerpt from any one programme that has been observed has been about seven seconds.'

'But, Professor Helmetz, why do you assume that these waves are *living* things, a life form. Why not just waves?'

'Because "just waves" as you call them would follow certain laws, just as inanimate *matter* follows certain laws. An animal can climb uphill, for instance; a stone cannot unless impelled by some outside force. These invaders are life-forms because they show volition, because they can change their direction of travel, and most especially because they retain their identity; two signals never conflict on the same radio receiver. They follow one another but do not come simultaneously. They do not mix as signals on the same wave length would ordinarily do. They are not "just waves".'

'Would you say they are intelligent?'

Professor Helmetz took off his glasses and polished them thoughtfully. He said, 'I doubt if we shall ever know. The intelligence of such beings, if any, would be on such a completely different plane from ours that there would be no common point from which we could start intercourse. We are material; they are immaterial. There is no common ground between us.'

'But if they are intelligent at all –'

'Ants are intelligent, after a fashion. Call it instinct if you will, but instinct is a form of intelligence; at least it enables them to accomplish some of the same things intelligence would enable them to accomplish. Yet we cannot establish communication with ants and it is far less likely that we shall be able to establish communication with these invaders. The difference in type between ant-intelligence and our own would be nothing to the difference in type between the intelligence, if any, of the invaders and our own. No, I doubt if we shall ever communicate.'

The professor had something there. Communication with the vaders – a clipped form, of course, of *invaders* – was never established.

Radio stocks stabilized on the exchange the next day. But the day following that someone asked Dr Helmetz a sixty-four dollar question and the newspapers published his answer:

'Resume broadcasting? I don't know if we ever shall. Certainly we cannot until the invaders go away, and why should they? Unless radio communication is perfected on some other planet far away and they're attracted there.

'But at least some of them would be right back the moment we started to broadcast again.'

Radio and TV stocks dropped to practically zero in an hour. There weren't, however, any frenzied scenes on the stock exchanges; there was no frenzied selling because there was no buying, frenzied or otherwise. No radio stocks changed hands.

Radio and television employees and entertainers began to look for other jobs. The entertainers had no trouble finding them. Every other form of entertainment suddenly boomed like mad.

'Two down,' said George Bailey. The bartender asked what he meant.

'I dunno, Hank. It's just a hunch I've got.'

'What kind of hunch?'

'I don't even know that. Shake me up one more of those and then I'll go home.'

The electric shaker wouldn't work and Hank had to shake the drink by hand.

'Good exercise; that's just what you need,' George said. 'It'll take some of that fat off you.'

Hank grunted, and the ice tinkled merrily as he tilted the shaker to pour out the drink.

George Bailey took his time drinking it and then strolled out into an April thunder-shower. He stood under the awning and watched for a taxi. An old man was standing there too.

'Some weather,' George said.

The old man grinned at him. 'You noticed it, eh?'

'Huh? Noticed what?'

'Just watch a while, mister. Just watch a while.'

The old man moved on. No empty cab came by and George stood there quite a while before he got it. His jaw dropped a little and then he closed his mouth and went back into the tavern. He went into a phone booth and called Pete Mulvaney.

He got three wrong numbers before he got Pete. Pete's voice said, 'Yeah?'

'George Bailey, Pete. Listen, have you noticed the weather?'

'Damn right. *No lightning*, and there should be with a thunderstorm like this.'

'What's it mean, Pete? The vaders?'

'Sure. And that's just going to be the start if –' A crackling sound on the wire blurred his voice out.

'Hey, Pete, you still there?'

The sound of a violin. Pete Mulvaney didn't play violin.

'Hey, Pete, what the hell –?'

Pete's voice again. 'Come on over, George. Phone won't last long. Bring –' There was a buzzing noise and then a voice said, '– come to Carnegie Hall. The best tunes of all come –'

George slammed down the receiver.

He walked through the rain to Pete's place. On the way he bought a bottle of Scotch. Pete had started to tell him to bring something and maybe that's what he'd started to say.

It was.

They made a drink apiece and lifted them. The lights flickered briefly, went out, and then came on again but dimly.

'No lightning,' said George. 'No lightning and pretty soon no lighting. They're taking over the telephone. What do they do with the lightning?'

'Eat it, I guess. They must eat electricity.'

'No lightning,' said George. 'Damn. I can get by without a telephone, and candles and oil lamps aren't bad for lights – but I'm going to miss lightning. I *like* lightning. Damn.'

The lights went out completely.

Pete Mulvaney sipped his drink in the dark. He said, 'Electric lights, refrigerators, electric toasters, vacuum cleaners –'

'Juke boxes,' George said. 'Think of it, no more goddam juke boxes. No public address systems, no – hey, how about movies?'

'No movies, not even silent ones. You can't work a projector with an oil lamp. But listen, George, no automobiles – no gasoline engine can work without electricity.'

'Why not, if you crank it by hand instead of using a starter?'

'The spark, George. What do you think makes the spark.'

'Right. No aeroplanes either, then. Or how about jet planes?'

'Well – I guess some types of jets could be rigged not to need electricity, but you couldn't do much with them. Jet plane's got more instruments than motor, and all those instruments are electrical. And you can't fly or land a jet by the seat of your pants.'

'No radar. But what would we need it for? There won't be any more wars, not for a long time.'

'A damned long time.'

George sat up straight suddenly. 'Hey, Pete, what about atomic fission? Atomic energy? Will it still work?'

'I doubt it. Subatomic phenomena are basically electrical. Bet you a dime they eat loose neutrons too.' (He'd have won his

226

bet; the government had not announced that an A-bomb tested that day in Nevada had fizzled like a wet firecracker and that atomic piles were ceasing to function.)

George shook his head slowly, in wonder. He said, 'Street-cars and buses, ocean liners – Pete, this means we're going back to the original source of horse-power. Horses. If you want to invest, buy horses. Particularly mares. A brood mare is going to be worth a thousand times her weight in platinum.'

'Right. But don't forget steam. We'll still have steam engines, stationary and locomotive.'

'Sure, that's right. The iron horse again, for the long hauls. But Dobbin for the short ones. Can you ride, Pete?'

'Used to, but I think I'm getting too old. I'll settle for a bicycle. Say, better buy a bike first thing tomorrow before the run on them starts. I know *I'm* going to.'

'Good tip. And I used to be a good bike rider. It'll be swell with no autos around to louse you up. And say –'

'What?'

'I'm going to get a cornet too. Used to play one when I was a kid and I can pick it up again. And then maybe I'll hole in somewhere and write that nov – Say, what about printing?'

'They printed books long before electricity, George. It'll take a while to readjust the printing industry, but there'll be books all right. Thank God for that.'

George Bailey grinned and got up. He walked over to the window and looked out into the night. The rain had stopped and the sky was clear.

A street-car was stalled, without lights, in the middle of the block outside. An automobile stopped, then started more slowly, stopped again; its headlights were dimming rapidly.

George looked up at the sky and took a sip of his drink.

'No lightning,' he said sadly. 'I'm going to *miss* the lightning.'

The changeover went more smoothly than anyone would have thought possible.

The government, in emergency session, made the wise decision of creating one board with absolutely unlimited authority and under it only three subsidiary boards. The main board, called the Economic Readjustment Bureau, had only seven members and its job was to coordinate the efforts of the three subsidiary boards and to decide, quickly and without appeal, any jurisdictional disputes among them.

First of the three subsidiary boards was the Transportation Bureau. It immediately took over, temporarily, the railroads. It ordered Diesel engines run on sidings and left there, organized use of the steam locomotives, and solved the problems of railroading *sans* telegraphy and electric signals. It dictated, then, what should be transported; food coming first, coal and fuel oil second, and essential manufactured articles in the order of their relative importance. Car-load after car-load of new radios, electric stoves, refrigerators, and such useless articles were dumped unceremoniously alongside the tracks, to be salvaged for scrap metal later.

All horses were declared wards of the government, graded according to capabilities, and put to work or to stud. Draught horses were used for only the most essential kinds of hauling. The breeding programme was given the fullest possible emphasis; the bureau estimated that the equine population would double in two years, quadruple in three, and that within six or seven years there would be a horse in every garage in the country.

Farmers, deprived temporarily of their horses, and with their tractors rusting in the fields, were instructed how to use cattle for ploughing and other work about the farm, including light hauling.

The second board, the Manpower Relocation Bureau, functioned just as one would deduce from its title. It handled unemployment benefits for the millions thrown temporarily out of work and helped relocate them – not too difficult a task considering the tremendously increased demand for hand labour in many fields.

In May of 1957 thirty-five million employables were out of work; in October, fifteen million; by May of 1958, five million. By 1959 the situation was completely in hand and competitive demand was already beginning to raise wages.

The third board had the most difficult job of the three. It

228

was called the Factory Readjustment Bureau. It coped with the stupendous task of converting factories filled with electrically operated machinery and, for the most part, tooled for the production of other electrically operated machinery, over for the production, without electricity, of essential non-electrical articles.

The few available stationary steam engines worked twenty-four hour shifts in those early days, and the first thing they were given to do was the running of lathes and stampers and planers and millers working on turning out more stationary steam engines, of all sizes. These, in turn, were first put to work making still more steam engines. The number of steam engines grew by squares and cubes, as did the number of horses put to stud. The principle was the same. One might, and many did, refer to those early steam engines as stud horses. At any rate, there was no lack of metal for them. The factories were filled with non-convertible machinery waiting to be melted down.

Only when steam engines – the basis of the new factory economy – were in full production, were they assigned to running machinery for the manufacture of other articles. Oil lamps, clothing, coal stoves, oil stoves, bath-tubs, and bedsteads.

Not quite all of the big factories were converted. For while the conversion period went on, individual handicrafts sprang up in thousands of places. Little one- and two-man shops making and repairing furniture, shoes, candles, all sorts of things that *could* be made without complex machinery. At first these small shops made small fortunes because they had no competition from heavy industry. Later, they bought small steam engines to run small machines and held their own, growing with the boom that came with a return to normal employment and buying power, increasing gradually in size until many of them rivalled the bigger factories in output and beat them in quality.

There *was* suffering, during the period of economic readjustment, but less than there had been during the great depression of the early thirties. And the recovery was quicker.

The reason was obvious: In combating the depression, the legislators were working in the dark. They didn't know its cause – rather, they knew a thousand conflicting theories of its cause - and they didn't know the cure. They were hampered by the idea that the thing was temporary and would cure itself if left alone. Briefly and frankly, they didn't know what it was all about and while they experimented, it snowballed.

But the situation that faced the country – and all other countries – in 1957 was clear-cut and obvious. No more electricity. Readjust for steam and horsepower.

As simple and clear as that, and no ifs or ands or buts. And the whole people – except for the usual scattering of cranks – back of them.

By 1961 –

It was a rainy day in April and George Bailey was waiting under the sheltering roof of the little railroad station at Blakestown, Connecticut, to see who might come in on the 3.14.

It chugged in at 3.25 and came to a panting stop, three coaches and a baggage car. The baggage car door opened and a sack of mail was handed out and the door closed again. No luggage, so probably no passengers would –

Then at the sight of a tall dark man swinging down from the platform of the rear coach, George Bailey let out a yip of delight. 'Pete! Pete Mulvaney! What the devil –'

'Bailey, by all that's holy! What are you doing here?'

George wrung Pete's hand. 'Me? I live here. Two years now. I bought the *Blakestown Weekly* in '59, for a song, and I run it – editor, reporter, and janitor. Got one printer to help me out with that end, and Maisie does the social items. She's –'

'Maisie? Maisie Hetterman?'

'Maisie Bailey now. We got married same time I bought the paper and moved here. What are you doing here, Pete?'

'Business. Just here overnight. See a man named Wilcox.'

'Oh, Wilcox. Our local screwball – but don't get me wrong; he's a smart guy all right. Well, you can see him tomorrow. You're coming home with me now, for dinner and to stay overnight. Maisie'll be glad to see you. Come on, my buggy's over here.'

'Sure. Finished whatever you were here for?'

'Yep, just to pick up the news on who came in on the train. And *you* came in, so here we go.'

They got in the buggy, and George picked up the reins and said, 'Giddup, Bessie,' to the mare. Then, 'What are you doing now, Pete?'

'Research. For a gas-supply company. Been working on a more efficient mantle, one that'll give more light and be less destructible. This fellow Wilcox wrote us he had something along that line; the company sent me up to look it over. If it's what he claims, I'll take him back to New York with me, and let the company lawyers dicker with him.'

'How's business, otherwise?'

'Great, George. *Gas*; that's the coming thing. Every *new* home's being piped for it, and plenty of the old ones. How about you?'

'We got it. Luckily we had one of the old Linotypes that ran the metal pot off a gas burner, so it was already piped in. And our home is right over the office and print shop, so all we had to do was pipe it up a flight. Great stuff, gas. How's New York?'

'Fine, George. Down to its last million people, and stabilizing there. No crowding and plenty of room for everybody. The *air* – why, it's better than Atlantic City, without gasoline fumes.'

'Enough horses to go around yet?'

'Almost. But bicycling's the craze; the factories can't turn out enough to meet the demand. There's a cycling club in almost every block and all the able-bodied cycle to and from work. Doing 'em good, too; a few more years and the doctors will go on short rations.'

'You got a bike?'

'Sure, a pre-vader one. Average five miles a day on it, and I eat like a horse.'

George Bailey chuckled. 'I'll have Maisie include some hay in the dinner. Well, here we are. Whoa, Bessie.'

An upstairs window went up, and Maisie looked out and down. She called out, 'Hi, Pete!'

'Extra plate, Maisie,' George called. 'We'll be up soon as I put the horse away and show Pete around downstairs.'

He led Pete from the barn into the back door of the newspaper shop. 'Our Linotype!' he announced proudly, pointing.

'How's it work? Where's your steam engine?'

George grinned. 'Doesn't work yet; we still hand set the type. I could get only one steamer and had to use that on the press. But I've got one on order for the Lino, and coming up in a month or so. When we get it, Pop Jenkins, my printer, is going to put himself out of a job teaching me to run it. With the Linotype going, I can handle the whole thing myself.'

'Kind of rough on Pop?'

George shook his head. 'Pop eagerly awaits the day. He's sixty-nine and wants to retire. He's just staying on until I can do without him. Here's the press – a honey of a little Miehle; we do some job work on it, too. And this is the office, in front. Messy, but efficient.'

Mulvaney looked around him and grinned. 'George, I believe you've found your niche. You were cut out for a small-town editor.'

'Cut out for it? I'm crazy about it. I have more fun than everybody. Believe it or not, I work like a dog, and like it. Come on upstairs.'

On the stairs, Pete asked, 'And the novel you were going to write?'

'Half done, and it isn't bad. But it isn't the novel I was going to write; I was a cynic then. Now –'

'George, I think the waveries were your best friends.'

'Waveries?'

'Lord, how long does it take slang to get from New York out to the sticks? The vaders, of course. Some professor who specializes in studying them described one as a wavery place in the ether, and "wavery" stuck – Hello there, Maisie, my girl. You look like a million.'

They ate leisurely Almost apologetically, George brought out beer, in cold bottles. 'Sorry, Pete, haven't anything stronger to offer you. But I haven't been drinking lately. Guess –'

'*You* on the wagon, George?'

'Not on the wagon, exactly. Didn't swear off or anything, but haven't had a drink of strong liquor in almost a year. I don't know why, but –'

'I do,' said Pete Mulvaney. 'I know exactly why you don't – because I don't drink much either, for the same reason. We don't drink because we don't *have* to – say, isn't that a *radio* over there?'

George chuckled. 'A souvenir. Wouldn't sell it for a fortune. Once in a while I like to look at it and think of the awful guff I used to sweat out for it. And then I go over and click the switch and nothing happens. Just silence. Silence is the most wonderful thing in the world, sometimes, Pete. Of course I couldn't do that if there was any juice, because I'd get vaders then. I suppose they're still doing business at the same old stand?'

'Yep, the Research Bureau checks daily. Try to get up current with a little generator run by a steam turbine. But no dice: the vaders suck it up as fast as it's generated.'

'Suppose they'll ever go away?'

Mulvaney shrugged. 'Helmetz thinks not. He thinks they propagate in proportion to the available electricity. Even if the development of radio broadcasting somewhere else in the Universe would attract them there, some would stay here – and multiply like flies the minute we tried to use electricity again. And meanwhile, they'll live on the static electricity in the air. What do you do evenings up here?'

'Do? Read, write, visit with one another, go to the amateur groups – Maisie's chairman of the Blakestown Players, and I play bit parts in it. With the movies out everybody goes in for theatricals and we've found some real talent. And there's the chess-and-checker club, and cycle trips and picnics – there isn't time enough. Not to mention music. Everybody plays an instrument, or is trying to.'

'You?'

'Sure, cornet. First cornet in the Silver Concert Band, with solo parts. And – Good Heavens! Tonight's rehearsal, and we're giving a concert Sunday afternoon. I hate to desert you, but –'

'Can't I come around and sit in? I've got my flute in the brief case here, and –'

'*Flute?* We're short on flutes. Bring that around and Si Perkins, our director, will practically shanghai you into staying over for the concert Sunday – and it's only three days, so why not? And get it out now; we'll play a few old timers to warm up. Hey, Maisie, skip those dishes and come on in to the piano!'

While Pete Mulvaney went to the guest room to get his flute from the brief case, George Bailey picked up his cornet from the top of the piano and blew a soft, plaintive little minor run on it. Clear as a bell; his lip was in good shape tonight.

And with the shining silver thing in his hand he wandered over to the window and stood looking out into the night. It was dusk out and the rain had stopped.

A high-stepping horse *clop-clopped* by and the bell of a bicycle jangled. Somebody across the street was strumming a guitar and singing. He took a deep breath and let it out slowly.

The scent of spring was soft and sweet in the moist air.

Peace and dusk.

Distant rolling thunder.

God damn it, he thought, *if only there was a bit of lightning.*

He missed the lightning.

Some other books published by Penguin
are described on the following pages.

Edited by Reginald Bretnor

SCIENCE FICTION, TODAY AND TOMORROW

This exciting anthology explores the role of science
fiction in the modern world. Extremely diverse as
writers and as personalities, the contributors are all
prominent in the science-fiction field. They include
Frederik Pohl ('The Publishing of Science Fiction'),
Theodore Sturgeon ('Science Fiction, Morals, and
Religion'), Thomas N. Scortia ('Science Fiction as the
Imaginary Experiment'), Poul Anderson ('The Creation
of Imaginary Worlds'), Hal Clement ('The Creation of
Imaginary Beings'), Anne McCaffrey ('Romance and
Glamour in Science Fiction'), and Jack Williamson
('Science Fiction, Teaching, and Criticism'). Read together,
their essays reflect the inexhaustible richness of science
fiction today. Isaac Asimov has called this book 'the most
interesting volume dealing with science fiction that I
have ever read'.

Not for sale in Great Britain, Australia, and New Zealand

Edited by Edward L. Ferman and Barry N. Malzberg

FINAL STAGE
The Ultimate Science Fiction Anthology

For this unique anthology, thirteen of today's best
science-fiction writers were assigned subjects that would
inspire each of them to create the definitive story of its
kind. Here is work by Frederik Pohl ('First Contact'), Poul
Anderson ('The Exploration of Space'), Kit Reed
('Immortality'), Brian W. Aldiss ('Inner Space'), Isaac
Asimov ('Robots and Androids'), Dean R. Koontz ('Strange
Children'), Joanna Russ and Harlan Ellison ('Future Sex'),
Harry Harrison ('Space Opera'), Robert Silverberg
('Alternate Universes'), Barry N. Malzberg ('The
Uncontrolled Machine'), James Tiptree, Jr ('After the
Holocaust'), and Philip K. Dick ('Time Travel'). In addition,
each author has contributed an Afterword on previous
treatments of his or her theme and a bibliography of
related writings. Edward L. Ferman is the editor of *The
Magazine of Fantasy and Science Fiction*. Barry N.
Malzberg is the author of several science-fiction novels,
including the award-winning *Beyond Apollo*.

René Daumal

MOUNT ANALOGUE

A Novel of Symbolically Authentic Non-Euclidean
Adventures in Mountain Climbing

Translation and Introduction by Roger Shattuck
With a Postface by Véra Daumal

Mount Analogue is René Daumal's last novel, written
when he was a pupil of the great G. I. Gurdjieff. In the
original French and in Roger Shattuck's beautiful
translation, it has come to be regarded as a classic
allegory of man's search for himself. Its characters are
artists and scholars who undertake a voyage on the
yacht *Impossible* and the partial ascent of a symbolic
mountain. Mount Analogue itself represents the way that
unites Earth with Heaven, a way to truth which 'cannot
not exist'. The writings of René Daumal, who died in
1944 at the age of thirty-six, are unique in twentieth-
century European letters. They succeeded in creating
totally new forms of the literature of consciousness —
forms that embrace completely the specific poignancy of
modern man's condition.

*Not for sale in Great Britain, Canada, Australia, and New
Zealand*

Olaf Stapledon

STAR MAKER

A man sits quietly on a suburban hillside. Then, a
moment later, he is whirling through time and space in
search of the Star Maker behind the cosmos. Like H. G.
Wells's Time Traveller, he visits many worlds, and
eventually he is joined by others to form a strange
mental community, reacting multidimensionally to a
mind-spinning range of experiences.

LAST AND FIRST MEN and
LAST MEN IN LONDON

Here are two science-fiction classics in one volume.
Last and First Men moves through five billion years of
human evolution, culminating in the extinction of the
sun and the dissemination among the stars of the seeds
of a new humanity. *Last Men in London* creates a
Neptunian, 'last man's' view of the twentieth-century
world.

SIRIUS

Thomas Trelone devotes his life to the attempt to produce
a superman by hormone injections into various mammals.
Sirius is the most successful of these experiments, for
he is the only dog ever born with the brain of a human
being. This is a moving story of immense and tragic
pathos.

P. D. Ouspensky

STRANGE LIFE OF IVAN OSOKIN

In turn-of-the-century Russia, Ivan Osokin visits a
magician and is allowed to relive twelve years of his life.
He is returned to the time of his stormy schooldays, his
early manhood, his first love affairs. What he does not
know — though he soon begins to realize it — is that he
will repeat the mistakes of his past. The problems of
duration, of infinity, and of eternal recurrence were
crucial to P. D. Ouspensky's thought. This, his only novel,
is the story of a young man caught in the coils of time.
Its exciting climax holds the answer to whether or not
he can escape.

*Not for sale in Great Britain, Canada, Australia, and New
Zealand*